MW01269099

LOVE WITHOUT A HOME

Shari Mong

She had everything and no time to give love to a man.

He lost everything and had only his love to give.

Published in 2013, by Gypsy Publications
Troy, OH 45373, U.S.A.
GypsyPublications.com

First Edition
Copyright © Shari Mong, 2013

Mong, Shari
Love Without a Home / by Shari Mong

ISBN 978-1-938768-22-4 (paperback)

Library of Congress Control Number
2013943861

Cover and Book Design by Tim Rowe
Cover Photo by David Joyce

PRINTED IN THE UNITED STATES OF AMERICA

The National Coalition for Homeless states that approximately 40% of homeless men are veterans and they estimate that on any given night, 200,000 veterans are homeless and 400,000 will experience homelessness during the course of a year.

This book is dedicated to them. Thank you for your service.

To learn more go to:
http://www.nationalhomeless.org/factsheets/veterans.html

CHAPTER 1

Elisa Drinnings walked into the conference room of Pose Magazine. She had worked for Pose Magazine as a designer's assistant in college and worked her way to Chief Editor, and nothing was finalized until she said so. She looked chic in a Chanel pin stripped suit with a matching hand bag. She had gone to The Art Institute of New York to get her associate's in fashion design.

Her fashion drawings while in high school got her recognition and landed her in New York, one of the fashion capitals of the world. Her drawings had been turned into reality and worn by Pose's models. She graduated from Troy High School and applied to The Art Institute of New York. At 37, she was still stunning. Many wondered why she had not modeled for Pose Magazine, but Elisa's main focus was more along the lines of drawing and the business side of fashion.

She had pursued her education further and got her Bachelor's and Master's in Fashion Merchandising and Marketing. An education along with skills, wits and a good eye pushed her to the top. She expected nothing less from her subordinates and was not afraid to voice her like or dislike for their work. She had auburn hair and violet eyes. She had creamy white skin. She got her Irish good looks from her mother's side.

Her sister, Cara had dark hair and dark eyes; she got that from their father who was Native American. They were only two years apart. Cara was their father's favorite. However, Elisa and her mother Mattie had always had a close relationship. Their father had worked for GM when things went downhill, he got laid off. With no job and the bills piling up, Mattie and

Lloyd Drinnings fought more and more. One night, when Lloyd came home drunk, he started in on their mother, while the whole time Elisa and Cara listened and cried.

Mattie told him that she found him coming home drunk unacceptable. Lloyd Drinnings left and never returned. Mattie held two jobs, a receptionist at a doctor's office and cleaning offices at night. There were many times where Elisa and Cara had to be home alone and fix their own meals.

The money that Mattie made barely covered the bills, rent and groceries. One night, Elisa was sitting in her mother's room, watching her cry, and said to her, "Mother, I promise you, I will always take care of you." Elisa kept her promise when the money from her drawings came in; she had sent her mother her earnings. Elisa also kept her promise when Mattie was diagnosed with Ovarian Cancer. Elisa hired a Hospice nurse and she would come home to see her mother.

By then, Cara was in Hollywood and had not even bothered to keep in contact with her mother. Cara still blamed her mother for their father leaving. Elisa could remember her mother's words on her death bed, "Please, Elisa I know that Cara has blamed me for her father leaving, but you two are sisters and all you have is each other. I hope that one day Cara sees that I did my best to give you both a better life. I would love to have my daughters here so I can say what I need to say to both of you. The doctor has not given me long. Call Cara and ask her to come."

Elisa was crying and kissed her mother on the forehead. Elisa walked out of her mother's bedroom to call Cara. "Hello," said a tired and wispy voice. "Cara, it is me Elisa. Mother wants you to come home and see her; she is dying and does not have very much longer to live, days only."

"Oh Elisa, I would but I have this movie I am working on and I tried too hard to get a part in it. I am the lead actress. They need me here."

Elisa was fuming. "Our mother needs you here Cara, that damn movie can wait." There was silence on the other end. Finally, Elisa spoke up again. "Mother asks for this last request before she dies, Cara. She wants both of her daughters here. How can you only think of yourself?"

"Oh Elisa, don't put this guilt trip on me," Cara spat. "I am not the one who caused daddy to walk out on us."

"She made him do no such thing." Elisa returned. "He made that choice on his own. Mother did everything she could to give us everything we needed and wanted. I know many nights we had to feed ourselves, but it was because of the sacrifices she made for us. It was not easy on her, either. She had to do what she had to do. Give her this, please." Elisa could not believe that she had to beg her sister to come and see their dying mother.

Elisa heard a sigh on the other side before Cara spoke up again. "Fine, I don't want you making me feel guilty for the rest of my damn life. I will try to make it on the next flight out." Cara hung up abruptly before Elisa could get another word in edge wise.

One week later, their mother passed away and Cara had not made it back. Elisa had stayed with her mother to the end. Her mother cried and cried every night for her sister Cara to be there. Elisa had called Cara back with the news. "I am so sorry sis, my director would not let me off to come and he said if I did, then I would lose the part in this movie."

"Well you can tell your heartless director that he can go screw himself. You have put your needs over us Cara, I will never forgive you. You can have all of the fame and fortune you want, but you will never have me back in your life. For all I care, you can stay out in California. I will not bother to tell you when and where the funeral is. You are not deserving of that. You are no longer my sister and you are dead to me." Elisa slammed the phone down and just sobbed.

Her body was racking with sobs as she sat on the couch. She put her hands over her face. She could not believe that her own flesh and blood would not even come back to give their mother her last wish, to have both of her daughters there when she died, and tell Cara her final words, hoping for Cara to forgive her.

Mattie died knowing Cara hated her, blamed her for their father leaving and could never forgive her. Elisa knew their mother died sad but at least she did not die alone, Elisa made sure of that. It was raining the day of the funeral as Elisa stood there only hearing half of what the preacher was saying. True to her word, Elisa never called her sister Cara about the funeral and Cara made no attempt to come or call.

The last time her and Elisa spoke was the day that Elisa slammed the phone down and told Cara she was dead to her. That was five years ago. Before her mother died, Mattie had given Elisa a letter for each of her daughters. Elisa still has them locked away to this day. Every once in a while she would get hers out and read it. She would begin sobbing all over again. Cara would never know her mother's final words nor did she deserve to.

Elisa put her briefcase on the table at work. Her fellow designers, her photographer Carl Drixel, and her assistant Sissy Epson were there. Sissy and Elisa had worked together, Elisa made Sissy her assistant when she became Chief Editor. Elisa knew Sissy was dedicated, hardworking and efficient, and Sissy was happy to be Elisa's assistant. Elisa sat down and began to speak. "I will be going over the third quarter profits. The last two quarterly profits were good, but I think we can do better. So far, the fall fashions for Pose magazine have propelled us. Next, we have a spring fashion show in Paris coming up in April and we need to get down to business on that.

"We need to come up with a theme, and I of course will have the final say. You designers will show me your work and from there I decide what fashions would be fitting of the spring show in Paris. Whomever designs I choose to use will accompany me along with my assistant Sissy here to Paris in April."

Brian Drugan, one of her designers for Pose Magazine, had accompanied her to London last fall for their fall show. He was hoping that he could accompany her to the spring show this April.

"Of course, you know that is only seven months away so

you all better get busy. We must continue to stay on top of our competitors and make this spring show the best, and even better than the last. I want this show to be talked about in the fashion world for months and even years to come. It is the middle of September; you have until the middle of October to get your designs into me."

She was flipping a pen around in her hand. Ellie Drisk was another designer and wanted to go to Paris in April. She worked hard last year for the fall show but was beaten out by Brian. "Carl Drixel, you will of course be responsible for the photo shoots and seeing that they are done." Carl shook his head in response. "Are there any questions?" Elisa asked as she looked around the room.

They all shook their heads no. "Well if that is all and there are no questions, then this meeting is adjourned. You all can get back to work now, start on the designs that you all have a month to show me. They all get up to leave."

Their theme for the fall show in London was Autumn Elegance and Fun. Everything had gone well and Elisa was very pleased. As Elisa was gathering up her belongings, her cell phone rang. Her employees knew better than to call her on her cell phone unless it was of the utmost importance. She answered it impatiently wondering who it could be.

"Hello," she said hastily. "Now is that anyway to treat an old friend?" It was Guy Drakes, the man she met at the London fashion show last year and she had been seeing occasionally. She had not heard from him in a while, so she was surprised. Elisa was not the one who had time for a relationship and to give all her time to a man; she was married to her career she so ardently pursued.

Guy Drakes had dark hair and stunning hazel eyes, he was bold, and handsome. He owned all the Drakes Jewelry stores around the world and provided the jewelry to the models. He and Elisa had spent many nights together in London. He was busy with the fashion shows, traveling around the world, and checking up on his business. He was one of Forbes top ten. Guy had racked in billions for his business. He was savvy.

"I am sorry Guy, but you know better than to call me when I am working. When I am at work I concentrate on that." Elisa was heading back to her office.

"Forgive me my Mon Cherie, but I am back in New York and was wondering if you would like to have dinner with me tonight?"

She had much rather just planned on spending the evening at her townhouse and snuggling up to a nice dinner by her chef Emilio and diving into her work. She had been working diligently night after night and it had paid off. She got back to her office and shut the door. When she did not answer, Guy spoke again.

"Well my Mon Cherie," he started calling her that in London. Guy had been married twice before and had many mistresses and Elisa knew that. She did not want a commitment and Guy said he would never marry again. She knew she was stepping in dangerous waters with him, but he was great in bed and when they were together, she had to admit, she had a great time.

"Yes Guy, I will have dinner with you. What did you have in mind?" Elisa sat down and looked out at her window in her office.

"I want it to be a surprise. So wear your best, I know you always do. You did in London." Guy said with sexiness in his voice. "I was wondering my Mon Cherie, I would like to take you on my private plane to the Greek Isles and then on my yacht. How does that sound."

"Very enticing," Elisa said with a modest tone to her voice. "But I have a lot of work and I have a fashion show in Paris coming up in seven months. I have my designers and my photographer working profusely on this. I cannot just up and leave for a weekend."

"Yes you can Elisa," Guy said. "We had a great time in London and you were able to leave your work for a while and enjoy all of what London and I," he laughed mischievously, "had to offer." Elisa knew he was right. She had such a good time in London. "You can tell me tonight at dinner and I will have my plane fueled up and ready to go if you decide you want to do this. Okay my Mon Cherie."

Elisa put her hand to her forehead and told him, "okay."

"Good it is settled then. I will pick you up at your townhouse at seven thirty. I have missed you Elisa and I look forward to seeing you tonight." He could be so vivacious and coy at the same time.

"Me too, I will see you at seven thirty." Elisa hung up the phone. She delved into her work as she tried to put Guy out of her mind. She called her assistant Sissy into her office.

"Yes Miss Drinnings," Sissy was cute with an "I love Lucy" attitude. She had been a dedicated assistant to Elisa.

"Hold my calls; I will be busy for the rest of the afternoon going over these pictures for the winter collection before I give my approval."

"Yes Miss Drinnings." Sissy said.

"I will have a decision by the end of the day on this." Sissy nodded her head and shut the door. For the rest of the afternoon Elisa fervently approved and disapproved things.

She called her photographer, Carl Drixel, into her office. "You called me Miss Drinnings." She looked up from the layouts. Her employees were to only call her by her last name. "Yes Carl, I have these ready," he walked over to her desk and she handed him her approved layouts for the winter collection of Pose Magazine. "I want this started on ASAP and even if you have to work nights and weekends. This must be done soon."

"Yes Miss Drinnings. I will get right on them." Carl said grabbing the layouts for the winter layout.

"Good Carl, our competitors have already pushed their publishing of their winter line. I want to astound people with ours."

"You know how to do that Miss Drinnings," Carl smiled. Elisa kept her business face. She was not amused by her employees coddling her with kiss ass remarks. She had no use for them. Carl took that look and left. After he shut the door, Elisa picked up her things and headed out of her office.

Many were still busy working and would be burning the "midnight oil." They all waved goodbye to Elisa and she waved back. She smiled at knowing her crew was doing everything they could to make Pose Magazine a huge success and keep it that way. She had to decline many who walked through the doors of Pose Magazine looking for a job.

She conducted the interviews and colleges who would send recruits to her. Even the colleges knew she wanted nothing less than the best. They would send their most prestigious designers to her. But Elisa had the final say in who got hired.

She walked outside. It was still sunny and warm. Her chauffeur was waiting. She ignored the man on the sidewalk. She got in, she wondered to herself how could people just beg off of other people and try not to even better their lives or work for what they want.

This was New York and she had seen her share of homeless people on the streets. She paid no attention to them. It was not her place to try and save every living soul, or provide for them. She had grown up with a hard life and worked her way up to success. America was the land of opportunity and she seized upon it, why couldn't they?

The car pulled away from the curb as the man standing there with the tin can in his hand looked on.

CHAPTER 2

Kyle Rimmer looked down into his can. Well, he thought, not bad for a day's work. He would go and get something to eat, and feed the birds in Central Park before heading back to spend the night in his usual spot under the bridge.

He had been in the military and knew how to survive. He had survived two tours in Afghanistan before heading back to the states for good. What he saw over there could mess anyone up. He was medically released from the military.

Surviving a shot to the head, he lost some of his vision and was unable to work. He would wake up many mornings with headaches and sometimes even migraines. However, he did not have the insurance to see a doctor. He had come back to New York to find his wife gone. She had cleaned out his savings and left him with nothing. She had left a note and divorce papers for when he arrived home from the war. She had run off with his best friend.

After his time in the hospital, and after his release, he had made his home on the streets of New York. Many people just walked by and did not give him a second glance; many would put money in his tin can to get him through another day.

He would sleep under the bridge and then find a street to make his money. He survived sleeping in the cold desert nights by his jeep with the clothes on his back and his gun to his side. He would wake up in the hot Afghanistan weather to be ready for his mission.

He would trudge up mountains in pursuit of the Taliban. He never complained, for he knew what he had signed up for. While many Americans back home were either sleeping in their warm beds, sitting at the dinner table ready to eat a hot meal, going on vacation, or having a family night, Kyle would be deep in the heart of Afghanistan fighting, and protecting the very freedoms that so many of us take for granted.

He had served his country and hell is what he had come back to. It was not fair, but Kyle made the best of what he had left. He headed to pick him up a few cheeseburgers and a shake. He had been craving that all day. He asked the waitress for some extra buns that they would just throw out. He said he would pay for them.

She was a kindly woman in her mid-sixties and just gave him the bread. She had seen him many times and felt sorry for him. He had told her his story and she had thanked him for his service and there would be tears coming from her eyes.

"Thank you ma'am, for the bread, now the birds will eat again." Kyle said kindly.

"You're welcome my dear." Mildred Hirth smiled through her grandma glasses. Mildred took the tips she had made today and gave some to Kyle.

"I do not want your tips Mildred. You worked hard for those." Kyle said his eyes watering.

"Not near what you have worked Kyle to protect our freedoms. What you have done for us is priceless." She put the money in his hand. Mildred had never married and had no family. She lived in a tiny one bedroom apartment upstairs from the hamburger shop.

"Have a nice evening, Mildred," Kyle hugged her.

"You too dear Kyle, I love you as my son." Kyle was thirty-nine and Mildred had loved him like a son. There were times when Mildred and Kyle would talk after Mildred's shift.

Mildred watched him walk out the door and back to where he would be spending another night. Her heart ached for him and wished that he could have a better life than the one he was handed.

Kyle sat down on the bench and started feeding the birds. He tried not to ponder on how his life ended up like this. He just spent every day doing the best he could to survive.

Elisa was finishing her bath and was getting dressed for her date with Guy Drakes. She had chosen an off the shoulder cocktail dress that accentuated her features and figure. It was red and had a slit clean up to her hip on her left side. She had worn the necklace, earrings and bracelet that Guy had given her from his store when they met in London.

She had her auburn hair swept up and donned with sparkling jeweled hair pins; also a gift from Guy. She wore her satin high heels and did her make up that made her violet eyes stand out more. She put on her expensive perfume that she got while in London. She took a once over in her full length mirror and was satisfied with the results.

Her housekeeper hollered up that Mr. Drakes was here to see her. "Thank you Cora, I will be down." Elisa grabbed her diamond studded hand bag and headed down the steps. Guy had his back turned, looking through the Pose magazines on her table in the hall.

He turned around as she came down. "My oh my," Guy said, "You look like an Audrey Hepburn or a Bettie Davis, no my Mon Cherie, you look better than them." Elisa smiled feeling herself being subdued by warmth. Guy grabbed her hand and kissed it. "Shall we, I have made reservations at New York's finest restaurant; nothing but the best for my Cherie."

Cora bid them farewell and would lock up when she was done. Guy and Elisa walked out into the cool night air to the limousine waiting in front of her townhouse. "Your carriage awaits my dear." Guy opened the door for her and she slipped in. He got in beside her and they took off. The restaurant where he was taking Elisa knew Guy real well and would make him reservations at the last minute. Even if they were booked up, they would find a way to get him in.

They got to the restaurant and they were taken right to their table. It was Guy's usual spot where he took all his dates. It was cozy and private, away from the eyes of the other patrons. They sat down and Guy ordered from the waiter their most expensive bottle of wine. "So how are things going with work and you, my dear?" Guy took her hand and kissed it.

"Busy as usual, I have the spring show in Paris in seven months and I had a meeting with my staff. I told them to start with the designs for the spring line and from there I would pick whose was the best, and I would take them with me to Paris. I gave them a month to do it. I am having my photographer right now getting the winter magazine in gear. Otherwise, I am doing fine."

"You are such a workaholic my Cherie." Guy smiled not taking his eyes off of her.

"It is a competitive business, the fashion industry. Just as your jewelry business is competitive against other jewelry stores." Elisa told him taking a sip of her wine.

"You are right on that my dear, but I also take the time to enjoy what free time I do have." The waiter came back and asked if they were ready to order. Elisa ordered the duck with wine sauce, the mixed vegetables, and a salad. Guy ordered his usual of lamb rare with very little mint sauce, caviar and asparagus. The waiter took their order and left.

"Well, my free time" Elisa said swirling her wine in her glass, "is spent looking at photo shoots and designs. I did not get to be Chief Editor of Pose Magazine by taking numerous vacations, being a wallflower on the wall, not keeping my opinions to myself. I am a go getter, I am a perfectionist, I do not take anything less than the very best, and I keep up with the fashion industry and what my competition is doing. When I am at work, I do not partake in pleasure mixing with business. I do not placate my competitors and I do not allow failure."

"I am sorry my Cherie, I did not mean to espouse that hard work does not pay off or make you successful, quite the contrary."

"No, you are right Guy," Elisa interrupted him, "I do engross myself in my work, but I had to grow up fast and realized that if you want to make it in this world you have to be aggressive and cut throat. My father walked out on my mother and left her to raise two girls alone and work two jobs. I vowed that I would not become like that.

"I made a promise to myself that I would go out and pursue my dreams of fashion and not let anything hold me back. I would always read fashion magazines and see the clothes that I wish I could have, or the kind of clothes that I could design that would one day make a mark on the fashion world, and models would wear down the runway. I accomplished all that Guy and then I went into the business aspect of design and here I am."

The waiter brought their food. They started eating. "My grandfather started the jewelry business, well in truth," Guy said between bites, "is that my grandfather was a jewelry designer, he could take any metal whether it was gold, silver, copper, and make the most beautiful jewelry that anybody could want. He passed that along to my father before he died, and when my father died, he had passed that along to me, but I never went into the design aspect of it. I learned everything about jewelry and how to run a jewelry business from them. They taught me everything I know. I hired only the best jewelry makers from around the world to make my jewelry. I have managers who run each store, but I am the overseer of them all. Nothing goes into my store without me inspecting it first, and making sure it is nothing but the best. So, like you Elisa, I run a tight business."

"I too make sure that only the best designs are picked for my magazine and nothing gets approved without my say." Elisa added.

"So I would say that you and I are a lot alike in so many ways," Guy smiled.

"Hmm, I guess we are," Elisa reiterated.

"Though, I want to ask you again if you would like to go to the Greek Isles with me. We would leave Friday and I would have you back in plenty of time for work Monday. We could sail on my yacht, make love and do some sightseeing, though making love may take away from a lot of that sightseeing," Guy smiled mischievously.

Elisa sighed; she had not taken a vacation in such a long time because of her career. She was contemplating it. It sounded scrumptious. "Please, Elisa my dear," Guy said when he saw her being reserved about it. "Just these two days. I will have my private plane all fueled up and we can be there in no time. It is faster than the Concorde."

He took her hands in his. "I want to spend this weekend with you before I have to go to San Francisco to take care of some business with my store there. I promise I will have you back in plenty of time for your work." How could she refuse, he was making an offer any woman in her right mind could not refuse. She contemplated it some more before saying,

"Okay, but you better have me back before Monday so I can be back at work." Elisa implied, pointing her fork at Guy while half smiling.

"Oh thank you my Mon Cherie. You have made me a very happy man." They finished their dinner and the waiter asked them if they would like anything else, like dessert. They said no and the waiter gave them their bill and took their plates. Guy left the money; with a generous tip for the waiter.

They headed back out to Elisa's townhouse.

⸺⸙⸺

Kyle Rimmer lay under the Central Park Bridge looking up at the sky. His thoughts running back to his tour in Afghanistan and before his ex-wife left him. It was a beautiful night. He thought of the beautiful woman who had just glanced at him coming out of her office building. She looked at him, disgusted. He wondered what she was doing now in her high priced fancy world.

He knew he could never be a part of her world. Getting with someone like her was harder than climbing the mountains of Afghanistan. He fell asleep, his thoughts running rampant through his mind.

⸺⸙⸺

Elisa and Guy got back to her townhouse and Cora as always, had everything locked up and tidy just the way Elisa liked it. Guy carried Elisa up to her bedroom and they ravished each other as if this night for them would be their last on earth. He undressed her and she undressed him. He kissed her throat and she held her head back.

He took the hairpins that were holding her hair up out and let her hair fall down. "You are so beautiful Elisa, I have missed you terribly. Those nights in London were spectacular." Guy said, breathing hard.

"Yes they were," Elisa mumbled into his hair.

He lay on top of her on the bed. He grabbed her breast in his hands and started kissing them. He moved his head down to her stomach and touched her navel with his tongue. Elisa moaned. It had been a while since she had a man's touch and felt his lips on her. He moved his tongue down to the V-shape of her womanhood. He grabbed her hips and brought her to him.

The moonlight was peeking into Elisa's window, emanating light into the room. Their bodies were moist with perspiration. The moonlight made their love making all that more romantic. It was shining on Elisa's auburn hair, giving it the glow of diamonds. Guy took his hand and ran in through her hair. Her violet eyes sparkled in the moonlight as she looked at him.

"I am a lucky man to have such a beautiful and lovely woman in my arms. You are the most beautiful woman I have ever seen." She took him passionately with her lips and she felt his hardness against her. He lifted her up to him and she wrapped her legs around him. He entered her with all the might of a jackhammer being forced into the concrete.

Elisa cried out. Their heavy breathing and the racing of their hearts could be heard. It was ecstasy that could tremble the very walls of Elisa's townhouse. They both climaxed and lay spent on her bed. Guy rubbed his hand on her cheek, "thank you, my Mon Cherie for giving me this night and for giving me the weekend to let me do this more often for you by taking you to the Greek Isles."

He slid his finger to her lips and she kissed them. She could not let herself get attached to this man. She vowed that her life and her commitment were to her career. He was a very charismatic and handsome man that any woman would be lucky to have, but like in the past with others who had come before Guy, she could not let herself fall in love and take her away from all that she had worked so hard to acquire.

"You're welcome my dear. You have given me much pleasure" Elisa whispered.

"I do my best," Guy said kissing her eyes, her nose and then her lips. Once again, these sensual feelings of touch, reinvigorated Elisa and they continued to make love through the night.

Chapter 3

"We are coming under heavy fire," one soldier says. Kyle was hunkered down behind a rock on the mountain. It had been an intense firefight with the Taliban. "KYLE!", his friend Garrett yelled, "You okay?"

"Yes sir I am," Kyle shouted back. They were in the mountains of Tora Bora. They had gotten word that the leader of Al-Qaeda was hiding there.

They trudged up the mountains like the Vietnam Veterans trudged Hamburger Hill. Kyle's good military friend Brett had been shot. He was bleeding profusely. Kyle had gotten up and started firing again while managing to get to his friend Brett.

"Come on man, you have got to survive. Don't leave me man." Kyle held Brett crying.

Brett looked up at Kyle and grabbed onto his arm. In Brett's choking words, he told Kyle, "Please, tell my wife Ellie that I love her. Tell my daughter Dolly that I love her."

"No man, you're not going to die, not like this man," Kyle cried. "We are going to get out of this and grow old. We are going to hang out together and share stories our kids can meet and be friends." At that time, Kyle did not know that he would never have kids with his wife.

"I am not going to get out of this alive," Brett choked, coughing up blood. "You have to promise me that you will tell my wife and child what I have asked you. Please, give my wife this letter and my daughter my dog tags, I want her to know that her father died with honor and courage. That he died defending her freedoms and to always remember that you have to fight for what you believe in." Brett took his dog tags off and handed them to Kyle and pulled a letter he had written out of his pocket and handed them to Kyle.

Kyle started shaking Brett, "No man no please." Brett took his last breath and died. Kyle held on to him tightly until he heard Garrett hollering at him.

"Hey man the choppers are here firing on the Taliban." The Taliban had fled and they airlifted the men out of there. They took Brett's body and loaded it on the chopper. Kyle stayed right beside him with his hand over Brett's. Kyle looked down at the mountains where the firefight had ensued. It was a battle he would never forget.

Kyle woke up sweating and breathing hard. The sun was just coming up. He sat up and put his hands over his face and rubbed it. He went over to the water and washed himself up. He ate the rest of his dinner from last night and headed to his usual spot for another day of collecting.

≈≈≈⊹≈≈≈

Elisa woke up and saw that the clock read six thirty a.m. "Oh my gosh I have to get up and get a shower and head to the office." She jumped out of bed waking up Guy.

He turned over. "Well good morning to you too my Mon Cherie." He smiled.

"I have to be at the office at eight and I need to get ready."

Guy leaned up and pulled the sheets away from him and got up to get dressed. Elisa could have jumped back into bed with him and made love again but duty called. Guy pulled on his pants and put his shirt on and was buttoning it up. "So will you have dinner with me again tonight Elisa or even lunch today?" Guy asked.

"Not tonight, I want to stay home and go over some reports." She was going over their quarterly reports for the magazine. "I am so busy that I may just skip lunch all together." She went into the bathroom and closed the door. He could hear the water running in the shower.

He walked over to the bathroom door and opened it. He walked in. He could see through the shower glass Elisa's toned and sumptuous body. He took off his clothes and stepped in. Elisa turned around, "Guy, what are you doing?"

"Taking a shower with you Elisa," he grabbed her and they made love in the shower.

⊷❖⊷

Elisa got to the office with her coffee and bagel precisely at eight a.m. She had seen the same man again that she saw yesterday leaving her office out on the sidewalk holding that same stupid can again, begging for money. He looked at her and she turned away in disgust. He had attempted to say "Hello" to her but she ignored him and went into the building.

She wished that he would find another sidewalk to do his begging of society. As usual, she was dressed to the nine and alert. Guy had left her townhouse and said he would see her Friday to take her to the Greek Isles. It was Wednesday today and tomorrow she was working diligently to be able to take the rendezvous with Guy.

No sooner did she get into her office when her photographer, Carl Drixel, knocked on her door. "Come in," Elisa said. She was sitting at her desk and was about to call her assistant to bring her in the quarterly reports. Carl opened the door and came in, Elisa looked up. "Yes, Carl" He hated to disturb her, but this was urgent and she would not like it.

"Um, Miss Drinnings, I am not sure how to tel--," Carl began but Elisa interrupted him.

"Just get to it Carl, I am going to be up to my neck in reports. Sit down." Her stern voice commanded that he do so and so he did.

"We have a problem Miss Drinnings," Carl was nervous and looking down at this hands.

"What problem is that Carl?" This is not what Elisa wanted to hear.

"Getting the winter edition of Pose Magazine is going to be late." Carl was rubbing his hands.

"Why is that?" Elisa asked sternly.

"You have the layouts I gave you so what is the problem? I

want that winter edition of Pose Magazine on my desk before let me say, winter. So whatever problem you have you need to resolve it and soon."

She threw her pen down and sat back. "Carl do you realize that in the fashion world not only is how you present your work important, but also timing is everything as well if you want to overcome your competition?" Elisa was sitting upright and rigid.

"Yes Miss Drinnings, but--," Elisa interrupted him again.

"Then you will find a way to get this winter magazine done in the time I have specified. I do not care if you have to work 24/7 on this.

I know you value your job Mr. Drixel, and I value Pose Magazine as the leader in the fashion world, what people will be talking about, and girls who want to model for Pose Magazine. Now, I trust you will have this done in the time that I have allotted you, Mr. Drixel, or I will just have to do some rearranging. Do we have an understanding?" Carl knew what she meant by rearranging. "Tell those publishers of Pose Magazine that too."

Elisa leaned forward and put her hands together. "Yes Miss Drinnings we have an understanding. I will be working around the clock to get this finished in time."

"Good Mr. Drixel, now if there is nothing left to discuss, then this meeting is adjourned." "Yes Miss Drinnings."

As Carl got up to leave, Elisa said again, "Timing is everything Mr. Drixel. Always remember that."

He shook his head yes and left her office. Elisa called her assistant in and told her she needed the third quarterly report. Her assistant got right on that. Elisa got up with her coffee in her hand and looked out her office window. She could see the guy that she saw coming into work. They lived in two different worlds and she wanted to keep it that way.

Her assistant knocked on the door and Elisa turned around. "Here are the reports that you asked for Miss Drinnings." Sissy said.

"Thank you Sissy, put them on my desk."

Sissy did as Elisa asked her. "Is there anything else I can do for you Miss Drinnings?" Sissy asked her.

"Yes there is," Elisa walked over and opened up her Louis Vuitton purse. She pulled out her pocketbook a one hundred dollar bill.

"Give this to the man on the street out there. Don't tell him who it is from, but ask him to please remove himself from the sidewalk and use another one."

"Who are we talking about Miss Drinnings?" Sissy was confused.

"Come here Sissy and I will show you." Sissy walked over to where Elisa was standing. She looked out the window. "See that man down there standing with that dirty plaid shirt on and jeans holding out a tin can?" Elisa asked her.

"Yes Miss Drinnings." Sissy answered her.

"That is the guy." Elisa handed Sissy the one hundred dollar bill.

Sissy took it. "I will do it Miss Drinnings."

"Good Sissy. I always know I can count on you." Elisa took another sip of her coffee. She had hoped this would work. A hundred dollars to a homeless man could seem like a million. She just hoped it would feel like it to him and do the job. Sissy walked out of the office. Elisa sat down and went straight to work.

⊰⧉⊱

Sissy walked out of the building and up to the man that Elisa had pointed out to her. "Excuse me sir," Sissy said. Kyle turned around and stared into the face of a curly haired blonde woman with what looked like a one hundred dollar bill in her hand.

"What?" Kyle asked her.

"I was told to give you this." Sissy put her arm out to give Kyle the one hundred dollar bill.

"By who were you asked to give me this?" Kyle asked her.

"I was told not to say who it was, but they would like for you to take this and move to another sidewalk and off of this one."

Kyle was furious. "Well, you tell whoever gave you that

one hundred dollar bill to tell me themselves. Until then, I will stay on this public sidewalk." Kyle said defiantly. "They cannot push me off of here just like I was some stray dog."

Sissy wasn't sure what to say to him or to Elisa for him refusing it. "Take it sir; I am sure that you could use it. I mean a hundred dollars to someone like yourself could get you through for a while. Maybe get yourself a hotel room, new clothes, or anything else."

"I am not taking it ma'am. If it were out of the kindness of their heart, if they even have one, then I would. But this, this is to try and get me off this sidewalk, a public sidewalk that I have fought for so people could walk on it, is insulting."

Sissy was not sure what he meant by fighting for this sidewalk, but she saw that he was not going to take the money. "Well then, I shall be going back to work. I will leave you to do whatever it is you do." Sissy piped.

"Good then," Kyle said angrily. "Continue with your work and I will continue with mine." Kyle turned his back to her and she walked back into the building still holding Elisa's money. Elisa was concentrating hard on the reports when Sissy knocked on her door.

"Come in please," Sissy walked in and Elisa was still looking at the paperwork on her desk.

"Miss Drinnings," Sissy said, "he would not take the money, he said he felt insulted." Elisa sighed and looked up at Sissy.

"How did he feel insulted?" Elisa asked almost with a laugh.

"Well I told him, without giving your name of course, to give you this one hundred dollar bill and to remove yourself from this sidewalk." Sissy said.

"And what was his comment to that Sissy?" Elisa asked.

"He said to tell whoever gave you that money to tell him yourself and that he will stay on this sidewalk. That it was a public sidewalk and one he had fought for so people could walk on it. I am not sure what he meant by that."

"Me neither," Elisa retorted. "I told him that it could get you a hotel room, more clothes, or anything else. He said if it were out of the kindness of their heart then he would. He said they are not going to kick him off as if he were some stray dog. So I told him that I would continue my work. And he said good and he would continue his work."

Elisa laughed hard. "Not only is he homeless, but he is a stubborn ass homeless man. What he would call work is not work; it is begging and taking advantage of us who do actually work for a living. He would not know what work was if it came and bit him in the ass. Maybe he is not really homeless, but he just does this to make people feel sorry for him. What a shame. What if he actually has a nice place somewhere here in Manhattan?"

"That could be true," Sissy said in response.

"Well thank you anyway Sissy, I will be busy for the rest of the day so hold my calls. I am not going to leave the office for lunch so could you order me some Chinese from that Chinese place in Soho?" Elisa asked Sissy.

"Sure Miss Drinnings. What time would you like me to order it?" Sissy had given Elisa back the one hundred dollar bill.

"Order it about one o'clock Sissy." Sissy was about ready to go. "Wait a minute Sissy," Sissy turned back around to face Elisa.

"Take this one hundred dollar bill that that stubborn pig on the sidewalk would not take and buy you some lunch too. Just give me back the change." Elisa handed her back the money.

"Oh thank you Miss Drinnings, I certainly will." Sissy took the money, in all the time that Sissy had worked for Elisa; she could count the number of times on one hand that Elisa bought lunch for her workers.

Sissy did not want to look a gift horse in the mouth. Sissy left the office. Elisa walked back over to the window to stare down at the man on the sidewalk. She could have sworn he was looking up at her. Elisa thought, *What a loser, people do not know generosity when they see it.* She went back to work.

Kyle had looked up at Elisa from where he stood. He could have sworn she was the one who sent the curly blonde haired lady down to give him the money and ask him to leave the sidewalk. Well, he would not give her that benefit. It was just as much his sidewalk as hers. Even if she came down herself and tried to give him the money and asked him to leave, he would still refuse.

He was not going to let some hot-headed, beautiful, high society woman wield her power over him. Someday he would show her. To him, she was as heartless as she was beautiful. The only question was, would that someday come when he could show her?

Chapter 4

Elisa was so engrossed in her reports, that she did not realize that it was late when she looked at her watch. She had gone over the quarterly reports until she could no longer see straight. According to the reports, the magazine was again doing well.

She put the reports away and got up to leave. She walked over to the window and did not see the man on the sidewalk. *Good she thought I do not have to see him or deal with him tonight.* She was tired and she had called her cook Emilio to have her dinner ready when she got home. She told him that she did not know how late she would be working. Emilio told her that he would have her dinner ready for her and leave it warming for her.

Cora said, when Elisa was ready, she would draw her a hot bubble bath. Elisa loved Emilio and Cora, they were good workers. Elisa had put an ad in the paper for a housekeeper and she had interviewed many different ones until she found Cora. She gave Cora a probation period and had been happy with Cora so she kept her on.

Emilio and his family had immigrated to America when he was nine from Guatemala. His mother had taught him to cook as a young boy. He had been looking for work as a cook when he responded to an ad in the paper by Elisa. She had interviewed him and let him cook for her. He had made her many of his family's recipe dishes. She loved them and hired him.

She had given Emilio an offer that he could not refuse. She and Emilio had become good friends along with her and Cora. She gathered up her belongings and left her office. Elisa's

driver was outside waiting on her when she walked out. It was
a beautiful night. She headed home after a long day.

⊰⊹⊱✽⊰⊹⊱

Kyle had gone back to his usual spot, feeding the birds.
It had become a daily routine besides being on the streets
collecting money to get him through another day. Mildred had
given him his dinner and they talked for a little bit. He had left
before the woman came out of her office. He tried not to think
about the blonde haired lady trying to give him the hundred
dollar bill or the woman who had ignored him the other day.

It was just as much his sidewalk to be on as it was hers.
He wanted so much to just walk into her office and give her a
piece of his mind, but she wouldn't listen and would have him
thrown out of her office by security. I am sure she had security
all over that place. He would stay on that sidewalk and if she
confronted him he would be ready to give her a piece of his
mind.

He got up to walk back to his spot under the bridge. The sun
was low in the sky and he wanted to get some sleep. He wished
that he could work. He had spent several months in the hospital
after his injury. The government basically told him good job
and gave him a purple heart. He had tried to get disability and
the government said they would see to it that he got it. Kyle
kept after them and they said they would get to it. Kyle kept on
them and hounding them. They gave him the same old story.

He never got the money.

"Sorry sir," the lady said behind the counter. "We have no
papers stating that you receive disability pay. There is nothing
on file."

"I don't understand," Kyle said, "I served two tours in
Afghanistan, watched my buddy die, I was shot in the head,
underwent extensive surgery, and spent months in the hospital.
I lost some of my vision! The physician gave me documents
that I gave to the military putting me on permanent disability
so I could receive my pay." Kyle was furious.

"Look sir, I appreciate your service to our country, but

again, without the papers authorizing this, I cannot do anything else. My hands are tied." The lady responded. "You will need to call the proper person or people to explain this to them, and when I get those papers; we can start the disability payments."

"I have tried profusely and they keep giving me the run around." Kyle spat.

"Again sir, I am sorry, there is nothing I can do." The lady looked back to her computer. Kyle slammed his fist on the counter and walked away.

Kyle was dumbfounded; the country he had served was treating him like crap. He remembers hearing about the Vietnam Veterans coming home to nothing, being spit on, called baby killers, and many becoming homeless. He remembers hearing this from his dad before his parents died. His father had gotten real sick years after he came back from Vietnam. Kyle was sure it had something to do with his father being in the war in Vietnam, but the government denied it.

His mother died of a brain tumor before he graduated high school. He stayed with his grandparents. Kyle had received his parent's life insurance and used much of that to put himself through Culinary School. He had a good job and married his high school sweetheart.

After 9/11, he signed up for the Army, he went to basic training and after that, was shipped to Afghanistan. His wife Janice and his best friend saw him off, the money he had left over from the life insurance, he had put in Janice's name with her being his wife. She had full access to their accounts.

His best friend from high school, Jerry Lites, had been a Business Major and him and Kyle talked about opening up a restaurant in New York when Kyle got out of the military. Kyle would be the head chef and half owner of the restaurant and Jerry would be half owner as well.

Kyle gave his best friend a hug; he held his wife and gave her a long and loving kiss before he headed to Afghanistan. He had served eighteen months, and then came home for three months. Janice did not like what was being reported over there and wanted him out.

"I want you out." Janice said to him. "I want to start a family and it is hard to do when you're over there. We can only talk by email and a lot of times you cannot even tell me where you are or what you're doing." Janice cried.

"I am so sorry my love, but you knew this before I signed up. I cannot desert my fellow soldiers. I will serve another tour in Afghanistan, do my time, and I will not reenlist so we can start a family. I promise you okay."

Janice sighed. "I have nightmares Kyle. I cannot take this anymore. I want my husband back. I am tired of being lonely, tired of lonely nights."

"I know I know," Kyle hugged Janice. "I will return as soon as I can." Kyle was sent back to Afghanistan, two years this time. In those two years, Janice and Kyle's best friend Jerry were having an affair. Janice sent him an email telling him that she could no longer take this.

After his stay in the hospital, he was packing up to go home when he was given a letter by his commander and a manila envelope from his wife Janice. He opened it. With some of his vision gone, he had to hold it closer to him so he could read it enough to know what it said. It read this:

Dear Kyle,

By the time you read this, I will be gone. I am no longer in love with you. Jerry and I are in love now and we want to be together. I am tired of the lonely days and nights. I am tired of being so lonely. I need someone by me Kyle. I watch the news and hear what is going on over there. Jerry and I have been having an affair now for a year and we want to marry as soon as the divorce is final.

You will find the divorce papers in the manila envelope along with this letter. Please do not try and find me and try to get me back, I will not come back. It would be futile; anyway, I found out that Jerry and I are going to have a baby. It is the family that I have been wanting. Now I will have it. Jerry has gotten a good job and will provide for us.

I have sold the house and everything in it. I hope that someday you will understand. Jerry and I are happy now. Please let us be.

Goodbye,
Janice

Kyle just stood there. He could not believe what he was reading. While he was away fighting a war and recuperating after his injuries, his wife was having an affair with his best friend, having his best friend's baby, wanting a divorce, and sold their house. He wondered about the money he had left Janice in case something happened to him.

He would make a trip to the bank after leaving the hospital. He opened the manila envelope and looked over the papers. He was seeing them but still could not believe it. He had come home to losing his wife, his best friend, his home, and some of his sight.

He walked out of the hospital and got into a taxi. He told the taxi where to go. He went to the bank first to find out about the money. The teller just looked at him funny when he asked her about the life insurance money. She said he would have to talk with the head of that department.

He talked to the man. "I am so sorry sir," the man said. The man was a little older than Kyle and had red hair and brown eyes. "The account is empty. Your ex-wife withdrew the last of it."

"I don't understand sir," Kyle said in disbelief. "She was supposed to get that money if something happened to me. I am alive and well."

"Sir, you gave her power of attorney over everything. You gave her full access to the accounts.

Here is the form you signed." The man handed the paper to Kyle. Holding it close to him, he read the writing on the paper. The man was right; he had given Janice full power to his money. Kyle felt defeated.

"Thank you sir for your time," Kyle got up and left. He got

back into the taxi and told the taxi to take him to his old home. The taxi driver took off. They pulled up to his old house. Kyle got out. He told the taxi driver that he would be just a minute.

He walked up to the house. He could see the sold sign in the yard. He tried the door, but it was locked. He peeked through the windows; the house was empty just like his heart. The house that he had purchased with his wife Janice would belong to someone else. He had pictured someday that he would have a family with Janice and they would raise their kids here.

But that was never going to happen. His wife, his ex-wife now and his best friend had betrayed him. He felt that his whole world was crashing down on him. He walked back to the taxi and left the house for the last time and never looked back.

After his first tour, he had gone to Brett's home to give his wife and daughter what Brett had given to him in the mountains of Afghanistan. He had knocked on the door hoping that she would answer. He heard the lock click. She opened the door and looked straight into the face of Kyle. Ellie was a short woman with a heart shaped face.

She had shoulder length strawberry blonde hair and had a little girl in her arms. "Kyle, hello, come on in." Kyle stepped into the house. It was a nice and quaint house. He saw pictures of her and Brett; the wedding photos, his military photo, and a family portrait.

"Please, sit down," Ellie pointed to a chair. Kyle sat down. "Would you like anything to drink?" Ellie asked him.

"Coffee would be great Ellie." Kyle said. She sat Dolly, her daughter in her playpen. Kyle smiled at her and made faces. Dolly just looked at him and smiled. His heart broke again knowing he would not have a family of his own.

A few minutes later, Ellie Docker came out of the kitchen holding a tray. She sat it down on the coffee table. "I have some sugar and cream here for you Kyle." Ellie smiled.

"Thank you kindly Ellie."

When Ellie had been told that Brett was killed in Afghanistan, she was devastated. The military had made sure she got the money from Brett's life insurance.

Brett, before joining the military, had taken out a half a million dollar life insurance policy too. After Brett's death, Ellie received the money and put half of it away, she wanted Dolly to have college money. The rest of the money from the life insurance paid off the house and was enough to substantiate Ellie and Dolly.

"How are you my dear Kyle?" Ellie took a drink of her coffee.

"I am okay Ellie, thank you." He looked over and saw the American flag on Ellie's fireplace that was given to her at Brett's funeral. "I am on leave for three months, but I will have to go back for another tour. My wife Janice does not want me to, but I promised her after this tour I would not reenlist so we can start a family."

"I understand," Ellie responded. "I did not want Brett to go but he was determined. Dolly here was born before he left, so thankfully he got to see her born before he went over there. He talked about you all the time Kyle, in his emails to me. You and him became very close in basic training."

Kyle took a sip of his coffee. "Yes we did," Kyle replied. "He was a great man Ellie and an outstanding soldier. We both missed our wives and we talked about after we got out that we would stay in touch and share stories and our families could spend time together, but unfortunately he doesn't have that chance."

Ellie's eyes started watering. Kyle took her hand. "Your husband, Ellie, died a hero. He died defending freedom and doing what he wanted to do. He loved you and talked about you all the time about how much he missed you and Dolly. I was the only one who saw him cry whenever he talked about you two. He saved all your emails and pictures of Dolly.

"He could not believe how fast she was growing. He talked about all the things he would do as a father, he joked about her first date and how he would screen the man she would date," Ellie laughed at that. "He talked about her first prom, her going off to college, and walking her down the aisle." Kyle continued. "He wanted more kids."

"Yes, we had talked after his time in the military and after his release about having more kids," Ellie said, she sighed. Dolly was laughing. Ellie looked over at her and smiled. "She will never know her father, but I will talk about him to her and show her pictures of him when she gets older."

"Before I forget," Kyle said. Kyle took out the letter and dog tags that Brett had given him. "Brett said to tell you how much he loved you and Dolly and that he wanted Dolly to know that he died defending her freedoms and to always remember that you have to fight for what you believe in. He also said he wanted her to know that he died with honor and courage."

He handed Ellie the letter and dog tags. Ellie took them in her hand and started crying. Kyle hugged her. "I will tell her everything," Ellie said through her tears. Kyle stayed a little while longer; he held Dolly and kissed her goodbye and told that her father was a brave and good man. He put his hands on Ellie's shoulder and gave her a kiss on the forehead.

He left her house to head back home. He told Janice what he would be doing and Janice was fine with it. He called Ellie before going back to Afghanistan. Ellie told him to stay safe and come back home. He never spoke to her after that. Kyle had kept his promise to his friend Brett.

Ellie had sold the house that her and Brett lived in and moved away before Kyle came back from his second tour. It was better that way anyway; he did not want Ellie knowing how his life had changed. He was too embarrassed and he knew that Ellie had moved on. She did not need any more heartache or sadness.

He had given up on getting his disability money. It was futile he thought, just like Janice told him that it was futile for him to try and find her. She would not come back to him. He had not only been betrayed by the one woman he had loved since high school, he had been betrayed by the government that sent him to Afghanistan.

But Kyle would never regret serving in the military. He loved his country and knew his father would have been proud. Even if had to do it all over again, he still would have signed up in the military and gone over. He just never thought that he would lose everything.

He lay his head down to go to sleep that night. He looked up at the moon. The tears fell from his eyes. He had not cried since his friend Brett died and after he read the letter from his ex-wife.

Blocks away Elisa had enjoyed her nice cooked dinner and had soaked in her hot bubble bath that Cora had drawn for her. Elisa put on her silk chemise and got into her nice warm bed with freshly clean sheets that Cora had washed and put on for her.

Elisa had everything. Blocks away the man sleeping under the Central Park Bridge did not even cross her mind. Elisa slept soundly until the next morning.

CHAPTER 5

Elisa woke up. She had slept so soundly. She got up to take a shower and start her day again. She remembers when she was told that she would be the Chief Editor of Pose Magazine. Elisa had worked late nights while putting herself through college. After getting her degree in business management, Elisa started taking on more tasks. She had become Maggie Bench's (who was the former Chief Editor of Pose Magazine) assistant.

Maggie was hard to work for and demanded nothing less than perfection herself. She had given Elisa a hard time. Maggie had called Elisa into her office, which is now Elisa's.

"Come in," Maggie said in a deep voice. Maggie was a heavy smoker. Elisa opened the door and walked in. Maggie was sitting down with her hands folded across her lap. Even sitting down, Maggie could be intimidating. Her deep green eyes could penetrate right through you. She had dark hair. "Sit down please, Elisa." Elisa sat down as Maggie commanded.

"You are probably wondering why I called you in here." Maggie said lighting up a cigarette.

"Yes ma'am," Elisa said softly.

"I know I have given you a hard time Elisa and for your benefit," Maggie said puffing on her cigarette. "But I like you. You are a lot like me I have seen. I remember the day you came to Pose Magazine Elisa. You were like everyone else walking through that door.

You thought that you were the right person for the job. You thought that you were what Pose Magazine needed. I watched you and you are probably wondering why I gave you such a hard time." Maggie puffed on her cigarette again and looked at

Elisa with a smile.

"No ma'am, never," Elisa said shaking her head.

"You're lying Elisa." Maggie leaned up on her desk and snuffed out her cigarette. Elisa could not stand the smoke and the smell but said nothing. "I watched you for a long time. I liked your work, your designs. You were dedicated, and possessed a refined personality for fashion. You were a go-getter.

"That is why I gave you a hard time Elisa, to push you because I saw the determination you had for Pose or otherwise you would not have spent any late nights working. Plus, when I needed anything, you were there. That Sissy at the time, she did not know what she was doing and nothing about fashion, but you did Elisa. Sissy was not a go-getter like you Elisa.

"I wanted to push you to your full potential. You had an eye for fashion. I could tell that by what you wore and what you drew. Pose Magazine got great a review from your designs and that is when I really knew Elisa that you were what Pose Magazine needed. When you went to get your business degree in Fashion Merchandising and Marketing, I knew you wanted to go even farther.

"I don't give out these remarks lightly Elisa, but I know loyalty and dedication when I see it. I do not know about your past and I am not concerned with it. My concern is the continued success of Pose Magazine. I have been with Pose Magazine for over thirty years now and I, like you Elisa, did not let anything stand in my way of getting what I wanted and achieving success.

"I made you my assistant because of this." She got up and walked over to where Elisa was sitting. She sat down on the corner of the desk. Her demeanor was overwhelming. She looked straight into the eyes of Elisa and Elisa was almost sure she could read what was in them. "That is why after some long and tumultuous thinking, I am resigning from Pose Magazine as Chief Editor and I want someone with the capability and poise to run Pose Magazine and keep it successful.

Why am I resigning is not important, but what is important as I have stressed before is the continued success of Pose

Magazine and being the leader in the fashion world." She put her hand on Elisa's shoulder. "And you my dear, I am giving you the position of Chief Editor of Pose Magazine." Elisa could not believe what she was hearing. All her time here at Pose Magazine as a designer's assistant and now the assistant to the Chief Editor, it was what she had dreamed of.

She had proven herself a viable candidate in Maggie's eyes. Her hard work and dedication had paid off. She had stepped on some toes she knows, but she had gotten what she wanted. She had gotten what she felt she deserved.

"Thank you Maggie, but I am not sure what to say." Elisa was still absorbing this.

"I don't want a thank you Elisa," Maggie lit up another cigarette. "I want you to continue to keep Pose Magazine a success in the fashion world. I trust you. When I am out and I look through a Pose Magazine and listen to the fashion world, I want to see Pose Magazine still being the top fashion Magazine. Do you understand me Elisa?"

"Yes ma'am," Elisa said. "I will not let you down Miss Bench, I promise." Just like Elisa, Maggie wanted her workers to call her by her last name and not her first.

"Good, that is what I want to hear," Maggie said puffing on her cigarette and blowing out smoke rings. "Don't let my decision be wasted Elisa."

"I promise you Miss Bench you will be proud of me and I will keep Pose Magazine a success." Elisa said with confidence.

"Good to hear Elisa, even though I will no longer be working directly with Pose Magazine, I will be indirectly involved with Pose Magazine.

Any questions Elisa?" Maggie asked her.

"Yes, what about the others, will you tell them?"

"I will hold a meeting in my time Elisa, do not worry about that. I have made my decision and that is final. You need not worry. This meeting is adjourned Elisa. You may leave." Maggie sat back down.

"Yes Miss Bench." As Elisa walked to the door and put her hand on it to open it, she turned back around. "I promise you again Miss Bench; I will not let you down."

"I am sure you won't Elisa." Maggie answered. Elisa left.

When Maggie did finally have the meeting with the other Pose workers, she announced her resignation from Pose, but would continue to be indirectly involved with Pose Magazine. Sissy Epson was distraught and upset; she felt that she deserved that position, not Elisa. Elisa looked over at Sissy and could see the disappointment and distraught look in Sissy's face.

"Well if there are no questions," Maggie said. "Elisa here will be your new Chief Editor of Pose Magazine starting as of now." They all got up to leave. Sissy grabbed her things and walked out of the room. Elisa followed her.

"Sissy, Sissy," Elisa called after her. Elisa had liked working with Sissy, but now she would be Sissy's boss. Sissy had been there at Pose Magazine before Elisa.

"Sissy wait up please," Elisa was chasing after Sissy. Sissy stopped and turned around to face Elisa.

"What Elisa," Sissy said sternly. Elisa sensed the tension and hurt in Sissy's voice.

"I did not know that Maggie would choose me for the Chief Editor position Sissy, you have to believe me. She called me into her office and we had a long talk. She told me and I was ecstatic yes, I have worked hard for this position."

"So did I," Sissy said vehemently, "I was here a hell of a lot longer than you and I have worked my heart out too for Pose Magazine. I deserved that position. You took it away from me. I should have gotten it."

"Look Sissy," Elisa said, with consternation in her voice. "I got the position; Maggie obviously saw a lot of talent in me. My designs received great reviews for Pose Magazine. Some of us, Sissy are meant to go to the top while others are more suited for the bottom step of the ladder. I am your boss now, and if you don't like it, you can leave Pose Magazine anytime. Just leave your resignation on my desk and pack your things.

"My concern and always has been Sissy to keep Pose Magazine on top and a success. If you do not want to be a part of it, I say 'sayonara'. I know we have worked together, but I moved up the ladder and if that is a problem for you I don't care. What will it be Sissy?"

Sissy just stood there with her lips in a tight line. Elisa had cut her to the quick. Sissy loved Pose Magazine and was not about to leave. "I will not give you the benefit of the doubt of me leaving Elisa. Pose Magazine is my love just as much as it is yours and I care about it too and its success. I will work even harder Elisa much, much harder." Sissy said defiantly.

"Good Sissy," said Elisa. "That is what I like to hear. I was told that you did not know what you were doing on anything and nothing about fashion Sissy, but I beg to differ. I liked that you stood up to me and did not walk out of here and give me your resignation. That shows me Sissy that you love Pose Magazine and want to see it stay on top.

"I have worked with you Sissy. I know by working with you what you say is true, that is why I want to make you my assistant. You do not have to give me an answer now Sissy, but think about it and let me know." Elisa walked away leaving Sissy speechless and watching Elisa walk away, her eyes wide.

A week later, Sissy knocked on Elisa's office door, now saying Elisa Drinnings, Chief Editor. "Come in," Elisa said. Sissy walked in. Elisa was looking through some Pose Magazines. She looked up. "Oh Sissy hello, please sit down." Sissy did as she was told. "What is it Sissy?" Elisa asked her taking a sip of her coffee. She did not like to be interrupted from her work unless she called her workers in or it was of the utmost urgency.

"I have been thinking about what you asked me a week ago Miss Drinnings, and I would be honored to be your assistant and whenever you need me I will be there."

Elisa smiled. "Well Sissy, I am delighted that you took the offer. You were my first choice and I know when I need you, you will be there. You have proven that to me when we worked together. I expect nothing less from you Sissy."

"Is there anything else Sissy?" Elisa asked her.

"No Miss Drinnings, unless you need anything right now." Sissy said, standing up to walk out of the office.

"Not right now Sissy, but when I do, I will let you know." Sissy smiled and left the office. Elisa smiled to herself; this was her office now, the office that she had so long dreamed about, Chief Editor of a very successful fashion magazine, and it was just the beginning.

That was five years ago, after her mother passed away. Her mother would have been proud of Elisa had she lived to see it. Elisa had come a long way from Ohio to New York and there was no turning back. She took another sip of her coffee and got back to work.

⊸⊹⊹⊹⊷

Elisa got to work and did not see the man on the sidewalk. She got to her office and Carl came up to her. "Miss Drinnings, I wanted to let you know that everything is fine and that the winter edition of Pose will be out and on your desk next week."

Elisa turned to look at him, standing outside her office. "Good Carl, I will hold you to that. And if not, I will hold you personally responsible and you can kiss your job goodbye."

"Yes Miss Drinnings." Elisa smirked and walked into her office. She put her briefcase on the desk. She called Sissy into her office.

"Yes Miss Drinnings," Sissy smiled.

"I want to move the showing of some new designs from next week to today. Call and get that taken care of and get back to me. I want it for this afternoon." Elisa would go and look at new designs and give her opinions. Nothing was set until she was satisfied.

"Yes Miss Drinnings. I will get right on that."

Sissy left her office. Elisa looked out her office window and still did not see the man on the sidewalk. She got right to work.

⊸⊹⊹⊹⊷

Kyle Rimmer woke up with a massive and blinding migraine. Everything to him was blurry. It took him a while to get his eyes adjusted. He could swear his eyesight was getting worse. He felt sick to his stomach and his body was aching. He decided that today he would just stay under the bridge. He had enough food to get him through the day.

He sat there and ate looking around and hearing the birds. It was just him and nature. He remembers before his dad got sick that they would go to upstate New York and fish. His dad taught him to bait the hook and know when to pull on the line.

"Hey there boy, you're doing great now keep it steady. Reel it in. Now you're doing it." Kyle reeled in his line. He had what looked to him the biggest fish he ever saw. His dad got a hold of the fish and took it off the hook. "Good job Kyle. I am so proud of you. I love you son. We catch some more of this; we will have some good eatin'." Kyle smiled up at his dad.

After Kyle's father got sick and died, Kyle never went back to that lake. It was too painful. He did not have a boy of his own to take there. Kyle remembers holding his father's hand before he died. "I am proud of you son. Take care of your mother for me." Kyle's mother was standing in the bedroom crying. "Whatever you decide to do with your life Kyle, do it with honor, courage, and determination."

"I will make you proud of me dad. I promise."

"That's my boy." Kyle's father died that night. If only he could see Kyle now, he would be so disappointed. Kyle homeless, can't work, and living under a bridge begging for money from strangers. Oh yeah, his father would be so proud of him; a failed marriage too. He was glad that his father had not lived to see this.

Kyle had tears coming from his eyes. He remembers his father's funeral. It had been a military funeral with a 21 gun salute. He remembers the American flag on his father's casket and them folding it up giving it to his mother. Before she died, she had given it to him. When Janice left him, she took the flag. Kyle did not even have that.

He would hope when he died that he would get a military funeral but he did not hold his breath on that. If he could not get his disability from the military, why would he think that he would get a military funeral when he died? He was a homeless veteran who would remain this way and die without so much as a tombstone.

He closed his eyes again with the migraine still pounding his head.

Elisa had gotten the meeting moved to that afternoon. She was leaving her office. She was anxious to see the new designs. Anytime there was any new or aspiring designers, Elisa wanted to be the first one on the scene to see them and see if they were good enough for Pose Magazine and worthy of Pose Magazine.

She got outside and the lowly man was nowhere to be seen. She got into the car and told her chauffeur where to go. She rolled up the window as the car pulled away from the curb.

CHAPTER 6

Elisa got to the location. It was a studio building in downtown Manhattan. Elisa walked inside. From the looks of it, it looked like it was not only a makeshift design studio but someone's home as well. Sissy and the others were already there. Sissy walked up to Elisa. "I hope that I am not wasting my time Sissy." Elisa said dryly.

"Oh no," said Sissy. "Marco Shoops is an upcoming and talented designer. I already did the background check on this guy."

Elisa looked at Sissy with an amazed, but yet reserved expression. Sissy continued. "He graduated from the Art Institute of California and came to New York. His father, Martin Shoops, is a Hollywood producer."

"So," Elisa interrupted "what brought him here to New York?"

"Well, he wanted to get away from the Hollywood scene and do his own thing. His father wished that he had become a producer like him, but Marco wanted no part of that.

Instead, he started drawing his own designs in high school. After high school, he left for college and the designs he is going to show today have never been shown to anyone else." Sissy stopped to catch her breath.

"Why?" asked Elisa.

"That is the mystery I cannot quite solve, but" said Sissy putting her finger up, "if I had to guess, he was saving it for now.

By the way, he is handsome, but there is one thing," Sissy paused.

"And what is that?" Elisa asked her.

"He's gay."

Elisa looked at Sissy like that does not bother me. "One," Elisa said. "That has no bearing on whether he is a great designer or not and two, how in the hell did you come up with this conclusion about him, did you use to work for the CIA or something?" Elisa was perplexed.

Sissy laughed. "I talked to some people who knew him and went to school with him and got my resources and information from some of his previous lovers." Elisa had to admit she was impressed with Sissy. "Here, I got you a seat up front." Elisa followed Sissy to her seat. Elisa sat down and waited.

Marco walked out and Elisa had to admit, he was handsome, but the way he talked and moved his hands, Sissy was right about his sexual orientation, but Elisa was more concerned with his work than anything else. Pose Magazine was always in the business of looking for new designers but not all made it.

"I would like to start with my collection now and share with you my designs." Marco smiled. The women one by one walked out with Marco's designs on. Elisa just sat there and Marco was nervous, he saw Elisa looking at the designs. He was not sure how to read her. Sissy looked over at Elisa. She knew Elisa was contemplating.

One by one the models came out. Some with evening gowns on, some with sexy lingerie, some with that rugged but sexy cowgirl look, and some with casual looks. Elisa stood up. Sissy got up as well. After the models left, Elisa walked over to Marco. "Hello I am Elisa Drinnings."

Marco took Elisa's hand and said, "I am so honored to meet you, I have heard so much about Pose Magazine. I hope you liked the show," Marco was not sure how to address her.

"Call me Miss Drinnings," Elisa said.

"Okay Miss Drinnings."

"I will say I was quite impressed by your designs Mr. Shoops." Elisa stood with her hands down holding her hand bag.

"Oh please Miss Drinnings, you can call me Marco." Marco

put his hand up to his chest and laughed.

"Okay Marco, I will be in touch with you soon." Elisa turned away. Sissy followed. "Thank you for your time Miss Drinnings."

When they were outside the studio, Elisa's driver was already waiting. Sissy walked up to her. "Well," Sissy said.

"Well what Sissy," Elisa opened the door.

"Are you going to give him a chance? Is he Pose material?"

Elisa took a deep sigh. "I will give you my answer when I get back from the Greek Isles this weekend on Monday morning, okay Sissy."

"Oh my," Sissy said excitedly, "the Greek Isles. With who, that nice man you met in London last year? What is his name?" Sissy put her finger to her head.

"Guy Drakes Sissy, and yes, it is him. I will be going now Sissy. See you back at the office." Elisa got into the car and left.

Sissy was smiling to herself as she headed back to the office.

⟞⟞◦⟠◦⟜⟜

Kyle was at the restaurant having one of his hamburgers and talking with Mildred. His migraine had subsided. Mildred had given him some painkillers. Mildred was on her lunch break drinking her coffee. She had bought Kyle his lunch and was sitting with him. "Why don't you go and see a doctor about that migraine Kyle dear?" Mildred was being her kind motherly self to Kyle.

"I would Mildred, but I cannot afford a doctor. I have no insurance. Hell, I cannot even get my disability from the military." He took a drink of his coffee and finished up the rest of this sandwich. Mildred put her hand on his arm. "I wish there was more I could do Kyle, I could at least pay for the doctor to see you."

"No Mildred, I will not let you do that." Kyle said a little too sternly.

"Kyle it will not be a problem. I have some money in a jar I could give you. I have been saving it for a rainy day, and this is one of them."

Kyle was so touched by Mildred, but knew he could not take the money. She was not making much as a waitress there and many times she had bought him lunch there. She was struggling like the many more out there.

"No really Mildred, I am touched and appreciate it. You have done enough by listening to me and buying me lunch. You have been like a mother to me. And besides, I am sure it is nothing. People get migraines all the time." Kyle brushed it off with a wave of his hands.

Mildred knew that Kyle had gotten shot in the head while in Afghanistan and knew all about his recovery, his ex-wife leaving him with his best friend, and the fiasco of trying to get the disability. "Tell me Kyle, when did the migraines start and how often?" Mildred asked softly so no one else could hear.

"Well," Kyle put both hands up to his face. "They started out as headaches over the years. And as time went on, progressed into migraines, you know I got shot in the head over there."

"Are you sure they removed the entire bullet from your head Kyle?" Mildred asked.

"They said they did." Kyle never really asked himself that question.

"Do you know for sure Kyle? I mean they could have said they did." Mildred had a feeling that they didn't.

"With me not having any health insurance and being able to go to the doctor's and have tests ran, I am not sure, but they had me at Walter Reed Medical hospital. I was in there for months." Kyle took another sip of his coffee. "I never questioned it." Kyle looked over at the door and a couple of more people walked in. Mildred's eyes were watering and she took Kyle by the hands and squeezed them.

"There's this woman who works in the office building that I stand in front of. She looks at me as if I am nothing more than a cockroach to be squashed." Kyle turned back to Mildred. She was looking at him. "Please don't cry Mildred, I am taking care of myself."

"You do not deserve this Kyle but I know that sometimes life deals you a bad hand."

"Yes Mildred and you can take that bad hand and keep it or turn it around." Kyle remarked.

"Now," said Mildred, "I have ten minutes left on my lunch break. Tell me about this woman you mentioned." Kyle told her about how she had sent her assistant down to give him a hundred dollar bill to get him to get off the sidewalk and go to another one.

He told her how he had refused and told her to tell her boss to come down there and talk to him. He said he fought for the right of that sidewalk and he was not moving. He had just as much right as she did to be there. He told her about the clothes she wore; she had a driver, and was beautiful.

When Kyle was done, Mildred said, "People like her Kyle, with their high society ways, their money, and exuberant life also have to deal with life's hard problems. They may not have it as easy as you think. Not even with all the money in the world can those people cheat death or be free from hardships of life that we all face." Mildred got up. "Don't let her get to you Kyle; she is as human as you are."

"Yeah with a place to live, nice things, she doesn't have to sleep under a bridge, beg for money, and wonder where her next meal is going to come from or if she is going to have one," Kyle said angrily.

"Those are just material things Kyle; they are not the most important things in life." Mildred patted his arm and got back to work. Kyle sat thinking about Mildred's words.

She was wise. Her parents had lived through the great depression. She had no other family. She never married and yet she always seemed to not let life bring her down. He wishes that he could be more like Mildred. He got up and walked out the door.

⊷⊶⊷

It was Friday afternoon, the day that Elisa had anticipated. Elisa had left the office early to pack. Guy would be there in two hours to pick her up. She was going through her things packing. She figured she needed this time away. It would do her some good and she had never been to the Greek Isles. Hell, she had hardly ever given herself a vacation.

She had given Cora and Emilio the weekend off. She would not be here to eat and Emilio had wanted to go and spend time with his family for the weekend. Cora lived with her sister. She put on a pair of brown dress slacks, a cream colored silk blouse, and her jewelry to match that Guy had of course gotten her, a cream colored silk scarf to match the blouse, and her Prada shoes to match, and a handbag to match.

She was finishing packing when the doorbell rang. She looked at her watch, he is early she thought. She went downstairs to answer it; she opened the door and stood there in total shock. It wasn't who she was expecting. Standing in her doorway was the man from the sidewalk. "What in the hell are you doing here and how did you get my address?" Elisa said angrily.

"Well ma'am, umm you had lost this and I was just returning it." Kyle pulled out her pocketbook. She realized that her ID was in it and that was how he knew where she lived. She snatched it from his hands. She had not even realized that she had lost it. She had become so inundated with trying to get things together for this trip and making sure that everything was in order before she left the office. She started to look through it. "It is all there ma'am," Kyle said unaffected by it.

"I just want to make sure, I never know with you people. Your kind may try and do nice things while at the same time steal from us hard working people of society." Kyle just remained silent. She looked through it and everything was there. "You're lucky; I would have had to call the law on you." Elisa seethed.

"How did you get here anyway?" she asked him.

"I took a taxi here ma'am."

"I am surprised that you could afford one." She saw the taxi waiting outside her townhouse.

"This sure is a nice neighborhood." Kyle remarked.

"And it certainly has no room for the likes of you," Elisa spat. "Here," Elisa threw some money at him to pay for the taxi fare back to wherever it is he came from. "I do not want to see you here again. Now that you know where I live, I do not want you to be stalking me. You will take this money, pay for your fare, and never return here.

If you do, I will have you arrested." She slammed the door in his face.

Kyle just stood there looking down at the money and uttered under his breath, "you can be sure I will not be back here you ungrateful excuse for a human being who doesn't deserve what she has."

Kyle left the money there where Elisa had thrown it and walked back to the taxi. He looked back and saw her. I guess she wanted to make sure he left. He got into the taxi and headed back to what he called his home.

Elisa watched the taxi leave. When it was out of sight, she opened the door and saw the money that she had thrown at him earlier. She picked it up and held it in her hand staring at it. She shrugged her shoulders and shut the door. That was twice now he had refused her money when she offered it to him. For a homeless man, a man that was down on his luck, she could not understand it. *Oh well,* she thought. *I am not going to stand here and ponder on it. I have a wonderful weekend planned.* She went back upstairs to grab her things. She just hoped that he would not be back.

❈❈❈❈❈

Kyle on the ride home sat and thought about the events tonight. She was just as beautiful when he saw her tonight as she was the first time he saw her. She had a heart of ice but a beautiful face. He did not get even so much as a thank you tonight and then the audacity of her throwing that money at him like she was doing him a favor.

He would take the sleeping under the bridge over anything she offered. He told himself that he would not be back there. He had done a good deed and that was that. He remembered what Mildred had said just days before, that not all those things the rich has is important. They are just material things.

But sometimes, he wondered how it would feel to live in that world.

CHAPTER 7

Elisa had all of her things downstairs when she heard the doorbell again. She wondered if it was that wretched soul of a man again. This time before opening it, she peeked through the hole, it was Guy Drakes. Elisa breathed a sigh of relief. She opened the door and hugged him hard.

"Oh my Cherie, wow, I am so happy to see you too. I have missed you. How about I leave again and come back." Elisa released him and laughed. They kissed long and hard. "I am all packed and ready to go."

Guy looked at her things. "With all your stuff you would think that we were going for a month." Guy started grabbing her things to take out to the waiting limousine.

"A woman can never have too much stuff." Elisa smiled and grabbed her purse and another bag and they headed out. They got into the limousine and Guy opened a bottle of wine and poured each of them a glass.

"I did not tell you my Mon Cherie how beautiful you look, but then again, you always look beautiful even with no clothes on." Elisa threw her head back and put her hand on her chest and laughed that supercilious laugh.

They clinked their glasses together and drank their wine. Elisa did not even think about the man who came to her townhouse and she never mentioned it to Guy as they drove to where his private plane was to head off to the Greek Isles.

⊶⊰⊱⊷

They pulled up to where Guy's plane was. Elisa got out of the limousine and looked at the jet. It was impressive. Her and Guy had been seeing each other since last fall at the fall showing in London, but they would get together for dinners and shows, but with the demands of her career, she never took the time to let Guy take her anywhere on his plane.

Now standing here, she was amazed at it and felt a twinge of pain at not letting herself indulge in this luxury. Guy came up behind her. "What do you think?"

Elisa turned around to him. "I should have let myself indulge in this before now." Guy laughed. They got her things and loaded them on to the plane. Guy was giving instructions to his crew. The plane was being inspected.

Guy and Elisa got onto the plane. It was massive. It had plush seats, a staircase going to the top, the carpeting matched the plush seats, and Elisa sat down on one of the plush seats. "They recline and massage," said Guy. He reclined the seat and turned on the massage. Elisa fell in love with it. She never had these seats even when she traveled first class on an airline.

"You know, I could have my manicure and pedicure done just like this," Elisa smiled with her eyes closed.

"Let me take you into the lavatory my dear." Guy took her hand and led her to the lavatory. He opened the door and it was not just your ordinary lavatory. It had a marble sink, a marble tub with jets, a marble floor, embroidered towels, and housecoats.

Elisa ran her hand along the sink and tub. She smelled the soaps and felt the housecoat and towels. Any woman in her right mind would be spoiled to this. Even the damn toilet was made of marble. "You like my Mon Cherie?" Guy asked her.

"Like, I love it!" Elisa exclaimed clasping her hands together.

"Let me take you upstairs my dear." Guy took her hand and led her up the stairs. Upstairs it had a wet bar, Guy led her into another area where the cooks prepared the food, and he led her to his bedroom. It was very masculine from the bed sheets, bed spread, all the way to the curtains and furniture.

"You leave nothing non-pleasing to the eye," Elisa was elated.

"I try my damnest. Just let my crew know whatever you want to eat and drink and they will get it for you. While we are up here, why don't we take advantage of this time and break in the newly clean sheets." Guy said nibbling on her ear.

"Well my captain, I surrender." He picked up Elisa in his arms and took her to the bed.

Just as he laid her down, his intercom came on. "Sir, the plane is ready for takeoff." The pilot said.

"Then let's roll." Guy spoke back into the intercom.

"Yes sir," and the pilot was off.

"Now where were we?" Guy asked.

"We were just getting started," Elisa said in whispered breaths. Guy grabbed the back of her head and pulled her to him and clasped his lips to her like he would never taste them again.

Elisa reciprocated with the same fervor. They were on their way to the Greek Isles. Guy kissed her all over her throat while Elisa moaned. He was unbuttoning her blouse as he was kissing her. He started kissing her breasts as he pulled off her blouse. He was undoing the clasp of her bra. He got it unclasped and took both of her breasts and started suckling on them. Elisa thrust her head back.

Guy took his tongue and started from the top of her throat all the way down to her belly button. Elisa shuddered. Elisa was pulling of his suit coat and unbuttoning his shirt. He was undoing the button and zipper on her slacks. She got his shirt unbuttoned and was taking it off. He was pulling down her slacks. Once off, he ran his hand up her leg to her thigh and put his finger under her panties strap and started sliding it down.

He put his finger on her womanhood and could feel the wetness. He was rubbing it and playing in it and Elisa was breathing hard. He laid her on the bed, took his hand, grabbed her leg, bent down, and starting with the toes, he kissed her all the way up to her thigh and then to her womanhood.

Elisa screamed out. "Shh my Mon Cherie," Guy said softly. He made her cum over and over. He took off his slacks and Elisa got on top of him and kissed him from his face all the way down to his manhood. She put her mouth over it and got him all worked up. She then slid up to him and put him inside of her. They were moving in synch with each other, oblivious to anything or anyone but them. When it was all said and done and they both had climaxed, Elisa lay down beside Guy.

They were both breathing hard and out of breath. "Hmm, I did miss this," Elisa said rolling over to face Guy. He took the back of his hand and rubbed her cheeks.

"You are so beautiful my Mon Cherie and wonderful in bed too."

Elisa grinned. "You're not so bad yourself stud." Guy laughed. They lay there for a little while longer before getting dressed and heading up to get something to eat and drink.

The rest of the way to the Greek Isles, Elisa and Guy spent their time making love, drinking fine wine, and they even had put on some music and danced. Elisa felt like she was on top of the world. She never dreamed in a million years that she would be living this kind of life, but she had worked too long and too hard to get here. It was all a reality now.

⋈⊶⋇⊷⋈

They landed in the Greek Isles; the pilot had gotten clearance to land the plane. Guy and Elisa got off the plane and got into the car that would take them to Guy's private cottage in the Isles. As they were being whisked away, Elisa was enthralled by the beauty of the Isles. She made a mental note to get herself back here again.

"I have so much planned for us my Mon Cherie; the weekend is ours to do as we please."

"I am looking forward to it." Elisa sat back and enjoyed the ride there. They got to Guy's cottage and it was set in a perfect location overlooking the Isles. Elisa snapped some pictures before grabbing her things to take inside.

"Oh no dear Elisa, let me help get your things and take them to "our" room." Elisa noticed how Guy had put much emphasis on "our" room.

Elisa let the servants take her things and put them inside.

She was leery of her things, but if Guy trusted them, then for the next two days she would have to too. With the time zone, it was in the early hours of the morning, while in New York it would be evening. Elisa and Guy sat outside in the gardens and watched the sun come up.

"After breakfast we will do some sightseeing and then I will take you out on my yacht." The air was warm and smelled of the ocean. Elisa had changed into a strapless sundress that had been part of Pose's summer collection this year. Against her creamy skin it was even more gorgeous and Guy told her so. She had to watch herself out in the sun, even though her father had been Native American, unlike her sister Cara, Elisa had to be careful about being in the sun.

She had more Irish in her and she was more prone to burn so she used the best sunscreen there was on the market. She was wearing her favorite perfume, Chanel 5; she had thought about Pose coming up with a fragrance line and would make a mental note of mentioning it at their next meeting. Not only would Pose be in the clothing industry, but in the fragrance industry as well, she would have her employees come up with a name for the perfume line.

She would have a male and female model commercialize it. Elisa took a picture of the sun coming up over the horizon and it took her breath away. She should vacation more, but her job was so demanding. "You want to capture memories of this I see," said Guy.

"There are some memories worth capturing and moments like this are one of them." Elisa leaned over and they kissed while the sun was turning the sky into daylight.

They had breakfast and Elisa grabbed her bikini, her sunscreen, and other personal items. They would have dinner on his yacht so she made sure she took an evening dress. They set out and toured the Isles and took in as much as they could. They tried the local cuisines and even danced with some of the locals. Elisa was having the time of her life. She could stay here, but her demanding career and life in New York would beckon her back all too soon.

But while she was here, she might as well live it up and that is what she was doing. Elisa got many pictures and souvenirs. She had left her personal items and evening dress at Guy's yacht so when they went back they would already be there. As the morning turned into the afternoon, they headed to Guy's yacht to go sailing and then Elisa would shower and put on her dress. She knew she would not have it on long.

She could already feel herself tingling inside at the sensation of having Guy touch her and kissing her. They got to the yacht and Guy's crew had the yacht all ready to go. Elisa went down and changed into her bikini. It was violet to match her eyes and the wrap to match. Guy saw it and whistled.

He already had on his swim gear. "You make the sun want to dance." Guy wrapped his arms around her and she could feel his warm skin against her. He took both of his hands and brought her face to his and brushed her lips. They were warm and soft. "I thought that we could go jet skiing. I have two jet skis." Elisa had only been jet skiing once and that was when her father took her to Indian Lake with some of his friends. He had taught her how to ride one but it had been years. She did not know if she could still do it.

"What is it my Mon Cherie?" Guy looked perplexed at her expression. "Are you worried about something?"

"Oh no Guy, it is just that the last time I went jet skiing was when I was little, before my father left us and with his friends back in Ohio. I do not even know if I remember how to ride one."

Guy laughed and Elisa just stared at him. "Is that all? It is nothing. You start it up, you steer it like you would a car, and the gas and brakes are on the handles. Here let me help you." Guy took her hand and brought her to where the jet skis were. He untied one. "I will let you in front and me in back until you get the hang of it again."

Elisa stared at the Jet Ski as if it were a shark. "Don't be scared Elisa." She took his hand and got on. He got behind her and told her to start it up. She started it up. "Now ease it on out."

She hit the gas a little too hard and almost knocked Guy off of it. "Oh, I am so sorry Guy." Elisa said nervously.

"It is okay." He put his hand over hers and gently eased the Jet Ski out and took off.

He helped her steer it and drive it. He eventually let go and let her take control. She almost knocked him into the water a few times but managed to keep it under control. "You are doing a great job Elisa," Guy said over the roar of the Jet Ski. Elisa was getting the hang of it again and was laughing. Her nervousness was gone.

They pulled back up to the yacht and Elisa stayed on the Jet Ski and Guy got the other one out. "Now," said Guy. "Let's go." They both took off and were racing each other across the water. Guy would get close and spray her with water. Elisa got him back by turning her Jet Ski so that water just splashed Guy. She was laughing. "You will pay for that later," Guy said, drenched now.

"Oh yeah," said Elisa. "You will have to catch me first."

"That will not be a problem." Guy said. They jet skied for what seemed like hours when they got back to the yacht and tied up the jet skis.

When they were back on the yacht, Guy grabbed her and Elisa screamed. "You see, I told you that getting you would not be a problem."

They were both wet as he carried her downstairs. They threw their wet swim wear on to the floor as their wet bodies clung to one another. He kissed her all over and he took her with all his might. He pulled her to him from behind and entered her. She cried out and he moved in and out of her until he ejaculated into her. He lay on top of her from behind caressing her thigh, his other hand holding up his head. Elisa laid there with her hand stretched out and her hair spread out.

"I have a surprise for you at dinner my Mon Cherie." Guy said softly.

"You have already given me this trip Guy." Elisa turned her head to him.

"I told you about it before hand, so it is not a surprise. I hope you will accept it."

Elisa's curiosity was alert and what did he want her to accept. She would find out at dinner. She got up to shower and get ready for dinner. Guy joined her in the shower and took her again.

They were at dinner and Elisa looked spectacular as ever. Guy had opened the finest wine and it was a beautiful evening on the water. Elisa was wearing a light blue evening gown that slit all way up to her thigh on the left side and had diamonds studded around the bodice. She was wearing the earrings, the necklace, and bracelet to match that Guy had given her.

"I know you were wondering what the surprise was, but I wanted to wait until we were done eating." Guy poured them another glass of wine.

"Yes Guy, I would be lying if I said I was not curious." Elisa took a sip of her wine. They had finished dinner.

"This is not easy for me especially since I know the kind of woman you are. You are dedicated, hard-working, and independent. You have made your career your life. I know I said that I would never do this again Elisa, but I cannot help it. When I am with you, I forget everything else.

You are the only woman in a long time that has made me feel this way. We have known each other for a year now and we have had great times together and great sex. You are married to your career I know, but I was hoping that for once Elisa you would give this a chance." Elisa had a feeling what he was going to ask her but remained silent to let Guy finish. "I have had many women in my life Elisa and I have had two bad marriages. But after being with you Elisa, I want you in my life, I need you, and I am in love with you."

He pulled something out of his jacket pocket. "I wanted to wait until the right time to do this." He opened the box and a ring with a diamond as big as a quarter shown. Elisa's eyes got wide. "Elisa Drinnings, will you marry me?" Guy asked.

CHAPTER 8

Elisa could not speak, she was surprised. She never expected this. Guy knew her feelings about marriage. She was married to her career. She had never let herself put a man before her career. She had never let herself, even before she met Guy, to fall in love with any man. Guy was a great man and surely any woman in Elisa's shoes right now would say yes, but Elisa was not any other woman and while she loved spending time with Guy, she was not in love with him.

"Elisa darling, I know this is a surprise to you." Guy was watching her.

"Oh Guy, we have known each other for a year yes, but you know where I stand on this."

"Listen Elisa, you do not have to give me an answer right away. You can have time to think about it." Guy told her putting the ring away. "I will not force you to do what you do not want to do, but I just wanted you to know Elisa while we had this time together to let you know how I feel."

"Guy I do appreciate what you have done for me and given me. This trip, the jewelry, the wonderful lovemaking, and I do not want to seem ungrateful, but I thought that we had an understanding. I made a vow that I would not end up like my mother and depend on a man. That is why I worked hard and put myself through school to get myself where I am today and get out of the miserable life that I was in."

"I am not asking you to give up anything Elisa darling. Your career or anything, but we could build a wonderful life together, with everything we have, we could travel and see the world. Like I said, I will give you time to think about it."

"I have thought about it," Elisa remarked.

"No you have not," Guy said indignantly. Elisa was taken aback. She got up. "Where are you going Elisa?"

"I am going to change and go to bed, I am quite tired."

"It is still early my dear, there is still so much left to do." Guy stood up.

"Do what you want Guy, I am going to bed." Elisa walked off and down the steps leaving Guy sitting there.

She changed into her chemise, washed up, and brushed her hair. She looked at the bed that they had made love in hours ago. She knew Guy had a guest bedroom so she slept there. Guy went down and did not see her in the bed. He looked and called out her name, but Elisa did not answer. He did not want to ruin this weekend with a fight. He looked in the guest bedroom and found Elisa sleeping. He wanted to walk up to her, to touch her skin, her hair, to kiss her but he did not dare.

Instead, he shut the door and went back out on the deck. He had his driver bring him some cognac and he drank thinking about tonight. The sun was setting and the sky was a mixture of blues and oranges. He would have loved to spend this night with Elisa. He sat there drinking and deep in thought.

The next morning, Elisa put on her robe and headed upstairs. She was sitting on the deck at the table drinking her tea and having a muffin. She was not really hungry. She sat there looking out at the other boats on the water. Guy came up and saw her sitting there. "Did you sleep well my Mon Cherie?" Guy sat down. His cook had asked him what he would like and Guy said to just bring him some coffee.

"I am sorry Elisa about last night. I sprung this on you." Elisa sighed. The cook had brought out Guy's coffee and left before Elisa spoke. Ignoring his question about how she had slept last night, she spoke.

"Please do not bring this subject up again or ask me." Elisa continued to stare out at the water without looking at Guy.

"If I give you more t—," but before Guy could finish, Elisa interrupted him.

"I do not need more time Guy, you have my answer. I have

been honest with you from the beginning." Elisa said sternly.

"Okay my Mon Cherie, I do not want to upset you anymore. We have a few hours to kill before we must leave. I thought that we would have lunch at my cottage and do some shopping before we leave. How does that sound to you Elisa?"

"I would like that Guy, but just as so long as you have me back before I have to go back to work." Guy ordered his driver to take the yacht back. They sailed back to the dock and Elisa had gathered up her items. Guy's limo driver took them back to his cottage. When they got there, Elisa went upstairs to freshen up for lunch. Guy told his servants how he wanted the table set and what they would be having.

When Elisa came down in white shorts, a pink off the shoulder silk blouse, a wide brimmed hat, and her sandals, Guy thought she looked like something out of a 1950's movie. Oh how he wished that she would marry him. "Oh my dear, you look exquisite. " He took her hand and kissed it. "I have already told my servants what to fix for lunch. Come please Elisa."

The table was decorated with a lace tablecloth, fresh cut flowers, engraved silverware, and embroidered napkins. The lunch was delicious and they talked, but Guy never mentioned again about marriage. He hoped that she would eventually come around. They finished eating and did some last minute shopping before heading home.

Guy bought Elisa an expensive oil painting and a beautiful vase. Elisa was going to buy some gifts for Guy but he told her, by her coming, that was all the gift he needed. They headed back to his private plane and set off back to the states. Elisa had a great time except for when he asked her to marry him, but the whole way home they never discussed it. They were too busy making love and relaxing.

They got back to New York and Guy drove her home. It was late. Her bags were carried in and Guy kissed her goodnight. "I had a great time Guy, thank you."

"I did too, thank you for coming." Guy kissed her one more time. "I will be in San Francisco all week; can I see you when I get back?"

"Sure," Elisa responded. Guy walked out the door and Elisa watched him leave.

She shut the door and walked upstairs leaving her bags there. She would have Cora unpack them tomorrow when she came in the morning. Elisa sat on her bed. The events of the weekend had exhausted her. Guy asking her to marry him brought back memories of her mother and she missed her more than ever. She wished that she was here for Elisa to talk to. Thinking about her mother made her open the drawer of her nightstand and pull out the letter that her mother had given her before she died.

Elisa saw the letter from her mother with Cara's name on the envelope. Since she and Cara stopped talking, she had never bothered to give it to her but had kept it all these years for reasons that were unknown to her. She opened the letter and reread the letter her mother had written her.

My dearest and sweetest daughter Elisa,

I do not want to leave you but there comes a time when our time is done and we must say goodbye. Know that I will always love you and know I have not truly left you. After your father walked out on us, I tried to do the best I could to give us a good life. Though we were not rich, we had each other. You and Cara were my life and I even now; do love your sister even though she blamed me for your father leaving. I wish that I could have made Cara understand and explain why her father left and that I did everything I could to keep him here. I couldn't. She was so angry and hurt and then she up and left.

I never saw her again after that but I never stopped loving her. In the letter I have written her, I hope she sees that I tried to do everything I could do to hold this family together. You grew up Elisa and made me very proud. You went on to college, worked hard, and made a good life for yourself. You kept your promise to take care of me. You have got to stay strong Elisa, even after I am gone. You need to remember that we all choose our own destiny that we all choose how we want to live every day we are given, and that life will throw us a few curveballs but we just have to learn how to hit them.

I remember when you were little how you would dress up and act like you were a model, or read those magazines and learn about the latest fashions. You grew up to be a beautiful woman Elisa. You became a successful woman. I wish that I could have been like you and gone to college and became successful, but I married your father right out of high school and then had you.

I always pushed you to be successful. I remember one evening we were out on the porch and you asked me this question: "Mother do I make you proud?" and I said, "Every day." Though you and I were closer than Cara and I, I loved you both just the same. Don't forget where you came from Elisa and where you are now. We all have battles to fight; we just have to know which ones to fight. When you get down or lonely Elisa, remember, someone else may have it worse than you. Remember this song I use to sing to you and your sister Cara, "Oh Star in the Sky" Oh, Star in the Sky, how you shine so bright, oh how you light up the sky, Oh Star in the Sky shine on me tonight. Blink, blink, blink so bright, oh star in the sky. Oh Star in the Sky you give off your beautiful light, Oh Star in the Sky shine on me tonight.

Elisa I am sure your career keeps you busy, but remember this: "Don't drive through life so fast that you miss the scenery." My time is almost up and I am getting weaker but I will always love you. I must go now.

Love,
Mom

Elisa was sobbing now. She wanted her mother here to talk to. She could make sense of what all was going on. Sometimes, things just didn't make sense. Elisa lie back on the bed with her mother's letter to her in her hand and fell fast asleep.

Elisa was in such a deep sleep that she did not hear Cora

come into her home. Elisa woke up and looked at her clock. It was ten a.m. "Shit," Elisa hollered. Cora came into her room.

"Is everything okay, Senorita Drinnings?"

"No, I am late for work. I am never late for work. I was so exhausted from my trip that I did not set my alarm."

"Would you like me to put away your things Senorita Drinnings?" Cora asked her.

"What, oh yes my luggage downstairs." She had forgotten that she had left her luggage downstairs. "Yes, thank you Cora." Cora left and Elisa saw her mother's letter on the floor. She picked it up and put it back in her nightstand drawer. She hurried and took a shower and got herself ready and headed out.

Her driver was already there. She got to work and saw the lowly man there on the sidewalk. She got out of the car and ran past him.

"Good morning ma'am." Kyle said to her.

She ignored him as she ran into the building. Sissy was at her desk as usual doing her work when she looked up.

"Miss Drinnings, good morning," Sissy said. She got up out of her desk. She had made sure that Elisa had her coffee each morning on her desk, hot and waiting for her. But with Elisa running late, it was cold by now.

Sissy did not even knock on Elisa's door, but walked right in. That was a no no with Elisa, but this morning she did not care. "Are you alright Miss Drinnings?" Sissy asked her. "I am sure your coffee is cold by now I can go and heat it up for you."

"Sissy you can call me Elisa, you and only you."

Sissy knew there had to be something wrong because Elisa would never let her call her Elisa, two she would have been furious with someone walking into her office like Sissy did, and three cold coffee.

"I do not care about the coffee right now. I cannot believe I am late. I have never been late in all my years with Pose Magazine. I am sorry." Elisa was talking a mile a minute and Sissy was trying to keep up.

"Whoa, Elisa, you are the Chief Editor of Pose, you can be late."

"No Sissy, this job is my lifeblood, it is the very essence of my life, it is the reason why I get up and make sure I am here every day and on time, and this is unacceptable."

Sissy did not know if Elisa was trying to convince herself of this or Sissy.

She took the coffee and left with Elisa standing there. Elisa watched as Sissy left. She could not believe Sissy had just walked out of her office like this. Sissy had never done this. Elisa plopped down in her chair. Sissy came back with Elisa's coffee heated up. Sissy shut the door to Elisa's office and sat down.

"Now you want to tell me what is unnerving you?" Sissy asked Elisa taking a sip of her coffee. Elisa took a sip of her coffee and sighed. "There is a lot of work to be done and I cannot believe that I am late for work." Elisa was going through her briefcase. Sissy put her hand on Elisa's arm. "Please Elisa, we have worked together for years, I have never seen you act like this. What is up?"

"Sissy I want you to call that guy, that new designer, what is his name again?" Elisa asked Sissy.

"Marco Shoops," Sissy responded.

"Oh yes, call him and tell him that I very much liked his work and that I want him to come and work for Pose Magazine."

"I will Elisa when you tell me what is eating you." Sissy said sternly.

"Did you just get stern with me Sissy and not do right away what I asked of you?" Elisa was irked by it.

"I will do as you ask as soon as you talk to me. I am worried about you Elisa. You did not get furious with me when I walked right into your office, you said nothing about the coffee being cold, and you are letting me call you by your first name after how many years of working together? I want Elisa and I want to know what you have done with her. The Elisa I know would not have allowed that. I care about you Elisa. We are best friends. We are like sisters." Sissy knew about what had ensued between Elisa and her sister Cara.

And Sissy had become her confidant, especially after Elisa

lost her mother. "Now talk, you have no scheduled meetings today Elisa. And I am caught up on my work." Anyone else, Elisa would have fired and thrown out of her office for this kind of behavior, but this was Sissy. The woman who she made her assistant, who helped her when she first came to Pose, the one whom she confided in, and the one who lost out on getting the Chief Editor position.

Elisa, like a deflated balloon, purged herself to Sissy of what was ailing her.

CHAPTER 9

"I cannot believe he asked you to marry him," Sissy said stunned. Sissy was older than Elisa and had never married. She too, had focused on her career with Pose Magazine and worked hard. She had dated here and there, but never committed. She was hoping to get that position as Chief Editor, but when she didn't she was disappointed.

She had fallen in love with a man, who was a lawyer, but broke it off when she found out he was married. He did not want to leave his wife, he was afraid that he would lose everything so he never asked Sissy for anything more.

Since then, Sissy had made herself immune to love. She had joked with Elisa about becoming a nun and Elisa begged her not to. "Yes Sissy, he asked me to marry him knowing how I felt about marriage. I am married to my career. He says that he would give me time, but I have already made up my mind. I was honest with him from the start. He is a great guy and he has been married twice."

"Are you still going to see him?" Sissy asked her.

"Yes, he is in San Francisco this week to take care of some business with his jewelry store there. He asked if he could see me when he got back and I said yes." Elisa and Sissy had ended up ordering their lunch and were eating in her office.

"Well, at least you guys are still talking and can get together. I mean I have seen this man Elisa and I must say he is a looker and a keeper. He is wealthy and you would be crazy to let him go. But if you ever do, send him my way." Sissy laughed.

"Oh Sissy, you have cut yourself off to love." Elisa threw her napkin at Sissy.

"Yes, but I could reconsider with someone like him. You do not realize how lucky you are Elisa." Sissy said taking a bite of her turkey sandwich.

"Why do you say that Sissy?" Elisa asked her noncommittally.

"You are Chief Editor of a very successful fashion magazine, you have a wonderful man who dotes on you, buys you beautiful things, flies you to the Greek Isles on his private plane, stay on his yacht, you live in a beautiful townhouse, have a housekeeper, a great cook, and you are beautiful, smart, independent, and can hold her own." Sissy said counting these things on her fingers.

"Are you jealous Sissy?" Elisa asked her slyly.

"Me jealous, oh no," Sissy waved her napkin. "Well," Sissy said putting her fingertips up to her chest and tilting her head, "maybe just slightly. But I am happy for you Elisa."

"Thank you Sissy." Elisa took another bite of her sandwich. "Someday Sissy you will be successful like me." Sissy almost choked on her food over that. "Me," Sissy said washing her food down with her drink.

"I have tried, unless I can go to another fashion magazine and get Chief Editor there, but I have a better chance of falling off the Empire State building and surviving." Sissy chuckled.

"Oh come on now Sissy, one day will be your day."

Sissy looked at Elisa funny and wondered why Elisa would say such a thing.

"Anyway, off with Guy for a while. You would not believe what else happened to me Friday while I was packing." Elisa got wide eyed.

"Oh do tell," Sissy said enthusiastically. Sissy leaned up in her chair.

"That guy on the street down there, well, I was so busy trying to get things together for my trip, being the last minute packer that I am, came to my home."

Sissy let out a whistle. "How did he know where you lived? Did he follow you, is he stalking you?"

"No that is the thing, you see after I left the office Friday, I was fishing through my purse, oh I cannot even remember now what I was searching for. But anyway, my pocketbook fell out with my ID in it. I heard the doorbell ring and I thought hmm Guy is early so I went downstairs. I opened the door without even thinking, I usually have Cora do it but I gave her the weekend off.

"There stood that wretched soul of a man. I asked him how in the hell he knew where I lived. He pulled out my pocketbook. Naturally with him being homeless or whatever, I looked through my pocketbook to see if he had stolen anything. Everything was there. I told him not to come back and if he did I would have him arrested.

"I saw that he had a taxi waiting outside for him and asked how he could afford one. I threw some money at him to pay for the taxi cab back to wherever it is he is staying. He did not take the money. That is the second time he would not take the money that I offered him. I do not understand it. I mean he obviously has no job, he begs for money on the street, his clothes need to be burned, and who knows where he stays when he is not out on that sidewalk.

"He got back in the cab and I watched him leave. I opened the door and picked up the money and put it back in my pocketbook. Why do you think with a person in his situation would refuse money to him?" Elisa got up and was standing at her window staring down at the man.

Sissy swallowed her last bite of sandwich and elicited a response to it. She wanted to say the right words. "Maybe at that time he was not looking for money but just a simple thank you. The first time you offered him money; that one hundred dollar bill, you wanted him to leave the sidewalk. He wanted you to do it out of the kindness of your heart. We do not know the reason why he does what he does each day, out there on that sidewalk Elisa. Have you ever thought about that?"

Elisa turned back around. "Are you kidding, all I am feeling sorry for this guy Sissy? He chose to be in this situation. He has opportunities just like you and me. I mean look at us Sissy."

"Yeah look at us Elisa," before Elisa could get another word in. "Look at what we have; a career, money, a home, nice clothes, and we go to the nicest restaurants. What if at one time Elisa, he had all those things? We all have choices Elisa, but what if something happened in his life that put him there?"

Elisa did not manage a response to that. Whatever the circumstances, it was not pertinent to her right now. Right now she needed to get back to work. "Remember Sissy, call that new designer and tell him I want him to start work tomorrow."

"His name is Marco and I will. If he was not gay, I would be all over him like the mayonnaise on my sandwich." Sissy giggled.

"Oh man, just go and call him Sissy," Elisa shook her head and laughed. "Oh Sissy, just one more thing."

"Yes Elisa," Sissy had her hand on the doorknob.

"Thank you for listening."

"You're welcome Elisa and thank you for not firing me and throwing me out for breaking the rules."

Elisa knew what she meant. "Don't tell anyone else and don't let anyone know you can call me Elisa."

"Got it," Sissy said saluting her and shutting her door.

Elisa looked out at the man again on the sidewalk and thought to herself, as hard as it was, she could at least thank him for returning her pocketbook with everything in it. She made a mental note to tell him that.

She sat back down and got right to work. It had been a fulfilling morning. Sissy came on the line and knocked Elisa out of her reverie of work.

"Yes Sissy," Elisa answered.

"It is Maggie Bench, she says it is urgent."

Oh my gosh, it is Maggie Bench, Elisa thought to herself. She had not heard from Maggie Bench in the five years Maggie made her Chief Editor.

I wonder how she is doing, Elisa thought. "I will take the call Sissy." Elisa picked up the phone. "Hello Miss Bench how are you? I have not heard from you since you appointed me Chief Editor." Elisa said.

"Oh cut the chit-chat."

Maggie is still her same old self, Elisa thought.

"I was in New York and I was wondering what you had planned for tonight?"

"I have nothing going on." Elisa responded and even if she did, she would have canceled it for Maggie. You did not refuse Maggie, even though Maggie was not working for Pose magazine anymore, her opinion still held water.

"Good, I want you to meet me at my favorite restaurant tonight at seven p.m. sharp and don't be late."

"Of course I will be there," but before Elisa could get all the words out, Maggie had already hung up. Elisa knew the place and knew not to be late. *Not that I don't have enough pressure in my life,* Elisa thought. She wanted to run the idea of her fragrance line for Pose that she thought of while in the Greek Isles. Maggie would let Elisa know if that was a good idea or not.

Yes, she would do that before she brought it up for her next meeting. Elisa finished up her work and headed out to get ready for dinner with Maggie. She passed Sissy on the way out, "everything okay?" Elisa knew why Sissy asked that. It was not just anyone on the phone, but Maggie, and Maggie did not like to be put on hold.

"Yes Sissy, enjoy your evening." Elisa was gone and Sissy shrugged her shoulders and got ready to leave herself. Elisa did not see the man there, and even if he was, she would not have had time to talk to him. She got in the car and headed home.

She told Emilio that a former colleague had invited her to dinner and she would be eating out. "Si Senorita. Then I shall leave for the evening." Emilio had his own apartment. Cora had her things all put away and her townhouse straightened up.

Cora asked her if she needed her for anything else. Cora had her dry cleaning picked up, her laundry done, and everything back to how Elisa liked it. The oil painting that Guy had bought for her was hanging up over the fireplace. "No that will be all Cora, Gracias." Elisa told her. "De nada," Cora smiled and gave a little bow.

She grabbed her things and left. Elisa went upstairs. She had called Cora earlier and told her about her dinner plans and told Cora what she wanted to wear. They were lying on the bed when she walked into her room.

She got a shower, got dressed, and took precision in getting ready. Even after all this time, she still wanted to make an impression on Maggie like she did the first day she walked into Pose Magazine. She took a once over herself, impressed, she grabbed her beaded handbag and walked out the door. The night was beautiful and a little chilly so Elisa had put on the jacket that matched her outfit.

She told the driver where to and he took off. She got to the restaurant and it was five till seven. She was five minutes early. Maggie was already waiting at her booth that she liked. It was in the back and away from everyone else. Elisa told the waiter who she was meeting and he took her right to Maggie's booth.

Elisa sat down and the waiter asked if Elisa would like anything to drink. Elisa ordered a Martini straight up with an olive. When the waiter left, Maggie responded, "I see you still like your Martinis that way."

"Yes," was all Elisa said. Maggie still had that aurora about her even though she had been away from Pose Magazine for over five years. "I am honored to be having dinner with you Maggie," Elisa responded when Maggie said not a word.

"I am impressed with you Elisa by the way you have kept Pose Magazine at the top. I have kept up with what is going on. I told you that I would still be indirectly involved with Pose Magazine even though I am no longer working for it. I have been around the world traveling but not all pleasure, no, I have been looking at different fashions and clothing from around the world. I must say that I was highly impressed. I brought some fabric samples back from many of these countries."

Maggie took out a notebook from her satchel. She put it on the table and the waiter came to give Elisa her martini. He asked if they were ready to order. Maggie ordered her usual and Elisa ordered their special with a watercress salad. Elisa opened the notebook and looked at the samples. She ran her fingers over them and loved the feel of them.

The colors, the feel, the designs were exquisite. Elisa would love to show these to her designers. She would not mind having these for Pose. "Do you like them?" Maggie asked her.

"Like them, I love them. I would love to show them to my designers. We are getting ready for our upcoming spring fashion show in Paris. How did you manage to get your hands on these samples?"

Maggie looked at her like you silly girl. "I have connections Elisa; remember I have been in this business longer than you have and I have many friends.

"That is why I came back. I wanted to show you these. Now I am not telling you that you have to use them for your spring fashion show, but what I can tell you dear Elisa, is that no other fashion Magazine I am sure has these." Maggie smiled her facetious smile and took a sip of her drink.

"How can you be sure of that?" Elisa asked her.

"You doubt me Elisa?" Maggie seemed disappointed.

"Oh no Maggie, I am sorry." Elisa felt like slapping herself.

"Oh do not worry Elisa, I am sure. You use these fabrics in your show and have your designers make their designs with these; you will make Pose Magazine even bigger."

Elisa told Maggie about how she made a contest for the designers to come up with designs for the spring fashion show and how she had hired this new designer by the name of Marco Shoops. "I have seen his work and I was impressed so I hired him."

"I trust that you made the right decision Elisa, that is why I made you Chief Editor."

"I like your idea of this contest for your designers, give them something to look forward to. Kind of like a reward." Elisa continued, "I also thought about for Pose, not just clothing line, but a fragrance line, something that a male and female model can commercialize." She saw the look in Maggie's eyes and wondered if she had said the wrong thing, that maybe this was not such a good idea.

"I like the idea, why some of the top selling magazines use fragrances in their magazines. I wish that I had thought of that while I was working for Pose."

"But this would not be just advertising any fragrance in our magazine, but Pose's very own fragrance for women and men. It would have the signature of Pose Magazine on it."

"Have you thought of a name for it yet?" Maggie asked her.

"No, I thought that at the next meeting I would give my employees the chance to give it a name. We could patent it so nobody else could copy it and claim the rights to it." Just then, their food came and the waiter asked if they would like anything else. They both said no and the waiter left.

"Have you got a backer for it Elisa, someone to patent it, a lawyer, and people hired to make the fragrance?"

"Um no, I just thought of the idea over the weekend." Elisa was not about to go into her love life with Maggie, even though she trusted Maggie and her opinions, Elisa did not feel it was viable to this meeting.

"How about you simply call it Pose? Many singers and actors or actresses simply name their fragrance after themselves."

Elisa thought about it for a minute and said, "That sounds great, sounds simple yet, robust. Pose perfume and cologne for men." Elisa took her fork and made an arch in the air with it.

"At your next meeting," Maggie interjected, "just tell your employees that this is what you want to do and that you already have the backing for it." Maggie took a bite of food.

"I don't understand," Elisa said, "we would partake of this as an industry."

"Yes Elisa, but your Chief Editor of Pose, you're in charge so take charge this is why I made you Chief Editor, you could put Pose Magazine even more on the map." Elisa contemplated it as she ate. She told Maggie she would do it. She would have an emergency meeting and bring this up at their next meeting.

"So," Elisa asked Maggie, "who do you know that could get this fragrance line going for Pose Magazine?"

"I not only have clout in the fashion industry but also in the fragrance industry as well. Do not doubt me Elisa, I have come through before just like with these fabrics. You leave this all up to me. I will work on the sidelines to get this going; all you have to do is present it to your employees.

"I will get this all set up, you need not worry, and I will be contacting you on this. Trust me Elisa." Maggie smiled at her.

"I do trust you and I have no doubt in you Miss Bench." Elisa smiled.

"You can call me Maggie."

"Okay Maggie, I have no doubt in you, besides if it were not for you, I would not be Chief Editor of Pose Magazine."

"No Elisa, you earned that position, and it seems you have not let me down even after five years." The waiter came back and they each ordered another drink. "But I would like to remain anonymous on this Elisa; this is your idea." Maggie said.

When their drinks came, they made a toast. "To Pose Magazine and her new fragrance line, may she ever stay successful." Maggie said and Elisa repeated it and they clinked their glasses together and smiled at each other. It had been a productive evening for Elisa.

CHAPTER 10

Elisa had called Sissy to her office. "You ran out of here like the Dickens. What is up?"

Elisa looked up from her work. "Sit down Sissy. I have something to tell you." Sissy sat down. "I had dinner with Maggie Bench last night." Sissy's eyes got wide.

"She is back in town?"

"Yes she is and it was a very productive dinner. I am calling an emergency meeting for everyone.

I want everyone in the conference room in five minutes." Elisa said. "I will let everyone know." Sissy got up and left her office. Elisa headed down to the conference room. Five minutes later, people had piled into the conference room. Brian Drugan, Ellie Drisk, and Carl Drixel were in attendance, along with their newest designer, Marco Shoops.

"Before we get started, I would like to introduce to you our newest member here at Pose Magazine, Marco Shoops." Elisa pointed to Marco who waved and everyone said hello.

"You are all probably wondering why I have called you in here," Elisa started out. There was some chatter and confused looks. Rarely does Elisa call an emergency meeting. This had to be something of the utmost importance. "I have come up with a new idea for Pose, as you know we are in the business of fashion as with most fashion magazines, but I am proposing that Pose Magazine start a fragrance line for men and women simply named "Pose." There was whispering.

Brian Drugan raised his hands. "Yes Brian," Elisa said.

"With this new undertaking that you are proposing, there is a lot involved such as legal issues, financing, patents, people to make the perfume and cologne."

"I have thought about all of that and I have that taken care of. I assure you all it will be done legally. I have someone working on that now." Elisa looked at Sissy who was writing.

"May we have that person's name?" asked Ellie.

"The person who is backing this has asked to remain anonymous, but I assure you, once the legalities and the okay is given, I hope to have the fragrance line for Pose Magazine up and running." "Why does this person want to remain anonymous?" Ellie asked.

"Because this person is not directly involved with Pose anymore, but has the resources to help Pose with this new line. That is all I will comment on about that." Elisa looked at Sissy. Sissy gave Elisa that look, she knew who the person was but would keep that between them. "And there is something else; this same person who is helping with Pose's new fragrance line has also introduced to me some of these fabrics from around the world." Elisa pulled out the notebook that Maggie gave her and opened it up. Brian, Ellie, and Marco all looked at and felt the fabrics. "I believe," Elisa continued, "is that with these new fabrics we can propel Pose even farther. Take a good look and feel my designers." Many of the fabrics were laced with pure gold. "I would like for Pose to start using these fabrics in our designs. I would like any opinions or suggestions."

Elisa looked around. "Do we have this in our budget?" Carl Drixel asked, "And what about the models who will be wearing them as far as allergic reactions?"

"Yes we do, and as far as the allergy thing goes Carl, the models that can wear these fabrics will be the ones to model it. I will order these fabrics and we can start testing it and start using it to design our clothes."

Elisa looked around the room. "Any more questions before I call this meeting adjourned?" When no one responded, Elisa spoke up again. "Good then, this meeting is adjourned. Thank you all." Everybody walked out of the room. Elisa walked back to her office with Sissy beside her.

"How do you think they took all of this?" Sissy asked her.

"I do not feel that they would object to Pose Magazine being propelled even farther. Everything is in order and all I am doing is waiting for the signal. Furthermore, if they do have a problem with it, they do not have to work for Pose Magazine."

Elisa walked off leaving Sissy to whisper, "Okay." Elisa got back to her office and called Maggie. "Hello this is Maggie Bench."

"Maggie hello, this is Elisa Drinnings. I am calling to tell you that I had that emergency meeting with my staff and it is all a go. I need you to order me those fabrics and start the ball rolling on that fragrance line."

"Good to hear Elisa, I will do that and you should hear from me in about one to two weeks. You did keep me anonymous right?" Maggie asked.

"Yes I did Maggie and your cover is not blown, I will be expecting to hear from you in about one to two weeks." The women said goodbye and hung up. Elisa turned her chair towards the window and smiled. Pose Magazine was about to go through the roof.

Elisa paged Sissy to take messages for her; she had to step out of the office for a little bit. Sissy said she would. Elisa walked out of her office and to the elevator; she pushed the button for the first floor. She walked out of the elevator and straight outside. She saw the man with his back turned to her and walked up to him.

"Excuse me sir," Kyle turned around and stared straight into the face of the woman he has tried hard not to think about.

"What?" replied Kyle, "you going to try and pay me yourself instead of sending your assistant down to get me to leave this sidewalk?"

"No." Elisa said with patience in her voice, something that to her was not a virtue.

"I know the other night I was a little harsh on you when you came to my residence to return my pocketbook. I just wanted to say thank you. So thank you."

"You're welcome," Kyle turned back around.

Elisa wasn't sure what else to say. "I know I have not been

very kind to you."

Kyle turned around. "Well ma'am, what is your name?"

"It is Elisa."

"Well Elisa, what you have just said is an understatement. You have tried to get your assistant to pay me to leave this sidewalk. I know it was you who sent her as I have already made that point clear." Elisa remained silent. "You have acted like I do not exist. Furthermore, when I did return your pocketbook, you thought I was stalking you until you saw your pocketbook, then you snatch it out of my hands and accuse me of stealing because of the position I am in without so much as a thank you.

"You threaten to have me arrested if I return to your place, you're afraid I will stalk you which I have not because I am not interested in you or where you live. I was just doing the right thing. Then you proceed to throw money at me for the taxi ride home and I do not accept it. I am sure you're wondering why I did not take your money. Well my dear, it is not from the heart. You have no heart. You treat people that are beneath you as if they are bugs to be stepped on. Well I am not a bug. I was not always in this position."

"I do not know what you want from me," Elisa retorted. "I have said thank you and admitted that I have not been kind to you. I am not sure what else you want from me." Elisa said staring straight at him.

Kyle got up. "Frankly my dear, I do not want anything from the likes of you people. You live in your own world and I live in mine. You would never accept me." Kyle turned back around. By now people were staring.

Elisa just smiled and waved. Many people just shook their heads and others walked off. "I was uh wondering, as a kind gesture of returning my pocketbook and not stalking me, if you would let me take you to dinner?" Elisa could not believe she had just asked him that.

Kyle turned to her. "If I do say yes to this, are you going to accuse me of taking advantage of you?"

Elisa was trying to hold herself back. "Look, I do not really care if you accept or not. I wanted to show my appreciation for you returning my pocketbook and being an honest h--.''

But before Elisa could get out the word, Kyle finished it for her. "Go ahead and say it Elisa," the way he said her name made her get tight lipped and squeeze her hands together. "I am an honest homeless man. You can say it without being embarrassed."

"Do you want to have dinner tonight with me as a token of my appreciation or not? I can have you get into my car and take you shopping, get you cleaned up and go to dinner. I am off work at five p.m. It is your choice." This was her last time she would ask

"What if I say no?" Kyle asked crossing his arms.

"Then so be it. I offered." Elisa turned to walk back into the building to her office.

"Five o'clock p.m. it is then my dear Elisa." Elisa turned back around fuming, Kyle was smiling. She headed back to her office. Kyle watched and turned back around laughing to himself. Who would have ever thought in a million years that the beautiful woman with a heart of ice would come down there to thank him and ask him to dinner?

Kyle had to pinch himself to make sure he was not dreaming. "Nope," I am not dreaming.

❦❦❦❦

Sissy was sitting at her desk when Elisa walked by her. "Did I have any calls while I was out Sissy?"

"No Elisa you did not." Sissy replied. Sissy was curious as to what Elisa had to do but did not ask. Instead she asked, "Why all of a sudden are you letting me call you by your first name after so many years working together?"

Elisa sat down at her desk. "I felt it was time to allow you to do that, but you and only you Sissy. I figured since you have been like a sister to me, it was only fair that I allow you to do that. But do not do it in front of anyone else. I do not want people to think that I am giving you preferential treatment. Understood?"

"Understood," Sissy repeated. Carl Drixel came to the door and knocked. "I shall be going." Sissy walked past Carl.

"Yes Carl," Elisa looked at him.

"I just wanted to say that the winter edition of Pose is done. We have worked diligently on it. I would like your opinion before we distribute them for sale."

"Put it here my desk Carl." Carl put the copy of the winter edition of Pose Magazine on her desk. "I will look over this and get back to you before the end of the day."

"Thank you Miss Drinnings." Carl started to walk out then turned back around. "I think that your idea for the fragrance line for Pose and the fabrics was ingenious." Elisa looked up at him.

"Number one Carl, flattery will get you nowhere, and two, may I remind you that you are only the photographer. Now if there isn't anything else, I will be busy going over this magazine here."

"Yes ma'am." Carl walked out. Carl walked past Sissy. "How can you be her assistant? It must get pretty demanding and tiring." Carl left before Sissy could answer. She just laughed to herself, if Carl only knew the relationship between her and Elisa.

It was almost 5 o'clock and Sissy asked Elisa if she needed anything else. "Yes Sissy, run this magazine down to Carl Drixel and tell him to get this edition on the shelves pronto."

"Yes Elisa I will do that." Sissy took the magazine from Elisa's hand.

"And then go home Sissy."

"Will do" and Sissy was out of the office with the magazine and grabbed her things.

Elisa grabbed her things and stuffed them into her briefcase. She looked out her window. He was still there. She turned everything off and locked up her office. She was about to have dinner with a homeless man. She walked out of the building and her driver was waiting on her. "Shall we?" Elisa asked the man. He grabbed his things and got into the car first with Elisa behind him.

She told the driver where to go and he headed off. "I did not get your name earlier," Elisa said to the man. She could tell he hadn't had a bath and desperately needed a change of clothing.

"My name is Kyle Rimmer." He looked out the window.

"My name is Elisa Drinnings and I am Chief Editor of Pose Magazine." Kyle said nothing. She was trying to break this monotony of silence.

They got to the department store and got out. She told the driver to wait there. They went inside. Everyone was staring, her in her a chic designer outfit and him in his dirty and smelly t-shirt, jeans, and holes in his work boots. She dragged him over to the men's department. One of the associates knew her and greeted her. "Hello Miss Drinnings. It is so nice to see you." The associate was dressed in a gray suit, white shirt, gray tie, and shiny gray shoes. He took Elisa's hand and kissed it.

He looked at her "friend" with a look of distaste. "What can I do for you Miss?" He asked.

"I need a nice suit and tie for my friend here." Elisa said, looking at Kyle who felt so out of place. He wondered how a person could maneuver around in this store.

"Right this way. I think we have something that will fit him." Elisa and Kyle followed the associate.

"Here we go, a jacket made of fine material." Kyle tried the jacket on. It was itching him. "If that is not suitable for you, we have many others here." They looked and looked and tried on until they finally found an outfit that fit Kyle and some shoes. "There we go," said the associate." The last time Kyle got dressed up was for his wedding and that seemed like eons ago.

Elisa paid for the suit and they left. "How do you like it?" she asked him.

"It is great if your use to wearing it." Kyle said.

"It is better than what you had on." Elisa remarked.

"They all looked at me with disgust. I was like a leper to them." Kyle said emphatically.

"Well for your information Kyle it is an upscale store and what you were wearing wasn't exactly upscale. All of us upscale people go there." Elisa retorted

"By the way," Kyle said. "Where are the clothes that I was wearing?"

"I had the associate get rid of them."

"You what," Kyle's voice getting loud. The driver looked back.

"Calm down Kyle. They needed to be burned. And besides, I have an outfit I can let you wear after dinner before I drop you off wherever it is you call your home."

They pulled up to her townhouse that only days ago Kyle had come to, to return her pocketbook. She let him in. Kyle could not believe what he was seeing. The immaculate shiny wooden floors, the fireplace, the staircase encircling to the upstairs, it made him miss his house before Janice sold it and left him. Cora came out and Elisa introduced Kyle to her and asked if she could prepare a bath for her friend.

Kyle just looked around. Cora saw her friend and said hello. Kyle said hello back. He looked like had hadn't seen a bath for weeks by his hands and face. Cora said she would and headed upstairs. Emilio came out and Elisa introduced Kyle to him. "Kyle, this is my cook Emilio, Emilio, this is Kyle."

"Nice to meet you sir," Emilio said.

"You too sir," Kyle would have shaken his hand but his were so dirty compared to Emilio's clean ones, so he didn't.

"Senorita Drinnings, I had your driver take me to the grocery store earlier to get some stuff and I just got done putting those away and organizing the kitchen. Since you will be eating out with your friend here," Emilio looked at Kyle and smiled. "I shall go. I bid you both a good evening."

"You too Emilio," Elisa responded and Kyle reiterated it. "I appreciate it Emilio." Emilio bowed and got his jacket and left.

"You have a beautiful place here Elisa." It had been ages since Kyle had seen the inside of someone's home, especially like this.

"Can I get you anything to drink while you're waiting?" Elisa asked him.

"I will have whatever you're having Elisa." She grabbed them both a club soda. She handed him one and he opened it and took a swig.

Elisa sat down. Kyle was afraid to sit down. He did not want to ruin her furniture. "So Kyle, where do you hail from?" Elisa asked him taking a drink of her club soda.

"I am from New York originally. I see here you have an oil painting above your fireplace."

Elisa was shocked that he knew it was an oil painting. "Yes, I got that while vacationing in the Greek Isles. I did not know you knew anything about art."

Elisa took another drink of her club soda. "I went to culinary school, but I took some art classes in high school and I just retained a lot."

"So why are you not working as a chef somewhere?" Before Kyle could answer, Cora came down to let them know that his bath was ready for him.

"Go ahead Kyle; I have another bathroom that I can take my bath in."

Kyle looked from Elisa to Cora. "I have everything laid out for you sir." He followed Cora up the steps and she showed him where the bathroom was. It was decorated in seashells and coral. Kyle just stood there. Everything was immaculate. He was afraid to touch anything. The mirror had lights going across at the top. "If you need anything, just let me know," Cora said to him.

"Thank you." Cora left and Kyle got undressed. Cora had even set down a razor and shaving cream. There was aftershave as well. Kyle smelled it. Mmm he thought, this has to be expensive. Something told him that Elisa had a male companion that stayed here, but it was not for him to pry. He did not want to look a gift horse in the mouth. This would be his first real meal in a long time. Kyle got in the tub and it felt good. It had been years it seemed since he had a nice hot bath. He laid his head back and enjoyed it.

Elisa had gone to her bathroom and was in her bathtub. Her bathroom had a sit down vanity in it and a whirlpool bath. It was decorated in ocean blue and light pink. She had the bathroom redone when she bought the townhouse.

Elisa did not want to think about it, but she was worried that Kyle might try to steal something. Before they left, she would have Cora double check everything. She did not want to do this to a man that did a good deed to her, but still he was homeless and she saw the way he was looking around at her living room.

In the other bathroom, Kyle felt like he was in paradise.

CHAPTER 11

Kyle got dressed, got shaved, and put some after shave on. He felt like a new man. He was not sure how to work the tie, so he left it off. He had put the dress shoes on that Elisa had bought him. He walked out of the bathroom.

Elisa had finished her bath and was dressed. She was putting some finishing touches on her makeup. "There, that should do it," she said. She went to check on Kyle. She saw him standing outside of the bathroom he had used. She could not believe her eyes. He looked totally different than the man who she saw on the sidewalk earlier.

"Wow, you do clean up good." Elisa said walking over to him.

Kyle smiled and said "thank you."

"I do not feel like myself," Kyle said lightly.

"That is because this is not familiar to you Kyle. Now let me help you with that tie." Elisa grabbed the tie and put it on Kyle and started to tie it. He could smell her perfume. It was the same one he smelled on her earlier today. It had been so long since he smelled perfume on a woman.

Her standing so close, it made him miss being with a woman. He had not felt a woman's touch since Janice left him. Her standing in front of him brought back those memories. "There we go," said Elisa. She had gotten his tie on and fixed. She saw his eyes watering. "Is something wrong Kyle?"

"Oh no, my eyes water once in a while," he did not want to tell her that being near her brought back memories of his marriage.

"My housekeeper Cora is good at cutting hair. We can

have her do that. We still have time." She looked down at his nails. "We do not have time to take you anywhere to get you a manicure done so I will clean your nails as best as I can. "Follow me." Kyle followed Elisa back into the bathroom. She had him sit down on the toilet seat. "I will get my housekeeper."

Elisa left. He felt like a king. He was not use to getting pampered like this even when he was married. A few minutes later, Elisa was back with Cora. "I need you to give him a haircut and I will clean his nails."

"Si Senorita Drinnings, I will." Cora grabbed a comb and scissors out of the drawer and started in on his hair. While Cora was cutting, Elisa was cleaning his nails.

Elisa's hands were soft and smooth. She had no flaws on her hands or anywhere that Kyle could see. She was beautiful all over. She was even more beautiful than his ex-wife Janice. Kyle's hands were rough. Elisa saw the calluses on his hands. Where Guy's hands were well manicured and soft, Kyle's was rough and rugged. Elisa could tell that these hands had seen some hard work and hard times.

When they were finished, Kyle's nails were better than they were before. Cora gave him a mirror to look at himself. Kyle let out a whistle. "Who is that man in the mirror? I do not recognize him." Kyle grinned.

Elisa laughed. "Alright, we better get going."

"I will clean up before I leave Miss Drinnings." Cora told her.

"Gracias Cora," "De nada," she responded.

Kyle walked out of the bathroom and Elisa had asked Cora to just check things and Cora said she would. Cora knew what she meant. Elisa and Kyle walked outside and the car was waiting. Kyle got in first and then Elisa. Elisa still could not believe that this was the same man whom she talked to a few hours ago on the street. If she did not know any better, she would think that he was a well to do man with a fortune.

Kyle knew this was a façade, after dinner, he would change and go back to his "home" under the bridge. His one night of feeling like Prince Charming going with Cinderella to the ball was all it was. Like Cinderella, after midnight the coach would turn back into a pumpkin, the driver would become a mouse again, his clothes would be back to being tattered and torn, and he would go back to his dwelling place.

Elisa was wearing a violet dress with spaghetti straps and a jacket over it. The dress came down to her calves. She had on heels to match. The jewelry she had on made the backseat of the car light up. "You look gorgeous tonight Elisa," Kyle said softly.

"Thank you Kyle and you look handsome." Elisa turned back around to stare straight ahead and Kyle turned to look out the window.

They got to the restaurant. Kyle watched as others walked in all dressed up in their suits and ties with women dressed as if they were going to the Academy Awards. Elisa put her arm through Kyle's and they walked in the restaurant. The waiter knew her well and took her to the table. They sat down. Kyle looked at all the silverware, dishes, and glasses. This is more dining ware than what he carried in his backpack.

"Just do what I do," Elisa said. Kyle looked over the menu. From his time being in culinary school, Kyle knew many of the items on the menu. If he and his ex-best friend now would have opened up their own restaurant, he could have cooked like this.

Kyle put down the menu and the waiter came over. "What can I get you two to drink?"

"Just give us a bottle of your fine wine." Elisa said.

"I shall do that my dear." The waiter smiled at Elisa.

"They sure do know you here," Kyle remarked when the waiter walked away.

"I have been taken here by many dates Kyle." Elisa remarked back.

"I see."

"And what is that supposed to mean Kyle?" Elisa asked him seeming offended by it.

"I did not mean to make it sound like it did Elisa. I am just saying with a beautiful woman such as yourself, I am not surprised that you would have plenty of men."

Elisa laughed. "Why is that a beautiful woman such as you is not married?" Kyle asked her boldly.

"We are having dinner for the first time."

"The first and only time Elisa." Kyle interjected. "You do not have to answer the question if you do not want to."

Elisa sighed. "I am married to my career. I have worked too hard to give it all up for a man."

"Oh, one of those types of women." Kyle looked at her.

"Is there anything wrong with that?" Elisa intoned.

Kyle held up his hand. "Oh no ma'am, that is alright by me."

"You think a woman should stay home and be a housewife?" Elisa said to him.

"I am sorry to have offended you Elisa."

"What about you Kyle? Did you have a wife? Anyone you use to love? How did you end up like this?" Before he could answer, the waiter came back with their wine, opened it, and poured them each a glass.

"Would you two like to order?" Elisa ordered her meal and Kyle ordered his.

When the waiter walked away, Elisa leaned up to him. "I am impressed. You ordered like you have been here before."

"Pretty good for a homeless man," Kyle said looking at her. Elisa backed up.

"I did not mean it like that and I was not insinuating that, sorry if I offended you."

"None taken, I can read and you forget I went to culinary school. I made many of these dishes."

"So why are you not working as a chef now?" It was the same question she asked him back at her townhouse. "You would not have to be living this kind of life now." Elisa took a drink of her wine.

"I did not choose to be like this Elisa. Sometimes things happen that are beyond our control. Life deals you a hand and sometimes you have to play the cards you are given."

"Not always Kyle. This is America, the land of opportunity.

We all have that choice. I chose to go to college, build a successful career, so I can have the kind of things I have and eat in places like this." Elisa said defensively.

"Yes Miss Elisa, I see that. I made my choices too and I took the opportunity I was given, but circumstances happened that were beyond my control. You think I want to live like this, that I want to wake up every morning having to panhandle my way through another day, to make enough to get enough to eat? I never asked for this. You see this is the problem with people such as yourself, you just assume that everyone should live in this ritzy lifestyle.

"Regardless of certain things that can be beyond our control; before this dinner and me returning your pocketbook you never had the audacity to even speak to me. If I had never returned that pocketbook to you Elisa, we would not be having this dinner together and we definitely would not be having this conversation. You would never have talked to me."

Elisa remained silent. Some people were starting to stare.

"Take a good look Elisa; I am not the only homeless person here in New York or America for that matter. I do not think that all of us chose this lifestyle. You had good luck come your way and you were able to be successful, as for me, until good luck comes my way or my circumstances change, I will forever be the man you see on that sidewalk."

Elisa put her hands under her chin. She had opened up a can of worms. "I am sorry Kyle," Elisa said softly. "

Stop apologizing Elisa and wake up." By that time, their food had come. They ate mainly in silence. Kyle was eating his food. "I could cook way better than this."

"Really?" Elisa asked him.

"Oh yes. Hell, I was cooking like this in school and I would have if I could have opened our own restaurant."

"What do you mean by opening our own restaurant Kyle?" Elisa asked him sincerely. Kyle put down his knife and fork.

He looked up at her. "I do not want to talk about it. It was years ago and just a dream."

"But…"

"I said I do not want to talk about it Elisa. It is in the past."
They finished eating and the waiter came back over.

"Can I get you two anything else?"

"No thank you sir that will be all. Please bring me the bill."
Elisa had her hands folded. The waiter nodded his head and
left.

"This was a wonderful meal Elisa. The best meal I have had
in years." Elisa looked at Kyle and smiled.

The waiter came back and Elisa paid the bill leaving him
a nice tip. They walked out into the cool night air. You could
feel fall in the air. Elisa took a deep breath. Elisa had called
her driver. They could hear the sounds of New York all around
them as the people rushed by them.

Her driver pulled up and they both got in. "I can give you
a place to stay tonight." Elisa said to him. "No, that will be
okay, just tell your driver where to take me." Elisa told her
driver what Kyle told her and he drove off. They rode the way
in silence.

"Stop here," Kyle told the driver.

"What?" Elisa asked him.

"I said stop the car." Kyle reiterated now with more
gumption. "I can walk the rest of the way."

"Kyle this is New York."

"Yes I know Elisa. I have walked this and lived this way for
years and I have survived. I have survived worse than this. I
am a survivor Elisa." The driver had stopped the car and was
waiting patiently.

"You will need a change of clothes Kyle." Elisa reminded
him.

"I have some in my backpack. I will give you back the suit,
tie, and shoes. I will have them in my backpack when you pass
me on the sidewalk tomorrow morning. You can pick them up
then."

He started to get out. Elisa grabbed his arm. "Driver, turn
the car around please."

"What in the hell are you doing Elisa?" Kyle asked her
angrily. "You will do no such thing driver."

"Hey, this is my car and my driver and I will make the calls. Turn the car around please."

The driver did as he was told. "Where are we going?" Kyle asked demandingly. Elisa said nothing. "You are a crazy woman," Kyle sat back against the seat.

They pulled up to her townhouse and Elisa got out. "Are you coming?"

"Do I have a choice?" Kyle asked her arrogantly. "

And with the same attitude he used with her, she used with him. "You can walk, but it will be a long walk."

"I am use to it." Kyle spat. "When you returned my pocketbook you took a taxi. You did not walk." Elisa said satisfactorily.

Kyle walked back up to her. "Why did you not walk to return my pocketbook but now you want to walk back?"

Elisa crossed her arms. "You are a stubborn and demanding woman."

Kyle seethed. "Is that all the response you can come up with to my question?"

"Look I paid with my own money to take a taxi to do a kind deed. You chose to take me to dinner. I can, for free, walk back."

"Please Kyle, out of the kindness of my heart; let you stay here for the night."

"Oh, so now you are inviting me to stay in your home at the kindness of your heart. Far be it for me to refuse."

Elisa turned around and Kyle followed behind her. She unlocked the door and they both walked in. "We will get you changed. I have some clothes that would fit you. There is an extra bedroom for you to sleep in. Don't worry about making the bed in the morning, I will have my housekeeper Cora do that."

He followed her up the stairs. She went into another room and gave him some clothes. He went into the bathroom and came out a few minutes later. "Well I guess this is where we say goodnight." Elisa told him.

"Yeah, goodnight Elisa," he walked out of the room to the

guest room. Elisa shut the door.

She turned and put her back against the door and sighed. It had been a long day; a long evening for that matter. She got out of her dress clothes and into her night clothes, brushed her hair, took off her makeup, and put some night cream on her face. She got into bed and turned off the light. Why she had invited him to stay she did not know, but she hoped that he was not a raging killer or a rapist. She would take her chances.

She lay there thinking about the events of tonight before finally falling into a deep sleep.

In the other room, Kyle lay with his hands behind his head. Instead of looking up at the sky, he was staring up at the ceiling. He had forgotten what it felt like to sleep in a real bed. In the military he would sleep in a tent on a cot or sometimes on the desert ground.

She had invited him to dinner for returning her pocketbook, why she had invited him to stay a night in her home was a mystery to him. He had hoped she did not think of him as a killer or a rapist. The bed was so soft and his head sank in the pillow. He closed his eyes with images of tonight in his head.

CHAPTER 12

The next morning Elisa got dressed for work. She walked to the guest bedroom and saw the door opened. She looked in but no one was on the bed. The bed had been made. The suit had been hung up and the clothes she gave him to sleep in were folded up on the bed but no Kyle. She looked around and everything seemed to be in order. She wanted to see if he wanted to have a nice breakfast before leaving.

His backpack was gone, she checked the second bathroom to see if he was using it and the door was wide open with no one in it. She shrugged her shoulders, sighed, and walked downstairs. She walked into the kitchen and poured herself a cup of coffee. Emilio had finished her breakfast.

"Buenos dias Senorita Drinnings." Emilio said to her.

"Buenos dias Senor Emilio. Did you happen to see Kyle the man I took to dinner last night leave?" Elisa asked him, sitting down to eat her breakfast.

"No, senorita, I did not see or hear anything. He must have left really early, even before I came."

"I checked the guest bedroom and the other bathroom but nothing. The bed was made, the suit was hung up, and the clothes I gave him to wear were neatly folded on the bed."

"Strange," said Emilio. "How did you meet him? Does he work with you?"

Elisa put down her fork. "He stands in front of my office building and begs for money. He's apparently homeless."

"I see." Emilio said and let Elisa continue.

"I have seen him a lot standing on that sidewalk." Elisa took another drink of her coffee.

"How did you end up taking him to dinner?" Emilio asked her.

"He found my pocketbook that I had lost without knowing it. It was the day I was leaving for the Greek Isles. There was a knock on my door and I opened it because I gave you and Cora the weekend off. And lo and behold it was him. I asked what the hell he was doing here and how he knew where I lived and that is when he produced the pocketbook that I had lost.

Of course it had my ID in it so he knew where I lived. He had taken a taxi and I wondered how he could afford a taxi to get here. I was very harsh with him and then yesterday I thanked him for it and got up the nerve to ask him to dinner as a way of saying thanks."

Emilio smiled. "You know Elisa, if it is out of love and goodness, it doesn't matter the means of how people do things."

Elisa sighed. "Well Emilio, this was a great breakfast. Gracias Emilio. I would like to have for dinner one of your Guatemalan dishes." Elisa said, grabbing her briefcase.

"Si Senorita Drinnings and one more thing," Elisa turned around. "My family was poor, we did not live like this," Emilio moved his hands around the kitchen, "but we were lucky to have found a way to come to America for a better life.

My family wanted me and my brothers and sisters to have a better life. They did it out of love. So they found whatever means necessary to get here. Have a good day Senorita Drinnings." Elisa smiled and told him to have a good day too. She saw Cora coming in. She told Cora about the guest bedroom, that her guest was gone, and to do some checking. Cora said she would get right on it.

Elisa gave Cora a hug and was out the door with Emilio's words dancing in her head. She got to the office and did not see Kyle. She takes him to dinner, lets him stay in her place for the night, and now he is nowhere to be found. Not surprising she thought. He did not even stay to say thank you for giving him a place to stay for the night. Elisa shrugged her shoulders and went to work.

For the rest of the week, Elisa did not see Kyle, every night she would go home, eat her nice home cooked meal that Emilio would fix her, and then take a nice hot bath. She would go to bed exhausted. Maggie had not called her back yet, but she would give her till next week to call her and then Elisa would phone her.

By Friday afternoon, Elisa was ready for the weekend. She was thinking about Kyle when her cell phone rang. "Hello." Elisa said going over some things.

"Hello my Mon Cherie. I wanted to tell you that I will be back in New York tomorrow morning and I wanted to have dinner and take my Mon Cherie to a nice show."

"What did you have in mind for a show?" Elisa asked hastily.

"Elisa dear is everything okay?" Guy asked concerned.

"Oh yes, just tired. It has been a busy week." "Okay, well, I thought that we would go to Carnegie Hall. There is a nice orchestra playing there this weekend. We would have a nice dinner and then relax with some music.

What do you say Elisa?"

"Wouldn't they be out of tickets by now?"

"Oh my Mon Cherie, you have been busy. You do need a nice weekend of relaxation with me. You forget it is me Guy. I am a regular customer there and have been for years, they know me. I can get tickets believe me and plus, the best seats in the house."

Elisa got up and looked out her window. No sign of Kyle. "That sounds enchanting. I would enjoy that very much Guy."

"Then it is settled. I will make dinner reservations and I will pick you up Saturday evening at seven. I shall go now. I need to tie up some loose ends and then I will be back on a flight to New York. Goodbye my Mon Cherie." Guy kissed into the phone. "I miss you."

"I miss you too Guy," Elisa said and made kissing sounds. She hung up her cell phone.

⊰⊱✴⊰⊱

Just a few blocks down, Kyle was in a florist shop looking

at some bouquet of flowers. "Can I help you," the lady asked him. She was wearing glasses with beaded straps going around her neck. She had her hair pinned up and came up to Kyle's shoulders. She saw the outfit he was wearing and wondered if he would even have the money to buy anything, or was this a rouse and he was going to rob her?

"Yes," said Kyle turning to her. "I would like to buy a bouquet of flowers to send to a friend of mine. I like this one." He pointed to the one that had yellow roses and carnations mixed in together in a beautiful basket.

"That is very expensive; we have some other ones that are not so expensive."

Kyle knew what she was getting at, he may be homeless, but he was not stupid. "No, I want this one." Kyle said adamantly.

"I see, um well let me get that for you and I will take you over here and I will ring it up. Would you like to have a card for it to say something? It will be extra." Kyle looked at her. She had barely made eye contact with him.

"Go ahead and add it, I will pay for it." Kyle said stiffly.

"What would you like the card to say?"

"Dear Elisa, thank you for dinner and letting me stay at your place for the night." The woman stopped writing for a few seconds. "Is there a problem?" Kyle was getting angry.

"Oh no sir," she finished writing it and put it in the flowers. "Now, you can deliver this yourself or we can sir. What would you prefer?"

Kyle wanted to just get the hell out of there; this lady was treating him as if he were less than human.

"I would like to have it delivered to her townhouse." Kyle remembered her address and gave it to the lady. The lady gave him the price and he paid for it. It took every last penny that he had to pay for it.

"Will there be anything else today sir?" The lady asked him, but before she got a response, Kyle was out the door. Kyle could not wait to get out of there. He headed to go and see Mildred.

⇒⊱⊰⇐

Elisa got home and walked into her townhouse. She walked into the kitchen. There was a note from Emilio telling her that her dinner was ready and he kept it warm for her and that he had a family emergency to tend to. Elisa hoped that everything was okay. She took her dinner, grabbed her a glass of wine, went into her living room, turned on some light music, and flipped through some of her competitors magazines.

Yes, even she read her competitors magazines to see what they had. Emilio had outdone himself again. The meal was exquisite. Cora came down the steps and said that everything is done and in order. "Cora, Emilio left a note saying he had a family emergency, did he say anything to you?"

"Oh no senorita, I was busy doing my cleaning and tidying up. I did not see him leave."

"Thanks Cora. Have a good evening." Elisa smiled.

"Buenos noches, senorita Drinnings, if there is nothing else, then I shall be heading out."

Elisa looked up from her magazine. "No Cora that will be all."

"Adios Senorita Drinnings,." Cora grabbed her jacket. "

Adios Cora." Elisa heard the door open and shut. She heard the lock click. Cora was just in the habit even with her there, to lock her door. Elisa finished her meal and put the magazine down. She took her hands to her face and rubbed it, then through her hair, and back down her face.

She had so much running through her mind. She did not have Cora run her a bath. It was okay. She sat back on her couch with her feet under her and drank her wine; the music helping her to calm down.

⇒⊱⊰⇐

Kyle had sat with Mildred after her shift. It was getting late. Kyle had told Mildred about the woman inviting him to dinner for returning her pocketbook after she nearly accused him of stealing and thinking he was stalking her.

He told her about her letting him stay the night in the guest bedroom. "After she talked to you like this Kyle, she did this all for you? Why do you think she did that?" Mildred had given Kyle some bread and again bought him dinner. He told her that all of his money went to buying those flowers for Elisa.

"I guess maybe her conscience got the best of her. Maybe her heart of ice is melting." Kyle laughed.

"Maybe so," Mildred said patting his hand. "Inviting you to dinner was one thing, but letting you stay there overnight was another. People can change Kyle."

"I made the bed, left the clothes that she got me there, and headed out. I haven't been back there. I am afraid that she would be angry with me for just up and leaving, so I sent the flowers hoping that may quell her anger.

"I have been working another sidewalk this week and looking to find the best way to thank her." Kyle took a sip of his coffee.

"Oh Kyle, with what you have told me, the flowers, the card you sent with them, and her having a change of heart, I am sure she will be delighted at the flowers." Mildred said.

"I hope so," said Kyle. "I mean it was rude of me just to up and leave without saying thank you, but I guess I got scared. It has been a long, long time since I have slept in a normal bed with clean sheets and fluffy pillows. Oh she is beautiful Mildred. Just being next to her made me nervous; it has been so long since I have been that close to a woman. She has everything Mildred.

"She has a cook, a housekeeper, and a driver. I wonder if she thinks I stole anything from her house. I am sure she was just as nervous having some homeless man under her roof. Probably thinking I could be a serial killer or rapist. I just wanted to get up, not bother her, and leave everything as I found it."

"She does not know the Kyle that I do. I am sure that everything you have described of her is true. I am sure that she does have everything to you because you feel you have nothing. You have so much to give Kyle." Mildred said softly.

"I wish that I could believe that. I mean I have nothing to

offer a woman like that. I mean we live in two totally different worlds, both socially and financially. There is nothing Mildred that I have to offer her." Kyle finished his coffee. It was getting dark out and Kyle got up to leave.

"Thank you again Mildred for the talk, the coffee, and the food. Someday I am going to pay you back."

Mildred got up and gave him a hug. "You owe me nothing Kyle. You have paid your dues. Take care Kyle."

"You too Mildred, goodnight," Kyle turned and walked out the door.

"Goodnight Kyle." Mildred said softly to Kyle's back. Kyle would save the bread for tomorrow for the birds.

He just hoped that the flowers would get there. He wondered how she would react to them. It was the only way he could pay her back for what she did. It may have taken the rest of his money, but it was better than nothing. He got to his place of dwelling and sat under the bridge watching the darkened sky. He thought that he could sense rain; he was far enough under the bridge that he would stay dry.

He wondered what Elisa was doing right now.

❈❈❈❈❈❈❈

Elisa had gotten her bath and was lying in bed. She was staring out her window. Emilio had a family emergency; Kyle did not even show up all week and had left without saying goodbye. She was tired but could not sleep. She lay there for hours thinking.

CHAPTER 13

Elisa got up late Saturday. She was sitting at her kitchen table drinking her cup of coffee when the doorbell rang. *Who could that be she thought?* Elisa knew it was too early for Guy to be there. She got up to answer the door. She opened and saw a man standing there with a bouquet of roses and carnations.

"Are you Elisa Drinnings?" The delivery man asked her.

"Yes I am." Elisa said, still looking at the flowers.

"Then these are for you." He handed her the flowers.

"Who are they from?" Elisa asked him.

"I do not know ma'am, but I need you to sign for them." She signed on the line and handed it back to the man.

"Have a good day ma'am."

"You too, thank you." Elisa reiterated and shut her door.

She set them on the stand in her foyer and saw the card. She opened it and read what was on it. She could not believe it. Kyle had sent these flowers and a card thanking her for the other night. These must have cost him a fortune or everything he had. She put the card in the drawer and went back into the kitchen. She still had not heard from her cook Emilio.

She had fixed her a light breakfast and put the dishes in the dishwasher. She went upstairs to pick what she would wear tonight. She settled on a black evening gown that had diamonds going down each side of it and with a low cut back. She grabbed her black suede boot heels and a jacket to match. The evenings were getting a lot cooler.

She had a black diamond bag to match. If she saw Kyle, she would tell him she appreciated them but a simple thank you would have been sufficient. How would she explain this to Guy? He would surely want to know where they came from and from whom. She would just have to make up something.

———✳———

Kyle was sitting on the bench feeding the birds. He wondered if Elisa got her flowers. She should have gotten them by now. He would be back on the sidewalk and she would see him. She would either mention about the flowers or not. Kyle watched the people walk and jogging by him. It had rained last night, but the sun quickly dried things out.

Kyle got up to go so he could have dinner tonight.

———✳———

Guy showed up at precisely seven p.m. Elisa was all dressed up in her clothes and answered the door. Guy looked handsome as ever. "Oh how I have missed you my Mon Cherie." He picked her up and kissed her hard. Elisa put her arms around him and he swung her around. He looked and saw the bouquet of flowers.

"Who are these from?" Guy put her down. Elisa knew this moment would come so she had prepared herself.

"Um, there was no card so I am not sure. They are beautiful are they not?"

"Yes they are, but it is strange that whoever sent them sent no card." Guy touched them. "I go to San Francisco for a week and come back to find my Mon Cherie with a bouquet of flowers in her house. Do you have a secret admirer?" Elisa could sense some hint of jealousy.

"Um, no not that I know of, I thought that they were from you. I knew you would be back today and I thought that you wanted to surprise me not only with dinner and a show but these flowers as well." Elisa hoped that she was being convincing enough.

"No Elisa, you know in the whole year that we have been together, when have I ever sent a bouquet of flowers to your house?"

Elisa did not know what to say, she knew he was right.

"Well you know there is a first time for everything." Elisa now wished that she hadn't of gotten them or at least hid them, maybe have thrown them away. She would definitely talk to Kyle when she saw him.

"Well anyway, we are going to be late if we do not leave now." Guy walked out in front of her and Elisa shut and locked the door. Elisa saw that he drove his sports car. "You brought your car tonight I see." Elisa was trying to ease the tension.

"Yes," Guy said walking around to his side of the car. Elisa opened her side and got in.

The drive to the restaurant was in silence. She could see the tension in his face. They got to the restaurant and the valet parked his car. They went inside and to their table. They ordered their wine and went ahead and ordered their dinner. "How was your trip? Is everything okay with your store there?" Elisa asked hoping to quell the tension between them.

"My trip was fine and everything is going well now." Guy answered her. Elisa could not understand his attitude. They were not engaged, they were not married, and she did not love him, but enjoyed being with him. She did not belong to him or any man. She could kill Kyle for sending those flowers, but how could she blame him, he did not know about Guy.

Their dinner came and Elisa thought that she would bring up about her idea of Pose's new fragrance line. She would hope that would change Guy's mood from upset to easy going. To go back to the man she knew last week before the flowers. "I have come up with a fragrance line for Pose. It would be for men and women. I thought of it when we were in the Greek Isles. I figured that we could be the first fashion magazine to have this." Elisa waited for a response. When she did not get one, she continued. "I know this sounds like a lot and you must be wondering how this is all going to be pulled off. But, I already have someone working out all the legalities, the patenting of it, and the financial aspect of it." She took a sip of her wine.

"So what do you think Guy?" Elisa asked him with her elbows on the table and her hands folded under her chin.

"That sounds like it would be successful if you can get it off the ground." Guy said somberly.

"I am glad you think so," Elisa said throwing her napkin on the table.

"Is this someone who is helping you with this the same one who got you that bouquet?" Guy asked her looking at her.

"Please Guy, let us not start this. We are having a nice dinner and I have not seen you for a week. Let us enjoy the rest of this night, shall we?" Elisa said, moving closer so they would not be overheard. "Is there someone else that I should know about Elisa?" Elisa was offended by that question. "Is this why you refused my hand in marriage?" Guy had pushed his plate away and grabbed his wine. The waiter came over and took their dishes.

When he left, Elisa was hurt and upset now. "There is no one else Guy and besides, you knew from the first time we met my feelings on marriage. We have had this discussion before and my feelings on it have not changed. I am married to my career and I have worked too hard to throw it all away. There is no other man in my life and I am adamant on not wanting to commit."

Guy called the waiter over and asked for the bill. "I am not asking you to throw anything away Elisa. I know how hard you have worked. You just fear marriage because of what your father did to your mother." That hit Elisa right in the heart. The waiter came back and Guy paid the bill.

"Well," Elisa said obviously hurt by this statement, "it looks like this evening is over. Please take me home now."

Guy and her walked out of the restaurant and he drove her back to her townhouse. When he pulled up to the curb, he did not even get out to open the car door for her. "I will be busy with my stores so I am not sure when I will be able to see you again Elisa." Guy kept staring straight ahead without looking over at her.

"That is fine, for I will be busy myself." Elisa got out and slammed the door. He pulled way leaving Elisa standing on her step. *To hell with all men,* she thought.

They all acted so childish. She didn't need them anyway.

She had done fine on her own. She walked in her townhouse and saw the bouquet that started this whole mess. She slammed her keys on the table and picked up the bouquet and threw it across the hall. The flowers and water went everywhere. She didn't care. Cora would clean it up.

She grabbed a glass of wine and went upstairs. She changed and got washed up. She sat in her bed drinking her wine. This had been a shitty night. She had too much going on with Pose Magazine and getting her idea up and running. She would not let this night get in the way of her success. She had to stay focused.

⇜⇝✳⇜⇝

On Monday morning, Cora came over and saw the mess. "What happened here Senorita Drinnings?" Cora put her hands to her face. She saw the mess all over the hallway floor.

"Nothing Cora," Cora looked at her and grabbed the broom, dustpan, and towels. Elisa walked into the kitchen. Emilio was in there.

Emilio had a somber look on his face. "I need to speak with you Senorita Drinnings. I am sorry I left out of here in such a hurry Friday but my family needed me.

My father called me. My mother is very ill. He is working two jobs right now and cannot take care of her as much as he wants to. My sisters and brothers are married and they all have family yes, and they are doing as much as they can too. It has become a burden. I am not sure how much longer they can hold out.

I am sorry Senorita Drinnings I am not sure how much longer I can work. I will need to be with my family. I have never married nor had kids. I would be in a much better position to help my family." This was another blow to Elisa. Emilio had become like Elisa's father. She had hired him after she got the Chief Editor's position at Pose.

She did not know what she would do if Emilio left, but she understood his situation. Emilio knew her family situation, they had long talks. Emilio's family was tight knit and she did not want to ruin that. "I understand Emilio and I am not upset. If you need to leave and take care of your mother full-time I will give you a good severance pay."

"Oh gracias Senorita, I have such a kind and understanding employer." Emilio hugged Elisa. She would miss him dearly when and if he had to leave. Emilio was the only man she had truly loved besides her father until he did what he did to their mother. Emilio thought of Elisa as his daughter and it would be hard to leave, but family came first.

"I am so sorry to hear that Emilio."

"Thank you Elisa."

"I will fix you a great dinner tonight Elisa." Emilio said to her and he could see the tears forming in her eyes.

"You always do Emilio. That is why I hired you." Elisa tried to smile.

"Oh do not cry Elisa. We can still stay in contact if I need to leave."

"That would be great Emilio. I would like that. I better head to work. I will have another busy week." Elisa hugged Emilio again and headed out. Cora had cleaned up the mess left by the bouquet. "Adios Cora and thank you for cleaning that up."

"You are welcome my dear and have a good day at work." Elisa waved and was gone.

※※※※※

She got to work and saw Kyle on the sidewalk. She walked up to him. "Well hello there," said Kyle. "How was your weekend?"

"Kyle, I know you sent the flowers." Elisa had her hands on her hips.

"Yes, as a way of saying thank you for dinner and letting me stay there at your place Elisa."

"A simple thank you would have been sufficient but you managed to disappear like Houdini without making a noise.

And then I do not see you all week. It is like I do this nice thing and you do not show up, not to mention that you sent me that bouquet which was nice, and I thank you, but it caused a rift between me and my lover. He got upset and asked if I was seeing someone else. Please Kyle, do not send me flowers again to my townhouse. Do you understand me?"

"Yes ma'am, I was just trying to be thankful for running out without thanking you or saying goodbye. I was on another sidewalk all week. I was scared. I was trying to make up for it." Kyle said offended. "I will not send you any more flowers again." Kyle turned back around.

"Can you not stay at a homeless shelter? I mean they have to be all over the place." Elisa waved her hand. "This is New York. It will be getting colder in a couple of months."

"Well I thank you for your concern Elisa, but they are only temporary and by the morning you have to leave. What good is that going to do me anyway? Even in the winter time I will still be outside."

"It would be better than wherever you're sleeping now," Elisa commented.

"I have survived many winters where I am at dear Elisa. Besides, homeless shelters fill up fast and I do not want my stuff getting stolen." Kyle said flatly.

Elisa looked around and wondered what he would have that someone would want to steal. "You live in New York, I am sure a homeless shelter would be more beneficial and safer than where you are at now." "Thank you for your concern Elisa, but I have done okay so far."

"Okay then do what you want, but please no more flowers sent to me." Elisa pointed her finger at him.

"Aye, Aye captain." Kyle saluted her.

Elisa walked away fuming. Elisa walked into her office and slammed the door. Sissy looked up from her computer startled. Sissy wondered what happened to her.

Elisa opened her door. "Sissy hold all my calls except for if it is from Maggie Bench. I will take that one."

"Certainly," Sissy responded. Elisa shut her door. Sissy got back to typing. She wanted to give Elisa time to cool down. Elisa slammed her briefcase down on her desk and sat down. She put her hands up to her face. She could feel the warmness of her tears touching her hands.

Everything that had transpired over the weekend had taken its toll, but she had a job to do and magazine to run. She could not let herself break down now.

⊰✵⊱

Kyle could not understand her. Every time he tried to do a nice thing for her she would get upset. It counteracted what she did for him. He did not need her. He did not need anything from her or want anything from her again.

CHAPTER 14

By lunchtime, Elisa had not heard from Maggie. She wanted to call her but thought against it. It was only Monday and she trusted Maggie to call her before the end of the week. Sissy had knocked on the door. "Come in," Elisa said looking up from her laptop.

"I was just going to go and get something to eat, would you like to come with me?" Sissy asked her. Sissy was going to her favorite deli.

"No thanks Sissy. I have so much work and besides, I am not hungry right now." Elisa gave a half smile and looked back down at her laptop.

"You alright Elisa?" Sissy asked, shutting the door.

"Yes Sissy. I am just not hungry today. I want to skip lunch today. I want to make sure I am here when Maggie calls."

Sissy looked at Elisa skeptically. "You seemed distraught. Is there anything you want to talk about?"

Elisa sighed. "I am okay Sissy and besides, it is nothing really."

Sissy wasn't buying that for a minute but she shrugged her shoulders. "Okay then. I will go and grab me some lunch. Is there anything you need before I go?" Sissy was hoping this would be the moment when Elisa would say "yes" and tell Sissy to sit down and tell her what is ailing Elisa.

But instead she told Sissy no. "I will be back before you know it. Bye," said Sissy.

"Bye Sissy," Elisa repeated. Elisa continued to work the rest of the day. She had worked late. It was after seven before she got out of the office. She headed out and walked right past where Kyle would have been. It was a good thing he was gone, she would not have even looked his way.

She got into her car and headed home. When she got there, Emilio had her supper all ready. She still wasn't hungry but she loved Emilio's cooking and did not want to waste it. She picked it up and tried to eat it. Every bite was harder and harder to eat. She finished what she could and grabbed her glass of wine to head upstairs to take a bath and look over some papers.

She ran her a hot bubble bath and sank into her bath inhaling the scent of the bubbles. She did not think about Guy, Kyle, or anyone.

⊰⊱⊰⊱⊰⊱⊰⊱

Kyle sat under the bridge. He had stopped by the hamburger shop to talk to Mildred. As always, she took the time to listen. He told her everything about how Elisa had invited him to dinner, bought him a new outfit, let him stay in her townhouse, about the flowers he sent her, and Elisa's reaction. Mildred being her usual motherly self listened until Kyle was done talking.

"It sounds like she wanted to make up for the way she treated you after you returned her pocketbook. But I must say, I do not think that it was so bad you sending her the flowers. You just wanted to return the favor of dinner and letting you stay there. How were you supposed to know that she had a lover?" Mildred said softly.

"I feel guilty by sending her those flowers and causing that rift, but I didn't mean to cause any problems. I felt offended by her outburst. It seems that when I try to do something nice for her, her stubborn and condescending attitude counters everything nice I do for her. I do not want anything from her again. I do not need her." Kyle said vehemently.

To Mildred, it seemed that this woman that Kyle talked about entrenched his mind and heart. She knew he had not been with another woman since Janice. She didn't want his hurt over what Janice did to him to boil over to this woman. Mildred would love to be able to meet her and tell her what kind of man Kyle was. There had to be another side to this lady.

"Plato had a saying my dear Kyle. *Be kind to everyone, for everyone is fighting some kind of battle.*"

"That is a nice sentiment Mildred, but it seems that this woman wants to start one." Kyle said getting up.

Mildred got up too. "Kyle my son," Mildred had called him that for years. Mildred put her hands on his cheeks. "One of these days, you may find out that you need each other. I know it sounds silly, but you never know."

"How could she need me?" Kyle laughed. "She has everything she wants."

"Yes you have told me that Kyle, but you never know what is going on in someone else's life. I do not care if they have a mansion to live in with a hundred servants, or a nice car, or loads of money. You just never know." Mildred gave him a kiss on the cheek and told him to be careful.

He hugged her and walked out the door. Now sitting under the bridge he still found Mildred's echoing words preposterous. He loved Mildred dearly and she was wise, but she had never met this lady nor ever had to deal with her. Kyle looked up at the sky. He would do this in the cold Afghan desert, just look up at the sky and wonder about home, Janice, and having a family and kind of life he wanted when he got out of the military.

He had dreamed of being part restaurant owner, but all his dreams were dashed. Looking up at the sky, there is no way that him and Elisa could ever possibly need each other or have anything in common. This was his life now.

⊰⊱⊰⊱

The rest of the week Elisa had kept her mind off Guy. He had not called and it was just as well. She had nothing to say to him. He had accused her of something that was not true. She did not care if he ever called her again. He was handsome and great in bed but that did not make up for his incessant accusations that were based on no evidence.

She did get some great news when Maggie called. "Hello Maggie." Elisa said enthusiastically. She needed to get out of the doldrums of everything that had gone on that week. She was so happy to hear from Maggie. "Meet me at the corner coffee shop at one o'clock sharp." Maggie told her.

"I will certainly do that." Elisa answered back. She looked at her watch. It was eleven thirty a.m. She had an hour and a half to be there. "I will be in my usual spot." Elisa knew where that was and reiterated again that she would be there. Elisa hung up the phone.

Sissy came in all bubbly. "I got the morning paper dear Elisa. They have given rave reviews about our winter edition of Pose Magazine." Sissy handed her the article. Elisa sat down and read it. Elisa slammed it down on her desk.

"Yes," Elisa clapped her hands together. "Wait until the spring fashion show. They will be raving about it even more. This is why Sissy I work so hard and I am so demanding. This!" she picked up the newspaper and shook it.

"This is why I push my crew so hard. You do not get talked about in the news without making some kind of splash."

Sissy was glad to see that Elisa was in a better mood than she was at the beginning of the week. "Why don't we go out and celebrate?" Sissy asked her.

"I would, but I have a meeting with Maggie Bench at one o'clock sharp. I am not going to be late."

"Is it about the fragrance line for Pose?" Sissy asked excitedly.

"That is all I can think of what it is for. You see Sissy, Pose is becoming even more of a phenomenon. I am proud to say that I am Chief Editor of it too."

"Well, I am glad to see that you are doing better Elisa than what you were before. Do you have anything planned for this weekend? You going to see Guy and go off on an exotic and romantic trip, a nice dinner, or a show?" Sissy asked. She could see the look in Elisa's eyes and her stiffening up.

"No." Elisa said shortly. Sissy knew she had hit a nerve.

"I am so sorry Elisa. I should never have brought it up."

"No Sissy it is okay. If I never hear from Guy again it will be all too soon. Men are such babies." Elisa laughed. Sissy laughed too.

"I take it that last weekend did not go well for you and Guy." Sissy gave Elisa that look.

"No Sissy." Elisa sat down and told Sissy everything.

When she was finished, Sissy let out a whistle. "I cannot believe he sent you flowers and Guy accused you of cheating. I am shocked that you let him stay in your home. Don't ever tell Guy that you took Kyle to dinner and let him stay a night at your place," Sissy warned her.

"Well Sissy, Guy and I have not talked since that night and whatever possessed me to do that is beyond comprehension. I let my heart make up my mind and I get burned in the end for it. I only took him to dinner to thank him because you made me feel guilty about not paying him back for returning my pocketbook to me and nothing being stolen."

"Me," said Sissy shocked, putting her hand to her chest. "I never told you to take him to dinner. I just told you that he just wanted a simple thank you, that maybe his circumstances that got him into this predicament were beyond his control, and that he wanted you to give him money out of the kindness of your heart. But dinner, no that was all you Elisa," Sissy said seriously.

She looked Elisa straight in the eyes. "There is a reason why you let him stay the night at your townhouse and sleep in the guest bedroom. Why you did not just drop him off after dinner on the side of the road and go on home.

"Why Elisa?" Sissy asked her.

"I do not know why Sissy. I was crazy that's why." Elisa shrugged her shoulders. "No Elisa, you did it out of the kindness of your heart and that is why he stayed that night and that is why he sent you those flowers. Those flowers may have cost him a fortune. It may have taken all the money he had.

He saw that night you going above and beyond. He sent those flowers as a token of his appreciation and nothing more. You got mad at him for it because it put a rift between you and

Guy. There is a reason why your paths have crossed."

"Oh Sissy, now don't go and get all philosophical and sound like a Hallmark card. We live in two totally different worlds. He will never be part of mine and I will never be part of his and I want to keep it that way. Our paths have just forked. I did my part to show my appreciation for Kyle returning by pocketbook and for falsely accusing him of stealing."

"Guy falsely accused you of cheating on him when he saw the flowers and you falsely accused Kyle of stealing from your pocketbook without hard evidence. You did the same to Kyle that Guy did to you." Elisa knew Sissy was right but would not let her know that.

"If you are done giving me a lecture Sissy, I need to get to that meeting with Maggie Bench." Elisa said, grabbing her things and her coat. The days were getting chilly.

"Yes, I am done. But remember my words Elisa," Sissy hollered to Elisa. Elisa just waved and walked on.

Elisa got to the café at the corner and saw Maggie talking to an older gentleman. Elisa had never seen him before. She never pried in Maggie's personal affairs. Maybe Maggie had met someone on her travels. Elisa got to the table. "Hello Elisa, this is Eric Delves. He is an attorney who has put together some paperwork for the fragrance line." Elisa shook his hand. He was tall, with salt and pepper hair, he had dark eyes, and when he smiled, his teeth were as straight and white as Elisa had seen.

He was handsome. "Nice to meet you Eric," Elisa said.

"You too Elisa. I have heard so much about you and Pose Magazine. I look forward to working with you on this." Eric sat down and Elisa too.

"Eric is a great attorney who handles patents and copyrights; I have known him since my days with Pose." Maggie smiled. "He will go over all the legalities of the fragrance line."

Eric opened up his briefcase and pulled out some paperwork. "First I will need you to read over these documents Elisa.

They are to say that Pose Magazine will retain the rights and any royalties shall remain with Pose with the sale of your fragrance line." Elisa looked at Maggie who smiled. "It also allows for you to release all of Pose's earnings for the last two years." Elisa took the documents.

"Before anything is finalized Elisa, we have to make sure that financially Pose can do this, if not, then we need to get a hold of some investors who will take the risk of going forward with this project." Eric continued. Elisa was reading over the documents. "The documents also state that if you should resign from Pose Magazine Elisa, the fragrance line stays with Pose and keeps the name." Eric continued.

"I understand," Elisa said. "I was never hoping to gain personally from this fragrance line but for Pose Magazine and for her to stay successful." Elisa told Eric looking up from the documents. "I knew when I gave Elisa here the Chief Editor position; I had made the right decision." Maggie said, giving Elisa a look of confidence.

"I will give you time to read over the documents and fax me. Here is my business card." Eric handed Elisa his card. Elisa took it. "What about the people who will be making this fragrance for Pose?" Elisa asked, looking at both of them.

"We already have the people lined up; we just need to get the legal and financial aspects out of the way first." Maggie told her, "not to worry my dear Elisa."

"I will need to have you fax me over the last two years of Pose's financial records." Eric stood up.

"When I get back to the office, I will do that right away." Elisa stood up.

"You will find my office number and fax number on my business card." Eric shook her hand again.

"It will be a pleasure doing business with you Elisa." Eric smiled and Elisa smiled back.

"Same here," Elisa reiterated.

"When you are done going over the documents Elisa, you can fax them to my office. Once I get the financial records from Pose and those documents signed by you, we can begin on getting the fragrance line started."

"Sounds good to me Eric, I will get right on that." Elisa sat back down.

"I must get going," Eric said. I have a two o'clock appointment with another important client.

"I shall wait to get those papers from you Elisa." He took her hand and kissed it. "Maggie my dear," Eric took her hand and kissed it. "Shall I be hearing from you again?"

Maggie laughed and said, "Oh you will my darling." Eric grabbed his things and left.

When he was out of earshot, Elisa asked Maggie, "So where did you meet him?"

"Eric and I go way back, even before Pose. We went to school together and we dated in school. He is divorced with two grown kids. We have always remained in contact, and when you mentioned about starting a fragrance line for Pose, I knew he was the one to contact." Maggie lit up a cigarette.

"So are you two dating now?" Elisa asked her finishing up her lunch.

"Let me just say dear Elisa, that Eric and I will be seeing a lot more of each other." Maggie puffed on her cigarette. Elisa did not need for Maggie to elaborate.

"Thank you so much Maggie for all that you have done. If it were not for you, I would not have even got this idea off the ground."

"My dear Elisa, you came up with the idea. There are still many hurdles to jump over, but I am confident that this fragrance line will be a huge success."

Elisa and Maggie finished up with their lunch and told each other goodbye. Elisa got back to the office to get everything needed to send to Eric. She was so excited she could barely keep hold of the papers. She still had some hurdles to jump as Maggie said, but she was confident that everything would fall into place.

CHAPTER 15

September turned into October and Elisa had prepared everything for the fragrance line. Eric had gotten back with her and told her with what he was seeing from Pose's financial aspect that it was a go. They could get the equipment needed for making the fragrance, the people who would be making it, lease the space to manufacture it, and the transportation to deliver it. It was astounding for Elisa to hear and she could not be more elated.

It was time for the designers to have their drawings in for the spring show coming up in six months. The drawings were on her desk and she was looking over them. Brian had come up with a theme for the spring show, he wanted to call it: "Spring ahead for Pose fashion." Elisa thought different, but she looked at what Ellie had come up with. Ellie wanted to call it: "Spring on the Pose Fever." Elisa liked that. It was catchy.

Ellie had really come a long way since last year's fashion show in London. She loved what Ellie had to offer, but Brian also had great drawings. It would be another close call. She had told them she would get back with them by next week. She wanted to call in Marco Shoops to see any of his new designs.

"Hey Sissy, call Marco and tell him I want to see him in my office pronto."

"I will get right on that Elisa." Sissy responded.

Five minutes later, Marco was in Elisa's office. "You wanted to see me Miss Drinnings." Marco asked standing in the doorway.

"Yes Marco, and please shut my door and have a seat." Marco took his seat wondering what Elisa had in store for him.

"I realize that I only hired you a month ago, but I wanted to see if you had any new designs. As you know, we are having a spring show in Paris next April and with what I saw of yours, I would like to give you the opportunity of accompanying me to Paris in April along with my assistant Sissy."

"Oh my," Marco said clapping his hands and throwing them up in the air. "I have dreamed of going to Paris all my life. Oh thank you Miss Drinnings. You will make my dreams come true if I can go."

"I have not gotten a chance to really talk to you Marco since I have been busy. What made you want to become a fashion designer and why New York.

"Your father is a Hollywood Producer, why not have stayed there?"

"Oh you see," Marco said waving his hands. "I have loved fashion ever since I was a boy. When other boys were reading Spiderman and Superman comics, I was reading the latest fashion magazines and discovering the new trends. After my father made me shut the lights out, I would take a flashlight and get under the covers to read fashion magazines such as Seventeen, Cosmopolitan, and Vanity Fair.

I would dress better than my schoolmates. Yes, I was teased because of it and my sexual orientation, but it never stopped me. I was determined to someday work for a prestigious fashion magazine and travel the globe. And now here I am, working for the most prestigious magazine and having a chance to go to Paris for a fashion show. I cannot contain my enthusiasm." Marco was just waving his hands.

"My father wanted me to become a Hollywood producer but I wanted no part of it. I did however design clothes for Hollywood's elite. But I have dreamed of New York and wanting to come here. So after college, I left and came here."

Elisa was listening intently. "Well Marco, bring me any new designs you have and I will consider you going to Paris with me, my assistant Sissy, and another designer."

"You got it, Miss Drinnings. I shall."

"Okay Marco, that will be all for now." Marco got up leaving Elisa's office on cloud nine. Elisa was thinking, *if his father is a Hollywood Producer, then I wonder if he knows of my sister Cara?* Why Cara crossed her mind she has no idea. They have not spoken in over five years.

Elisa had not heard from Guy. It was just as well. She was too busy and engrossed in her work. With the new fragrance line under way, the fashion show in six months, and new designs to look at, she had no time to even think about Guy. She spent the rest of the day and week going over designs.

⊶⊷

Elisa was sitting at her kitchen table one night when Emilio said he needed to tell Elisa something. Elisa was dreading what he had to say. He sat down next to her. "My dear Elisa, you have been like a daughter to me and I have enjoyed working for you and the talks we have shared immensely. This is why this is going to be hard for me to say, but I need to."

Elisa had just finished her meal that Emilio cooked and was sipping her chamomile tea. She needed it to unwind with the stressful and busy week she was having. "My mother has taken a turn for the worse. The doctor says she is really sick and has not much longer to live. The cancer has spread throughout her body. There is nothing left that they can do. They are giving her six months, a year at the most. The chemotherapy has bought her time but not much.

"I have given up my apartment to move back in with my family and take care of her. The medical bills are outrageous even with my father having medical insurance. I love you Elisa as my own but I will have to leave."

"Elisa's eyes were watering. She knew that Emilio's mother had been sick for a while and she anticipated this moment with hesitation. She had told Emilio that she wanted him to be with his family, especially in a time like this, and take care of his mother. She had taken care of her mother in her final days of suffering from ovarian cancer. Pose had given her the time off. That is the only time she had taken an extensive amount of time off from her career to take care of her mother.

The hospice nurse had taken good care of her mother but

Elisa wanted to be there in the last few weeks of her mother's life. She knew what Emilio was going through. "I deeply understand Emilio. I wanted to be there for my mother and for her remaining days and take care of her. I will give you a substantial severance pay. When will be your last day Emilio?"

Emilio looked up at Elisa with sad eyes. They had been together ever since Elisa got a promotion at Pose. "I will not be back Monday Elisa. I will be back in the morning to fix you breakfast though. I wanted to tell you earlier than this, but with my mother on my mind and with everything else and your schedule, this was the only time I could tell you when we both had time.

"I am so sorry to give you such a short notice Senorita Drinnings. I hope this does not hinder our working relationship or the friendship that we have obtained throughout the years together. I know I did not give you enough of a notice to find another cook." Elisa reached over and touched his hand.

"Oh no Emilio, never, you have been like the father I never had. I will find another cook eventually.

I will give you a good reference if you ever need one to find another job. I want you to be with your family. I had the opportunity to be with my mother in her final days and hours of her life. I never had the strong family bond that you have had Emilio. You know we have had extensive talks about my family, me and my sister Cara, and what happened there."

"Yes Elisa. I know your mother is gone and your father walked out on you. So you have no close relatives and your sister is in California as far as you know, but Elisa we do not know how much time we have left as in the case with my mother. I want to remain in contact with you. I hope one day that you and your sister can reconcile things and be close again as you were when you both were younger.

I hate to see something happen to either one of you and never have the chance to forgive, love each other, and spend time together as sisters should." Elisa was crying now. Emilio hugged her and let her cry. She was letting go of another person she dearly loved but knew they would keep in contact so that made her feel better.

Emilio promised he would keep her updated on his mom's condition. She got up to get her purse. She came back and wrote him out a nice check. "You can use me as a reference if you ever look for another job Emilio and I will mail you a letter of recommendation." Emilio had given Elisa the address of his mom and dad's house.

She would write it as soon as she could and send it out. She would put an ad in the paper Monday morning for a cook. Elisa did not cook, so in the meantime it was either eating out or TV dinners. "You are Elisa a good and warm hearted person. I know how much your career and being successful means to you, but someday Elisa you will see that all of these things are superficial."

Emilio and Elisa talked for the rest of the evening and finally went to bed. Elisa had her driver take Emilio home. Elisa lay awake in bed thinking. Pose's fragrance line moving ahead, she would next week announce who would accompany her to Paris, and she had to find a cook. She was thinking of all the things that she and Emilio had talked about and what he said to her about her sister Cara. She did not know if she could ever forgive or have a relationship with her sister again.

Elisa could picture her father screaming at her mother while she and Cara listened from their bedroom. Cara was crying and Elisa was holding her and telling her things would be okay. "Dammit Mattie, I am the man of this house and I will find another job. I do not want you working. I want you home taking care of this house and our daughters. I want food on the table when I come home." Lloyd Drinnings hollered, throwing things around. Elisa and Cara could hear things breaking from their bedroom and their mother crying.

"Lloyd, the bills are piling up and they are threatening to turn off our phone and electric. We need to do something. There is hardly food in the house. You spend all your money on alcohol. The girls need shoes and clothes."

"Shut up woman about my alcohol. I made the money and I will do with it what I please. Our kids have food and they have clothes and shoes."

"I do not want you coming home like this Lloyd. I do not

want our daughters hearing this or seeing this. You have no job Lloyd and one of us needs to bring in some money."

"Fine woman," he hit Mattie and she screamed. Elisa ran out of the room to see her mother on the floor. She ran over to her.

"Get back in bed young lady before I lay into you." Lloyd said.

Elisa looked up at her father. "I HATE YOU FATHER! I HATE YOU!" Elisa screamed at him.

"You ungrateful little brat," he grabbed Elisa and dragged her back into her room. Cara was wide eyed. Cara loved her father. He had always treated her like a princess and gotten her things. She would sit on his lap and he would read her a story.

Elisa would help her mother in the kitchen. Cara never had to help with the dishes. Lloyd would always let Cara get out of it. Elisa would come home from school and do her homework, do the housework, and many nights they would have TV dinners, peanut butter and jelly sandwiches, or nothing at all after her father left them. Cara would refuse to help.

"You do not want me coming home like this that is fine Mattie. I am out of here. I will leave." Cara ran out of the bedroom before Elisa could stop her.

"NO DADDY! PLEASE DON'T LEAVE! I LOVE YOU! DADDY!" Cara was sobbing. Mattie was sitting on the couch. Lloyd had his things and was heading for the door. Cara ran up to him. "Daddy please don't leave. I love you daddy. I want to go with you."

Cara was hugging him. "There, there my little native princess, Daddy loves you, but you need to stay here with your sister and mommy and take care of them.

"Your mother doesn't want me to come home like this anymore. Your mother wants me gone so I am leaving." Lloyd opened the door and Cara was crying.

"Daddy no, please no daddy stay here." Elisa grabbed Cara and pulled her back. Lloyd walked out the door and out of their lives for the last time.

Cara turned around and looked at her mother with hate in her eyes. "You caused him to leave mother. You wanted him gone. I hate you mother and I will never forgive you for this." Cara ran back into their bedroom and slammed the door.

Mattie was sobbing and Elisa sat down next to her mother and hugged her. Mattie had a black eye from where Lloyd had hit her. "I am so sorry Elisa. I am so, so sorry."

"It is not your fault mother. I do not blame you. I love you mother. I will never forgive dad for doing this to us." From then on until the girls grew up, Cara had never forgiven Mattie and was rebellious. As soon as Cara could, she left home and never looked back.

Elisa went on to college and stayed in touch with her mother. Elisa would never forget that night that her father walked out on them. That is when Elisa had made a vow that she would never go through or be treated as her mother did. She worked hard and made a good life for herself and helped her mother until Mattie died.

Elisa cried herself to sleep. Things were going good for her in her career, but yet in her personal life, it was storming.

⇒⊱⊰⇐

The next morning Elisa walked with Emilio to the car after fixing her breakfast. She gave Emilio one last hug. "I will not forget you Elisa and I promise to keep in contact with you." Emilio said pushing a lock of hair from her face.

"Me too Emilio, I will never forget you either."

"Remember what we talked about last night Elisa."

"I will Emilio. I do not know if I can ever forgive or talk to my sister again."

"Please try Elisa. When everything else is gone Elisa, family is all we have." Emilio hugged her again and got into the car. He shut the door and the driver pulled away. Elisa stood there waving with tears in her eyes. It was a cold October morning. Elisa had on her silk pajamas with her house slippers. Soon, it would be winter and the snow would be falling.

She went back inside and fixed her a cup of French vanilla coffee. She sat down and began to work on the ad she would be putting in the paper for a cook. She would have the weekend to herself since Cora was off and Emilio was now gone. The townhouse was eerily silent and empty except for the ticking of the grandfather clock.

She wrote the ad the same way she did before, with saying cook needed, and the pay. She only put a phone number. She did not put her address. When the person called, she would meet them somewhere and interview them. She would look up their credentials and references, if she was not satisfied with them or they did not check out, she would tell them thanks for inquiring but they were not what she was looking for.

When she interviewed Emilio, he had impeccable references and credentials. She had checked them before letting him cook for her and hiring him. She did the same for Cora. Cora had worked for another family before they moved and they had given Cora a wonderful letter of recommendation. That is when she knew that Cora and Emilio would be right for the job and what she was looking for. Now, she had another task on top of everything else; to do it all over again and find a cook with good references, credentials, and someone she could trust. But where would she find this person, she would just put the ad in the paper again and see what happened.

⊷⊶⊹⊰⊱⊹⊷⊶

Across town, Kyle was eating his breakfast and drinking his coffee. It was a cold morning, but Kyle felt invigorated. He had another migraine yesterday but it was gone today. He knew winter was coming. He was preparing himself for it. He had gone to the library with people staring at him and checked the farmer's almanac to see what kind of winter they would be having.

According to that, it would be a severe winter. They were usually pretty accurate so he took no chances. If it got too bad, he would take Elisa's advice as much as he would hate to and stay at a homeless shelter. In the morning he would leave and do his usual thing. Would he ever catch a break?

He finished his coffee. It was Saturday and Mildred had the day off. He would go and visit her. He got up, put his things away, and headed to see Mildred.

Mildred was home at her table when she heard a knock at the door. She wondered who it could be since she never had visitors. She answered the door and it was Kyle. "Oh Kyle dear, I am so glad to see you." She gave him a great big hug. "Are you hungry? I can fix you something to eat."

"Oh no thank you Mildred, I already ate."

"Have a seat and warm up Kyle." He sat down on the worn couch. "Can I get you anything to drink?" Mildred had heated up water for tea.

"I will take a cup of tea Mildred thank you." Kyle said taking his coat off.

"Coming right up," Mildred went into her kitchen. There was only one picture of Mildred with her mom and dad. The living room had a three cushioned worn couch with a scratched up coffee table in front of it. There was a stand beside the couch where the lamp was sitting.

There was a rocker diagonal from the couch. A ceiling fan was above the table with the string hanging down. "Here we go," Mildred said coming out with a tray consisting of a tea kettle, cups, sugar, and tea bags. Mildred sat it down on the scratched coffee table. This was home to Mildred and it suited her. She was not fancy and this was all she needed. Kyle knew that Mildred was a humble person who did not need or want anything extravagant.

She was a simple person. She made Kyle a cup of tea and they talked. "How are you doing Kyle?"

"Well Mildred, I had another migraine yesterday but it is gone. I went to the library and looked in the almanac. It is going to be a severe winter according to that, so I may stay in a homeless shelter at night and then in the daytime go about my original routine."

"Oh Kyle I wish you would go to the doctor for that. I do not want you staying in a shelter. You can stay with me at night during the winter and then you can do what you like." "Mildred thank you, but I do not want to inconvenience you at all." Kyle smiled at her.

"Oh nonsense young man, why stay in a shelter when you

have a place to stay here. I am giving you the offer of staying here. I know that the couch is not the most comfortable thing, but I will give you clean sheets, a nice pillow, and a blanket to sleep with.

"It is better than what they will give you at the shelter. I will even make you a nice hot breakfast in the morning before I go to work." Mildred drank her tea. They were calling for the worst winter ever this year. Kyle had survived many winters where he was. He thought about what Mildred had told him.

"I will think about it Mildred and let you know." Kyle put his hands together.

"Oh what is there to think about Kyle? Mi casa es su casa."

Kyle laughed. "Well, if you insist, and it will not be any trouble for you, I guess that I can stay here this winter."

"Oh good I knew you would use that smart head of yours and relent." Mildred patted him on the hand.

"Unless something else happens that comes my way and changes things, but what are the odds of that?" Kyle said shrugging his shoulders and leaning back.

"You never know Kyle; something else could come your way. Something could pop up and change the course of things."

"I seriously doubt that Mildred. It has been years and nothing has popped up for me to change the course of things." Kyle waved it off.

"This year could be different for you Kyle." Kyle knew Mildred was trying to be positive about it, but even Kyle had to admit, she was wrong. He stayed for a while longer and Mildred even fixed him lunch. It was like having a son to Mildred. For Kyle, having Mildred around was like having his mom back again. They would be about the same age had his mother lived.

Mildred had fallen in love with a man and she loved him dearly, but when he was killed in a job related accident, Mildred never fell in love again.

She did not want that for Kyle, to not find someone and fall in love again or have something good come his way. But sometimes, things were just beyond your control.

CHAPTER 16

Elisa had put the ad in the newspaper and had called a meeting to decide who would accompany her and Sissy to Paris in April for the spring fashion show. "Thank you all for coming to this meeting. As you know, I am calling this meeting to decide who will accompany me to Paris this April. It was a tough decision. I liked both of Ellie and Brian's designs and themes for the upcoming show. However, I thought that Ellie's theme was catchier with "Spring on the Pose Fever." I loved Ellie's use of color that would be conducive to a Spring show and her designs have made me elect Ellie as being the one to accompany me and Sissy to the spring fashion show in Paris.

Like I said, it was a tough decision just like it was for the fall London show, but I have made my decision. You are all exceptional designers. Don't ever forget that." Ellie was screaming and jumping up and down. Everyone was excited for her, even Brian who was hesitant but happy for her nonetheless. "I cannot believe this!" Ellie exclaimed. "I am going to Paris in April. I am so thrilled. This was my dream. Oh thank you Miss Drinnings and thank you all."

"I would also like to add that the Pose fragrance line is a go. I want you Carl to find me some models, a male and female, to commercialize our fragrance line. I want you working on that right away Carl. I hope that after the spring show, our fragrance will be not only selling around the nation, but the world as well."

Carl looked at Elisa and said that he would get right on that. Brian came up to Ellie after the meeting and congratulated her. "Thank you Brian." Ellie said. Brian would just work harder for the next fashion show. The rest of the week went without a hitch and Elisa had already gotten three calls concerning the ad in the paper for a cook.

Elisa had managed to find time to interview them. There was one young lady she had interviewed, but found out she had fibbed on her references. So she thanked her for inquiring but told her no. The next one, a young man, had a felony record so Elisa stopped right there. The third one had canceled saying she was no longer interested. Elisa thought that she would never find a cook. She got home and threw a dinner in the microwave, well she thought, at least I know how to use one of these.

She had mailed Emilio a letter of recommendation in case he wanted to find another job. Emilio mailed her back thanking her. Emilio had never converted to the twenty-first century so he still used the old fashioned way of sending correspondence. Emilio thanked her profusely for the letter and said each day was a struggle for his mother. There would be some days that she would be her funny self and others where she would just lie in bed and stare at the wall.

It was hard on this family, but Emilio had told her the money had helped his family substantially. Elisa was happy and yet saddened at the same time. Happy that the money was helping, but saddened that his family was going through this. She finished her somewhat of a meal and poured her a glass of wine. She leaned against her counter and took a sip. She took a look around her kitchen.

It was not the same without Emilio. She missed his smile and the great smells that would emulate from her kitchen. She sighed and took another sip of wine.

⊷⊱✢⊰⊷

Kyle never got the newspaper or ever read it anymore. He figured that there was nothing good in it. He had already served in a war and gotten injured. He figured since he fought in Afghanistan that the world had not gotten any better or the news. He glanced at a table and saw a newspaper that someone had left. It was on the jobs hunting section. I guess he wasn't the only human being trying to find a job.

He held it up and that is when he saw it. He saw an ad for a cook. He read on. It only had a phone number and the pay. This may be his lucky day he thought. He remembered what he and Mildred had talked about in her apartment. This could change the course he was on. He doubted it but maybe Mildred had been right about this after all. It could get him some money to get off the street, to stop having to beg for money, and hopefully get him some health insurance.

"Hey Mildred, I need to use the phone." Kyle ran over to her.

"Of course Kyle, in the back." Kyle found it and dialed the number. For a while, it just kept ringing and he was wondering if this wasn't some kind of joke, but when a lady with a Hispanic accent answered he knew it wasn't.

"Hello, may I ask who is calling and why?" Cora asked.

"Yes, this is Kyle Rimmer and I am inquiring about the cook job. I saw it in the newspaper." Kyle answered.

Cora knew the first name sounded familiar but thought nothing of it, she did not know Kyle's last name. "Yes sir. My employer is looking for another cook. Her cook had to quit due to a family situation. I will let her know you called."

"Thank you so much ma'am," Kyle said. He hung up the phone and was smiling. Finally, he may catch a break. Mildred came back and asked him what he was excited about. He handed her the paper.

She read it. "Oh my gosh Kyle. You see, this could be the opportunity that you have been looking for. You see, you were so pessimistic, but I told you that something could happen to change the course of your life."

Mildred hugged him. He was so excited that he did not tell the lady how her employer could reach him. He hurriedly called back and gave the woman Mildred's phone number. She said again that she would tell her employer.

Kyle and Mildred, with their big juicy specialty cheeseburgers and milkshakes toasted each other. "To my opportunity knocking," Kyle said to Mildred as they clinked glasses. It would change his life.

⊶⊙⊱⊰⊙⊷

Elisa got home from work late and Cora had stayed over to make sure that Elisa had everything she needed to settle down for the night. "Senorita Drinnings, a man called to inquire about the job in the paper."

Elisa looked up. "Did he leave his name and number?"

"Yes, his name is Kyle Rimmer and he gave me this number to contact him."

Elisa about fainted and Cora grabbed her. "Are you alright Senorita Drinnings?"

Cora asked her. "Um, yes Cora. It is just that the man who called. I know the name." Cora looked perplexed. She did not realize that the man she had talked to on the phone was the same guy that Elisa had to her house over a month ago and took to dinner.

"What do you mean?" Cora had sat her down on the couch and was sitting opposite her.

"Cora that is the same man I brought here over a month ago and took to dinner; the same one who returned my pocketbook that I thought that I had lost."

Cora looked shocked. She knew the first name had sounded familiar but Elisa has never told her the man's last name. Elisa had remembered saying he had gone to a culinary school, but of course, if she went ahead and gave him this chance and interviewed him, she would treat him like everyone else and check his credentials.

Would she call this number back? She would see him on the sidewalk. Did she want to give him a chance? This job? What would it be like to have Kyle working for her after the way she was with him? It would be so awkward. Elisa got up to head upstairs to take a bath. Cora followed her. "Do you want me to call him back and tell him yes or no?" Elisa sighed, standing on the bottom step with one hand on the railing.

"No Cora, I am sure I will see him tomorrow on the

sidewalk. I want to take a few days to decide this."

"Yes, Senorita Drinnings, as you wish. I will leave now. Everything is ready for you."

"Gracias Cora." Elisa headed up the stairs and Cora left. She got undressed and sank into her bathtub. Kyle's call was the only call she had gotten about the job since the two interviews which turned out bad, and the one cancellation.

Would it hurt to give him a try? She would wait and see if she had any more willing participants to call and how the interviews would go. She had him over to her townhouse and let him stay the night, took him to dinner, but she could not fathom how it would be having him cook for her and maybe if need be, living there.

≈‡÷‡÷‡÷‡≈

Kyle was still smiling and could not wait to have Mildred tell him that he got a call back about the cooking job. He looked up at the bright blue sky. It was nearing November and the days were crisp and the nights colder. He had started a fire and was warming himself. The voice on the phone sounded familiar to him but he did not ponder too much on it. Just getting a phone call back, getting an interview at least, and maybe a job appealed to him.

But what would he wear if he gets the call for an interview? He didn't exactly have the most luxurious or even close to an accepting wardrobe. He knew the first impressions could make or break you. The old slogan of "You get one chance to make a first impression." He knew it had to be someone who had lots of money. Why else would they need a cook? The lady on the phone said she would talk to her employer, so that told Kyle it was someone with money.

But what if he didn't get the call, and then he would be right back to square one. He tried not to think about that as he kept himself warm.

≈‡÷‡÷‡÷‡≈

You could feel winter in the air as Elisa got into the car

to head to work. She saw Kyle on the sidewalk and said not a word. She still wanted to think about it. She walked to her office door and turned around to Sissy. "Sissy, please send me Marco Shoops to my office."

"Yes Elisa." Elisa put her briefcase on the table and took out her laptop ready to get to work. She tried not to think about Kyle when Marco knocked on her door.

"Come in," she said. Marco walked in. Twice now he had been called to her office. Wonder what she wanted this time.

"You called Miss Drinnings?" Marco said shutting the door.

"Yes Marco, please sit down. I was wondering if you had your designs for me to look at." Elisa sat there drinking her coffee and looking at Marco.

"Yes I do Miss Drinnings. I left them at my desk." Marco had his hands overlapping.

"Well Marco, you can bring those drawings to me later today okay. You mentioned that your father was a Hollywood Producer."

"Yes Miss Drinnings. He is the best in the business."

Elisa folded her hands together and leaned up. "I was wondering if he knew a Cara Drinnings?"

Marco's eyes got wide. "Oh why Miss Drinnings? Is she a relative of yours?"

"As a matter of fact she is. She is my sister." Marco was shocked. He may have remembered Cara working on a couple of his father's movies, but he never talked to her. He said nothing for a minute.

"Well," Marco started. "I do remember him putting her in a couple of his movies, but I have never talked to her. Why?"

"Without going into the aspects of my personal life, I was wondering if you could contact him and get her contact information."

"I am sure I could Miss Drinnings, but I do not know if my father could get her contact information without violating an ethics law about private information."

"I would never ask your father to do something Marco that would jeopardize his reputation in the Hollywood industry. I just want to know if he remembers her and if she is still in the Hollywood business."

"What would I say if he asks me who is inquiring about this?" Marco asked Elisa.

"Just say it is an old high school friend who wants to set up a high school reunion. Maybe he could put me in touch with some people out there who could send her an "invitation" to this reunion." Elisa was smiling and Marco had a worried look on his face.

"I will do it, but I have a question to ask you." Marco stood up.

"Yes Marco" Elisa said.

"Did you hire me for my designs or because my father was a Hollywood Producer?"

"I hired you for your designs of course Marco. I liked what you presented. Now, you can show me your new designs before the day is out. That will be all Marco."

Marco left the office nervous. He would do what Elisa asked of him, but deep down inside he did not like to lie, even tell a little white lie. He went to go and get his designs for Elisa. Sissy looked up and watched him walk by. Sissy got up and walked to Elisa's office. She walked in. Elisa was tapping away on her laptop.

"What did you say to Marco?" Sissy asked her.

"Why?" Elisa asked her.

"Well, he looked as nervous as a sheep surrounded by wolves."

"Sissy it was nothing, he will be fine. Now, I have something to tell you since you're here. Sit down." Sissy sat down not sure what Elisa had to say. She had known Elisa for years but Elisa could still be unpredictable at times. You will not believe who called inquiring about the cooking job I put in the paper." Elisa laughed.

"No who?" Sissy asked, her curiosity getting the best of her.

CHAPTER 17

"You're kidding me," Sissy got wide eyed and laughed.

"I am not Sissy I swear." Elisa held a hand up.

"Well, are you going to give him a chance?" Sissy smiled.

"I am pondering it still Sissy. I want to give it some time. I want to see if I get anymore inquiries about the job before I do. I may find someone by then."

"Oh Elisa that is a cop out and you know it." Sissy said half-jokingly.

"It is not Sissy," Elisa said defending herself.

"Yes it is Elisa. You do not want to give him a chance. You cannot do this to him. You have to give him some kind of response. I am sure he is waiting on it. I know you have no love for him and you wish that he would just disappear but you could at least elicit him a response to his call."

"Oh Sissy, why did I tell you this. I knew you would say that and make me feel guilty." Elisa leaned back looking up at the ceiling.

"Well you should Elisa. What you are doing to this man is wrong. I do not care if you do not give him the job, at least give him an interview, who knows, maybe he will surprise you." Elisa groaned. Sissy laughed.

"Changing the subject," Elisa said. "When Marco Shoops brings his designs up, please tell him to come on in. I will be busy, but I will put aside time to look at this drawings."

"Will do Elisa," Sissy smiled and shut the door. Elisa did not like what Sissy had to say. She would wait.

Marco came up after lunch with his portfolio and as Elisa said, Sissy sent him in to her office. Elisa was writing stuff down with her laptop beside her. "I have the designs you asked for Miss Drinnings." Elisa looked up. "Oh yes, just sit them here on my desk. I will look at them as soon as I am finished up here." Marco just stood there.

"That will be all Marco. Thank you." He walked out. Unbeknownst to Marco, he did not know that Cara had never graduated high school. He would call his father tonight. Since California is three hours behind New York, it would be two o'clock in the afternoon in California when he made the call. He was still uneasy about this, but he wanted the chance to make it with a top selling fashion magazine and go to Paris.

He would get right on that and get back with Elisa on the information.

⊹⊱┈⊱⊰┈⊰⊹

The days flew by. Carl Drixel had rounded up a female and male model to advertise the new Pose fragrance line. She had liked them. The woman was from Brazil and the male was from Italy. *Diverse, I like that* Elisa thought. Elisa wanted some fresh faces and she had interviewed them. She told them that when Pose had their fragrance line ready she would get back with them. When she was done, they all shook hands and left. It had been almost two months since Guy and her had spoken to each other.

Her nights were spent eating out or throwing TV dinners in the microwave. Ever since Emilio left, she had made practical use of the microwave. No one else had called to ask about the ad in the newspaper for a cook. With the rate of jobless people, Elisa would think that people would jump at this. She had decided to talk to Kyle as much as she tried to prolong it. Sissy had a point though, even though Elisa was being hesitant about it.

She would not call Kyle back; she would talk to him in person. Do the interview there on the sidewalk. Maybe she could eliminate him as a possible candidate, but then again, she was tired of eating out and TV dinners. She left her office. She walked outside. It was cold. She saw Kyle there.

She took a breath of the cold air and got the gumption to walk over and talk to him. "Kyle Rimmer." He turned around and saw Elisa. "Wow, this is a surprise. After so long of not talking to me, the great Elisa Drinnings wants to talk to me."

"I have no time for smart ass remarks Kyle. I am here to talk to you about the phone call you made to my housekeeper. The one inquiring about the cook position in my home."

Kyle stood up. "So, that was your ad? That was you who needs a cook. What happened to your other one? Emilio I think his name was."

"That is none of your business. I am not at liberty to discuss my former employee's personal business. However, I was wanting to, hard as this is, to give you a chance to interview for the job." Elisa bit down on her lip. Someday she may regret those words and eat them.

"Oh the lady who treats me as a leper and a disgrace to the human race wants to give me an interview and maybe a potential job. Hmm, let me bask in that. Anyone else I may jump at the chance." Elisa was mad now. It was cold and she did not like his attitude since she was going against her own feelings and giving him the dignity of an interview at least.

Kyle looked at her. He needed a job. It was an opportunity knocking. He needed to make money in some other way than how he was making it now. He needed a place of his own to stay. He needed insurance and the pay looked good. He did not care for Elisa's personality, and yet he needed this job. If he did not jump at this chance he may regret it someday, and if he did he may also regret it. It was a catch 22.

He did not like the idea of Elisa being his boss, but if it got him off the street, a place to live, and some insurance why not? "Okay Kyle. I was willing to give you a chance, but if you are going to be like this, then you can consider this interview over. I don't care anymore what you do."

Elisa started walking away. "Wait," Kyle hollered. Elisa turned back around. "I know that we are two different people living on the same planet, we have not been the friendliest towards each other, but please, and this may be my only chance of changing my life. I mean, that newspaper ad was an answer. I know what you think of me Elisa. You have expressed that with a profound hatred for me.

"I never read the paper or get it, but something told me to look at that table and that is when I saw it. The ad in the paper and I called. My dream of ever working in a restaurant or owning one as a chef is only that. It will never come to fruition. I cannot believe I am doing this, but please give me a chance."

Elisa just stood there. "Let us go somewhere where it is a lot warmer." Kyle picked up his things and they walked to a diner. She had picked that because it was not as fancy as the other places and Kyle was not dressed for it. They got to a table and ordered something to eat.

"Now Kyle, you had mentioned before that you went to culinary school. What school is that? I will be checking this out. I can guarantee that you have no references for me to check.

"I barely know you Kyle and without references, there is no way for me to validate anything. When I interview for a position, I like to be able to check the references of the person I am interviewing. I want to make sure that the person is being completely honest with me. I hope you understand." Elisa told him as their food came.

Kyle dug in he was so hungry. "I went to the Institute of Culinary Education here in New York. I graduated at the top of my class. I can give you the name of my teacher if he is still there. He gave her the name of his teacher. You can check my credentials."

Elisa took the paper. "So Kyle, what happened as to the reason you are not in the profession that you studied?"

Kyle put down his sandwich and looked around. It was going to be hard to tell a complete stranger, well someone he did not know very well and had only talked to a few times here and there his reasoning for why he ended up like this. He needed this chance. "I graduated at the top of my class as I said before. I married my high school sweetheart and had a good job and after 9/11 joined the Army."

"You were married before Kyle?" Elisa asked him taking a drink of her tea.

"Yes Elisa, I was married before. It is hard to talk about and especially with someone whom I haven't known for very long. But if it helps with me getting this job and makes you feel somewhat better about me, I will. My best friend and I from high school planned on opening up a restaurant right here in New York after my military service.

"I served eighteen months for my first tour in Afghanistan and watched a buddy of mine from basic training die in my arms. I came home for three months and my wife Janice wanted me out. I told her as soon as I could, I would get out and we could have our life. I got sent back to Afghanistan for two years this time. I was shot in the head and spent months in the hospital recovering.

"All this time my wife and my best friend Jerry Lites, the one whom I was going to open the restaurant with, were having an affair. When I was finally able to leave the hospital, I got a letter from her stating that she wanted a divorce and was in love with my best friend. She said it would be futile to try and find her. She was pregnant by Jerry and wanted to marry him as soon as the divorce was final.

"She sold the house and everything. I got nothing. I had some money left over from when I went to school and bought our house that my parents left me when they died. She took that too because I left her as the executor of the accounts. She wanted a family and she got it Elisa. The doctor put me on disability and the government and military denied my benefits. I had no job, no money, and no home Elisa. I have been living like this ever since.

"Everything was taken from me. I lost some of my vision from getting shot in the head and I am lucky to be alive. When I read the letter from my ex-wife, and saw the divorce papers, I wish that I would have been killed in Afghanistan. At least now, I would not be where I am. Having to beg and live off that and living under a bridge.

"So you see now that I did not choose this life, but I have

made the best of it. I do not work because of my disability, and I am on the streets because of not being able to have a job, and being denied the money owed to me." Elisa was running her finger around her cup. She did not know what to say. She had a hard life growing up, but nothing like what Kyle had. She had worked and become successful; Kyle had served his country, went to school, and was homeless.

"You can check the school I attended and ask about a Kyle Rimmer. Tell them that you are an employer and that you need to check my credentials. And I have someone else you can talk to, her name is Mildred Hirth. She has known me for years and is like a mother to me. She can tell you what kind of person I am. Here is where she works." Kyle handed the information to Elisa. Elisa took it.

She remained silent. She just looked at Kyle. She would have everything checked out of course, the school, his military, and of course this Mildred. He had given her everything she needed. "Thank you Kyle. I will check this out and get back with you. I am sorry Kyle for everything. I had no idea."

"I do not want you to be sorry for me Elisa. I want you to wake up and realize there are others out there like me. There are other homeless veterans out there like me. They sign up to serve their country and may go to war, then come home to a government that no longer cares about them or forgets them." The waitress came over and asked if they would like anything else. They both said no and she gave Elisa the bill.

Kyle got up to leave. "Thank you Elisa for giving me this lunch." Kyle grabbed his things and left. Elisa paid the bill and just sat there for a while going through what Kyle had told her. Her eyes were watering. She was not crying for herself, but for Kyle and others like him. She grabbed her things to head back to the office. She would get to work on the information that Kyle gave her. She took a taxi back to her office. She did not see Kyle anywhere or when she got back to her office.

What Kyle said to her tugged at her for the rest of the day. She was busy making phone calls. She got a hold of the school he attended and they confirmed his time there. She talked to his old teacher and he told her that Kyle was a great student and a great person to work with. Elisa then had a harder time trying to get information concerning his military service.

She had to jump through rings of fire, but she got a hold of who she needed to and told them who she was. She did not tell them that she was going to be his employer; but that she was going to be his landlord and she needed to know who she was giving this apartment to.

The man sounded gruff on the phone but finally gave her what she needed. It confirmed everything that Kyle had told her. She would take the evening and hoping to catch this Mildred Hirth; to talk to her. She looked over the address that Kyle had given her. It was a place that Elisa never visited. It was not in her neck of the woods and not her kind of neighborhood, but if she could help her with Kyle, she was willing to traverse there.

She was studying the paper in her hand so intently and her mind was wondering that the sound of her phone broke her out of her reverie. "Yes," Elisa answered. "It is Marco Elisa, he says that he needs to talk to you and that it is urgent." Elisa sighed and said send him in. Marco was in her office in a flash and out of breath.

"What is it Marco?" Elisa asked him.

"I um, got a hold of my father and he says that he knows of your sister Cara. She had been in some of his films. I told him that there was a high school friend looking for her to let her know about a high school reunion and needed to get a hold of her." Marco was silent for a minute.

"Continue Marco." Elisa broke the silence.

"Well, he has some clout in Hollywood and was able to find out that she still is in California and under a different agent. He was able to get the name of the agent and the phone number to reach this agent." Marco handed Elisa the information. She stared at it. She could not believe that after five years, she was a phone call away from contacting a sister that she said was no longer her sister and dead to her.

"Thank you Marco you have done well." Elisa put the paper in her purse.

"Um, I was wondering about the other thing," Marco pointed out.

"The other thing, oh yes, your drawings; they are exquisite and for your "hard work" and dedication, you will accompany me, my assistant, and Ellie to Paris in April."

"Oh thank you, thank you Miss Drinnings. My dream has come true. I am just in jubilation over this." Marco was jumping up and down and waving his hands.

"You're welcome Marco and that will be all if you do not need anything else."

"Oh no," Marco said. "You have made me a happy man." Marco left her office just dancing. Sissy had heard it and looked up at Marco as he came out of the office.

"What is wrong with him?" Sissy asked Elisa walking into her office. Marco looked like he could fly out of here.

"I just told him that he would be going with us to Paris in April." Sissy gave Elisa the look of okay.

"Sissy I need to leave. I have something to do tonight." Elisa was packing her stuff.

"Would this have anything to do with that Kyle guy?" Sissy said smiling.

Elisa turned back around and said smiling back, "in a roundabout way, yes."

Before Sissy could say anything else, Elisa was gone. She got into her car and told her driver to take her to the address that Kyle had given her of a Mildred Hirth. The driver pulled away from the curb and Elisa was on her way.

CHAPTER 18

Elisa's driver pulled up to the address. Elisa got out. It was a hamburger shop located in a run down side of New York. Elisa was thinking now I know why I never venture this way. The close sign was showing on the window but Elisa walked up to it anyway. She saw an older lady with her back turned doing something. Elisa knocked on the door. The lady turned around. She saw Elisa.

"Sorry ma'am we are closed."

"I need to speak with a Mildred Hirth. My name is Elisa Drinnings." At that, Mildred stopped what she was doing and unlocked the door. Being the closing waitress, she had a set of keys to the shop. Her boss would fire her if he knew she was doing this, but he had already left for the evening and would not be back until tomorrow.

Mildred unlocked the door and stood face to face with Elisa. "I am Mildred Hirth." Elisa saw a kind and motherly woman. Elisa had nothing to fear. This must be the woman that Kyle had talked about so much. She was all decked out in a designer suit that Mildred would have no idea who the designer was. She was wearing expensive jewelry from what she could see and her hair pinned up.

What would she be doing in a neighbor like this and especially at this hour? "Come in dear. It is quite cold." Elisa stepped in and saw black and white checkered floors, red bar stools, and booths. It looked like something out of the 1950's or a roadside diner. "Can I get you anything dear?" Mildred asked her.

"Um, no, I am not hungry. I would like something hot to

drink if you have it." Elisa said.

"I will get you that. Have a seat and I will bring it to you. I was just finishing the cleaning and closing out the register. Are you sure I cannot fix you anything to eat dear?" Elisa was looking around. She wondered how often Kyle came in here.

"Um yes, I am sure." Elisa replied. Mildred brought her over a nice hot cup of steaming coffee and had her one too.

"You are Elisa Drinnings. The Elisa Drinnings that Kyle has talked so much about. You are beautiful. He was right."

Elisa blushed. "Yes, I am Elisa."

"So what brings you to our neck of the woods dear?" Elisa was looking down at her coffee. "For a woman of your stature, you are in the wrong neighborhood." Mildred said kindly. Elisa laughed.

"Well I came here because Kyle called about the cook job. It was me who put that ad in the paper."

Mildred's eyes sparkled. "You may have saved his life dear Elisa. He did not think that anything good would come his way."

Elisa smiled. "I took him to lunch and we talked. I always vet people before I hire them. You never know who you are going to get. I had three callers before him and none of them worked out.

He was the fourth. I waited a few days. No one else called about it, so I talked to him about it. As you probably already know, by the way Kyle speaks of me, that you know that I have not been very kind to him."

"Yes, he has mentioned that Elisa, but I am sure you can put that behind you. You are giving him a great opportunity Elisa." Mildred took a sip of her coffee admiring this beautiful uptown woman.

"I have worked hard to put myself through college and become successful. Kyle spoke to me when I asked him why he was like this and how he became this way. I wanted to know him better before I would give him the job officially.

I do this with all potential candidates for a job. I work for Pose Magazine so my life can be demanding. It is a very successful magazine. Anyway, Kyle told me about him going to school, being married, joining the military, getting injured, and losing everything. I asked for references to check them out. He told me about you. He said you are like a mother to him."

"Ah yes," Mildred said softly. "I have known Kyle since he got his honorable discharge from the military. It was more like a medical discharge. Kyle did come home to nothing. He had lost everything he loved. His wife Janice left him for his best friend, his money gone, he couldn't work, and no place to live, he made a living panhandling.

"His father died years after the Vietnam War was over and he lost his mother to a brain tumor before he graduated high school. He lived with his grandparents until he graduated and then took the money his mom and dad left him to go to school. He put the rest back for a house and savings. He married, used the money to buy his house, but then 9/11 came and he joined the military. Newly married, out of college, and just bought a home.

"He signed up for the Army and got sent to Afghanistan twice. His marriage of course as you know failed and he came home to nothing. He left Janice all his money and she sold the house, left him, and took off leaving him with nothing. Kyle is a good man Elisa. He has seen a lot. He has been through a lot. He came in one day and got hooked on our famous mom and pop cheeseburgers and from there on he was a regular." Mildred laughed.

"We would sit for hours and talk. I became like the mom he had lost. He became like the son I never had. I never married. Kyle found in me someone he could trust. Kyle would help anyone he could Elisa. He has had so much bad luck." Elisa was listening intently with her eyes watering. Mildred put her hands on Elisa's.

"Him meeting you Elisa and that ad in the paper was the best thing he could have found. He is a wonderful cook. He has cooked for me in my apartment. I live just right above this hamburger shop. That man can cook a hell of a meal."

Elisa smiled. "He is a good hearted man. He is not proud of the life he is living. He did not ask for this nor did he want it. Well, I better get finished and head upstairs unless there is anything else you need dear Elisa." Mildred got up and took the coffee mugs.

"No Mildred, thank you. I think I have made my choice." Elisa got up and headed to the door with Mildred following her. They both said goodbye and Mildred locked the door. She watched Elisa get into the backseat and leave. She thought to herself, *what a beautiful young woman. Kyle would be so lucky.*

❈❈❈❈

When Elisa got home she did not realize how late it was. She went upstairs and sat down on the bed. She was exhausted. Tomorrow she would tell Kyle he had a job as her new cook. She did not know about saving his life but she was giving him a job. And knowing he was homeless, she would allow him to sleep in the guest bedroom and live there so as long as he worked for her.

She took out the paper that had the number and name of Cara's movie agent. She stared at for what seemed like forever. She got up the gumption to listen to Sissy and walk up to Kyle and talk to him about the job and was even giving it to him.

After five years, would she get up the gumption of taking Emilio's advice and patching things up with Cara? Would she make that phone call and try and talk to the sister she said was no longer her sister. Would Elisa make that phone call that could make another change in her life? She put the paper by her on her nightstand and got ready for bed.

She lay there wide awake for what seemed like hours. Finally sleep over took her and before she knew it, she was fast asleep.

❈❈❈❈

Kyle had lit another fire and was covered up. He remembered him and his buddy Brent sleeping in the desert underneath the Afghan sky. "Hey dude, this is just like camping out when I was little." Brent said.

"Yeah," said Kyle.

"My dad," said Brent "would take me out to our backyard and camp out. I remember going out west one year and we did not get a hotel. Oh no, we slept under the Arizona desert sky. It was so peaceful."

Kyle smiled at his buddy's telling him that story. Kyle missed those times. He did not miss the war, but the times he and Brent spent under the Afghanistan sky. They would have their most memorable talks. They would talk about their families, what they wanted to do after the military, and Kyle told Brent when he opened his restaurant, he would give Brent a job.

Kyle's eyes were watering. He missed his buddy. He wondered if Elisa would give him a job. He knew she was checking everything he said. He could not sleep; he had too much adrenaline running through him. He continued to warm up by the fire.

⸻⸙⸻

Elisa got up for another day at work. "Good morning Cora," Elisa said as she came down the steps to pour her some coffee.

"Buenos diaz Senorita Drinnings. How was your sleep?"

"It was good Cora. I am going to hire that man who called here inquiring about the job."

"Oh," was all Cora could say.

"Yes, he is the man you met that night whom I took to dinner." Elisa took a drink of her coffee. "I will let him know today he is hired if I see him."

"That is great. I am sure he will be happy to hear that."

"I hope. I will let him start tonight if he wants to. Oh and another thing Cora,"

"Yes Senorita Drinnings,"

"I want you to prepare the guest bedroom as you did for him that night. I will let him live here and he will sleep in the guest bedroom so as long as he is working for me."

"I shall," Cora replied.

"Good, I will see you later." Elisa walked out the door. She saw Kyle and walked up to him. "You are hired. If you can start tonight you will leave with me. But before you enter my house, you will rid yourself of these belongings and I will buy you new clothes. You will also stay with me so as long as you are employed by me. You will stay in the guest bedroom.

Are there any questions?" Elisa asked him.

Kyle could not believe what he was hearing. "Um yes, no I mean no, I have no questions."

"Good, before I come out of that building tonight you will be ready and have nothing on you but the clothes on your back until I can rid you of them. If you are going to work for me and live there, you will look decent. Now if you'll excuse me, I have to go to work."

Kyle watched her walk away. He was so ecstatic. He was jumping up and down and screaming. The people on the street stopped and stared at him. He did not care. He had a job and a place to live. After so many years of not having those, he was finally going to have them. Good luck was coming his way. He knew Elisa was tough and could have a heart of ice, but he would not look a gift horse in the mouth.

Kyle could not wait until her work was done. He left the sidewalk to rid himself of his personal belongings that he would no longer need and tell Mildred about this. He would say goodbye to sleeping under that bridge. He wanted to do a good job so Elisa would not fire him. He would show her that he was not the kind of man she thought he was.

⚜

Elisa walked into her office. Sissy followed close behind her. "So did you talk to Kyle? Does he have the job as your cook? Did you tell him no? What?" Sissy was going a mile a minute.

"Slow down Sissy, yes I talked to him and interviewed him. I checked him out and he is good to go. He has no criminal record thank you. I told him that he can start tonight. I told him to get rid of all of his belongings except for what he is wearing, for which I will get rid of that when I buy him all new clothes.

I told him if he is going to work for me that he will look decent. I also told him that as long as he is working for me he can stay with me. He will have the guest bedroom that he slept in before. I have my housekeeper getting it ready. I figured since he was homeless I could give him a place to live as long as he is my employee."

"Oh Elisa I am so proud of you. I knew you would do it." Sissy said excitedly.

"You did?" Elisa asked her confused.

"Oh well, I mean that I was sure you would. That you would come around and ask him, just like you would thank him for returning your pocketbook."

"Now do not go and get any crazy thoughts in that head of yours Sissy. He will just be my cook."

Sissy put her hands up in defense. "I am not thinking anything like that. But I am sure he is happy about it." Sissy said.

"Who wouldn't be in a position like his Sissy? I mean the man is homeless; and he has no other means of living and can't get one. He would have been crazy to say no to my offer today."

"So," Sissy said, changing the subject. "What are you doing for Thanksgiving?" Elisa had not even thought about it. She usually just had Emilio fix her a turkey dinner. She did not know what she would do this year.

"I am not sure Sissy. I haven't really thought about it. I have been so busy with so much on my mind that Thanksgiving was not at the forefront of my mind."

"What about Guy? Has he called you? What if he does? What if he asks you about Thanksgiving?"

Elisa looked up. "In response to your twenty thousand questions Sissy, "I don't know, no, I don't know, and I don't know."

"Hmm," Sissy said.

"Okay. Well, if not, maybe Kyle can and if not, you can join me and my family this year for Thanksgiving."

"I appreciate that Sissy thank you." Elisa replied. The

holidays were more or less days on a calendar to her like any other.

After her father walked out on her mother, Mattie struggled to give her daughters a good Thanksgiving and Christmas each year. Elisa hated the holidays after that. She stopped celebrating them. Sissy walked out and went back to her work.

❄❄❄❄

Across the way, Kyle got rid of his belongings. He said goodbye to Central Park Bridge where he had slept for years. He told Mildred and she was so happy for him. She told him of her meeting Elisa and their talk. Kyle promised that he would not forget Mildred and he would come and see her still.

Mildred gave him a big hug and kiss. "You tell Elisa that she has made me happy too."

"I will Mildred." Kyle walked out the door as Mildred watched him. He was walking back to where it all began and walking his way to a new life.

Chapter 19

Kyle was waiting on the sidewalk when Elisa walked out of the building. "Are you ready Kyle?"

"Yes I am." Kyle said excitedly. They both got into the car and Elisa told the driver where to take them.

"I will go over some things with you before you get to my townhouse about the job." Elisa stated. "One, the salary is as stated in the add, two, since you will be staying there while employed, you will work seven days a week and if you want to have a weekend off or the holidays you will get permission from me, three, you will have the guest bedroom and use the bathroom that you used when I took you to dinner, four, whenever you need groceries let me know and I will have my driver take you to the store, five, any laundry you need done tell Cora my housekeeper, six, when I have guests over for dinner or a date, which if ever I have guests over, you will cook of course and serve but that is all, seven, if I go out to dinner, then you will have the night off, eight, you are free to fix yourself something to eat but you eat after cooking for me, nine my bedroom, and my bath are off limits, and finally ten, you will be paid by cash weekly. Do you understand and are there any questions?"

Kyle was taking this all in. "What about medical insurance?" It was something he desperately needed as well.

"I will deduct so much from your pay each week towards your policy. I did the same for my last cook and for my housekeeper. My employees have the best insurance. But, I will not start deducting that until thirty days after your employment. This is a probation period in which I see how well you work."

So," Kyle interjected, "I will not have medical coverage for thirty days after my starting period?"

"That is correct. If you do not work out, I cannot see wasting money on medical coverage. Will that be a problem Kyle?"

Kyle did not tell her about the migraines, for right now he would just keep it to himself and see how things work out. "No, whatever is best." Kyle said with a half-smile.

"Oh and one other thing, you will address me as Miss Drinnings. I will be your employer so you will give me that title. Understand?" Elisa said straight forwardly.

"Yes I do."

They got to the department store and got out. Elisa told the driver how long they would be and he would be back. They walked into the department store and people stopped and stared. "Pay no attention to them Kyle." Elisa said as they were walking to the men's department.

"They act like they have never seen a homeless man before." Kyle said to her quietly. "This is New York Kyle, I am sure they have, just not in this department store dressed like you with someone dressed like me." Kyle waved to them and they turned away and shook their heads and started whispering to one another.

"Here we are," Elisa said, waving her arm like a game show host. A man in a tailored suit came up to ask if they needed any help. "Yes," Elisa answered him politely. "I am Elisa Drinnings and I need some clothes for my new cook here. He will be working for me and I want him to have some decent clothes. I will be paying cash of course so treat him well."

"Ah yes Miss Drinnings, I remember you. I certainly shall. Come this way young man."

Kyle looked at Elisa as he was being led away and mouthed, "young man" and pointed at himself. Elisa smiled and shooed him on with her hand. What seemed like forever and with Elisa's approval, two hours later they finally had a suitable wardrobe for Kyle. Elisa told the salesman to take his old clothes and throw them out. She paid him extra for that. He gladly accepted.

Elisa and Kyle got back into the car. "How do you feel Kyle?" Elisa asked him.

"Like a new man Miss Drinnings. Thank you."

"You're welcome Kyle and you do look like a new man and thank you for remembering to call me Miss Drinnings." They got to her townhouse and she led Kyle to the kitchen. He stood in awe. It was the most beautiful kitchen he had ever seen, even the one when he had his house.

It had an island in the middle with a grill on one side and the other side had burners. There were pots and pans hanging above it. The cabinets were done in cherry wood. Everything that a chef would need was in Elisa's kitchen. It looked like something you would see out of a magazine or a chef show.

Elisa showed him where everything was in the kitchen. "I will make a menu each day for you to cook for me, unless I call you beforehand and tell you that I will be eating out, otherwise, you will have it prepared for me before I come home. My last cook, he would leave it warming for me so it would stay warm. With you going to Culinary School, you should be able to cook pretty much anything I ask you to. Are there any questions about anything here?"

"No, Miss Drinnings. I should be able to find my way around and cook you some of the best meals."

"Flattery will get you nowhere with me Kyle. Now let me take your stuff upstairs. Cora is gone so I will take you to the guest bedroom."

They went upstairs and Kyle noticed that the sheets were different from the last time he was here. Elisa walked over to the closet. "This is your closet and this will be your dresser." She pointed to it. "My housekeeper Cora will wash your sheets and put new ones on. When you are ready to have them change, just ask Cora and she will do it for you.

"Now to the guest bathroom, you of course will have your own closet here with your towels. Please take any dirty towels and put them in a hamper for Cora to wash. I made sure that Cora went out and got you some shaving cream, razors, and everything that a man would need to keep up with his hygiene. Any questions?" Elisa had her arms crossed.

"No, I understand." Kyle said.

"Good, now you can go back to your bedroom and start putting your clothes away. I would have Cora do it but since she is gone, you will have to do it. I will let you get cleaned up. Since this is your first night, I will let you get settled in. You start tomorrow. I will get myself cleaned up and order some Chinese, do you want anything?"

Kyle was so hungry he could eat a horse. He loved Chinese food though it has been awhile since he had it. "Oh yes Miss Drinnings I would love some. I love the crab ragoons and the Kung Pao Chicken."

"Done then, for tonight only you will eat when I do, otherwise, you will eat after I am finished."

"Yes ma'am," Kyle said smiling.

"Um, Miss Drinnings will do." Elisa reminded him.

"Oh yes, Miss Drinnings." Elisa left Kyle to get his things unpacked. He went back to his bedroom and started putting his new clothes that he hadn't had in years in the closet and dresser. The closet was bigger than Mildred's kitchen and the bedroom was bigger than her whole living room. He folded and put his clothes away as if he were still in the military. The clothes she bought him cost more than what he could make in a year on the sidewalk.

Elisa ran her bubble bath and sank in it. She had ordered the Chinese and they said it would take an hour as they were very busy. Elisa said that was fine as she was tired and needed to soak. She had hired Kyle, she just hoped that he would work out and Mildred had not been wrong about him.

An hour later, the Chinese food was there and Elisa had sorted it out. She poured each of them a glass of wine. Kyle accepted gladly. With the dinner she had taken him to, and now tonight, he was getting a glimpse into her lifestyle. He was so hungry that he dug in before Elisa had hers opened. She saw him. "I am so sorry Miss Drinnings, it is just that I love Chinese and I have not had it forever and I am so hungry."

"It is okay Kyle, I knew you would be hungry, and it is late so that is why I ordered out."

He took a sip of his wine. He could not get over this kitchen.

This was the kind of setting he would have had for the restaurant him and his ex-best friend would have had, but of course much bigger to hire more chefs. "I love your kitchen Miss Drinnings, it would have looked the kitchen in the restau…" but before he could get out the word he stopped. He looked at Elisa and then back down at this food.

"Tell me Kyle, why did you stop? You were going to say restaurant but you stopped why?" Kyle stopped eating. He had not mentioned the restaurant again until now. He was not thinking and he was so entranced with her kitchen that it came back to his mind.

"I do not want to talk about it Miss Drinnings. It is in the past. It was a long time ago and just a dream. It is not important."

"Well it must be or you would not have mentioned it again around me." Elisa said taking a drink of her wine.

"Look, I just do not want to talk about it. It was a pipe dream." Kyle said angrily looking at Elisa. "It will never come true anyway."

Kyle got up and told Elisa thank you for dinner. "Do you want me to clean this up for you?" He asked her.

"No Kyle, I will do it."

"Thank you for dinner Miss Drinnings. I will start work tomorrow just let me know what you want for dinner." Kyle left the kitchen. Elisa watched him walk away. She could not figure out why he stopped himself from saying the word. He had already opened up to her about it in their interview and about his past life.

She was lucky enough that her dreams came true. It was obvious that Kyle's never had the chance to get his off the ground. She cleaned up the table and went upstairs. The door to Kyle's room was closed. She stood in front of it for a few minutes and walked away to her room. She got into bed, let the talk go, and fell fast asleep.

In the other room, Kyle lay there wide awake. He was starting a whole new life. Elisa had been able to fulfill her dreams, but his got flushed down the toilet. He could be living like Elisa was, with a nice place to live, nice clothes, and recognition. He would take what he could get now and be Elisa's employee. It was all he could ask for.

❦

The next morning Kyle was up before Elisa. Elisa walked into the kitchen. "Good morning Miss Drinnings. What would you like for breakfast?"

"Good morning Kyle, I would like a cup of coffee, scrambled eggs with cheese, and toast on rye bread."

"You got it." Kyle said. He got out the stuff and started making her breakfast. "I am sorry about last night Miss Drinnings. It is just something that I do not like to talk about much."

"It is okay Kyle. I just thought that maybe since you brought it up again that you wanted to talk about it." Elisa said softly.

He brought her cup of coffee and she put her cream and sugar in it. "It is just that some people can fulfill their dreams while others get their dreams snuffed out before they can pursue it. It is not fair, but being in the situation I am in or was in, even though I hated it, I learned to accept it."

She watched him make her scrambled eggs. He looked good in his clothes with his apron on she had him wear and was working the stove like a pro. She would see how his dinner would turn out tonight. She had planned on lemon herb chicken, with red potatoes, and mixed vegetables. Kyle put her eggs with cheese mixed in on her plate and the toast. He got her, her butter that she used and she spread it on there.

She tried the eggs. "Mmm, I must say this is delicious Kyle. I hope dinner is just as good. Speaking of dinner, here is the menu." He took the menu and looked at it. He laughed. "What is so funny?" Elisa asked him.

"I have made this dish before. It is no problem. I use to cook it for my wife, my ex-wife I should say." Kyle put the menu down on the counter and continued cleaning. His mood changed when he mentioned about his ex-wife.

Elisa finished her breakfast and Kyle took the dishes. "Just put the dishes in the dishwasher. Cora will be here today. I know you have met her once. I have to leave for work. I told her that I was hiring you so everything should be okay."

Elisa got up and grabbed her briefcase and purse with her laptop in it. "She seems nice Miss Drinnings. I will have your dinner ready before you get home."

"Good Kyle, I usually get home between five thirty and five forty-five, if I am running later I will call you ahead of time okay."

"Okay Miss Drinnings, have a good day at work." He heard the door close. He looked around. He would do what he could not to mess this up.

⊕⊖⊗⊘⊙⊖⊕

Elisa got to work. She got into her office and had not been there long when her cell phone rang. It could not be Kyle; she had not given him her cell number. She looked down to see who it was. It was Guy. He had not called her in almost two months since the bouquet incident.

She hesitated, sighed, and then answered it. "Hello."

"Oh my Mon Cherie, how I have missed you." Guy said with a sweet voice. Elisa was thinking, *yeah right that is why you haven't called me in almost two months.*

"Hello Guy, what do you want?" Elisa asked him punching on her laptop.

"Oh Elisa, please don't be angry. I am so sorry for the way I treated you. I want to make it up to you dear Elisa. How about we have dinner and I make up for not taking you to the orchestra?"

Elisa did not know if she wanted to. "I don't know Guy. I am busy."

"Please Elisa; I have been busy with my store which is why I have not been able to call you."

Liar, Elisa thought. "I know why you haven't called me. I still remember your remark you made to me at the restaurant about my father leaving my mother."

"Elisa I did not mean that. I was upset about the bouquet but now it all seems so trite and menial. Please forgive me." Guy was begging her on the phone.

"I promise you I will not say that again." Guy sounded like a scolded child on the phone.

"Let me think about it and I will get back to you." Elisa said without feeling.

"Okay my Mon Cherie. I will let you think about it, but please give me this second chance."

"I will get back with you Guy." Elisa reiterated and hung up.

Her office phone rang. "Yes," Elisa said over the intercom. It was Sissy.

"Brian wants to speak with you Elisa."

"I am a little busy right now what does he want?"

"I am not sure, but he sounded upset." Sissy said. *Another upset man, let the world stop.* Elisa thought.

"Tell him whatever it is to get over it. If it has nothing to do with the urgency of Pose Magazine then it is a waste of my time."

"I will." Sissy said. Elisa did not have time for childish antics from her designers or anyone who worked at Pose Magazine. Whatever there was nerving them they needed to get over it or look for another job.

⚜

Back at the townhouse, Kyle was preparing the chicken for Elisa's dinner when Cora walked in. Kyle turned around. "Hello," Kyle said. "I am Kyle Rimmer and I am Miss Drinnings new cook."

Cora had just gotten to work. Cora shook his hand. "Oh yes, I remember you now. You were here almost two months ago when Senorita Drinnings took you to dinner. She told me she would be hiring you. I am Cora Hernandez."

I hope we can become friends as we work more together." Kyle said politely.

"Oh yes, I am sure we can Senor Kyle."

"It is just Kyle."

"Okay Kyle. I shall get to work." Cora left the kitchen and Kyle smiled and shook his head.

Chapter 20

It was the middle of the afternoon when Elisa heard a knock on her door. "Come in please." Brian walked in. Elisa was looking at some photos.

She looked up and saw Brian. "Oh Brian, I see that you did not take my advice that my assistant gave you."

"No Miss Drinnings and I am sorry, but I could not let this go."

"What is so overwhelmingly pertinent Brian that you had to come to my office and could not let go. Does this adversely affect Pose Magazine in anyway?" Elisa leaned back with her arms crossed.

"Well yes and no." Brian said. He shut the door. "I don't understand it." Brian started.

"What do you not understand Brian that I need to explain to you?" Elisa said impatiently.

"I heard that Marco is going to Paris with you in April. He has been talking non-stop about it. He has only been here less than two months and I have been here with Pose and dedicated myself to her for years. How can he go over me? I understand that Ellie won the contest but I do not understand why Marco Shoops gets to go with you to Paris."

Elisa stood up, "sit down Brian." Brian sat down. Elisa walked over to him. "You went to London last fall with me. I thought that Marco's drawings would also be good for the spring show in Paris; my decision to let him go is none of your concern Brian. I suggest that if you have a problem with it, then you can hand me your resignation today. Pose Magazine is a successful fashion magazine and I have not the time or the inclination to be boggled with your incessant whining of why I made the decision I did. Do you understand me?" Elisa was sitting on the corner of her desk looking Brian right in the eye.

"Yes I do Miss Drinnings." Brian said, but was fuming inside.

"Well then, this unwelcome meeting is adjourned."

Brian got up. He turned back around. "Could this be because his father is a famous Hollywood Producer? I know about that. Is he going to get special privileges and preferential treatment because of this?"

Elisa was angry now. "This has nothing to do with that Brian. I have made my decision and that is final. If you do not like it, I have already told you what you can do."

"You will have my resignation today before I leave. I will not let my talent go to waste on someone who doesn't appreciate good taste."

That made her even angrier. "FINE," Elisa shouted. "I expect it on my desk soon and get all your belongings out of here. You are no longer employed here at Pose Magazine." Brian opened the door and slammed it. Elisa threw her pen down on the desk.

Sissy heard the commotion. She came in. "Is everything okay Elisa? I heard you and Brian fighting. I told him what you said and I tried to tell him not to bother you but he pushed me away."

"It is okay Sissy; it is not your fault. Brian no longer works for Pose Magazine as of today." Elisa sat back down and continued her work.

"Well if you need anything, I will be at my desk," Sissy replied.

"Thank you Sissy. How about you and I go have a drink after work?" Sissy was surprised. Elisa had never gone out for a drink after work. Sissy knew something had to be up. But she was game.

"Sure if you like Elisa. I will be ready. Just pick the place."

"I already have the place. I will have my driver take us there."

"Great," Sissy said. Elisa called home.

Cora answered. "Hello, this is Cora speaking how may I help you?"

"Cora this is Elisa, could you get Kyle on the phone please?" A few minutes later Kyle was on the phone.

"This is Kyle."

"Kyle this is Elisa, I will be late from work tonight. I am not sure when I will be home so just keep my dinner warm for me okay."

"I will Miss Drinnings." "Thank you Kyle." Elisa hung up. It had been a rough day and it was not even over. Guy calling and wanting to take her out after not calling her for almost two months, and she got into a fight with one of her designers and asked for his resignation,

Nothing that a "few" martinis could not clear up. By the end of the day, true to his word, Brian gave her his resignation. He walked out with his stuff. Elisa told him, "Good luck and good riddance." She had a magazine to run not a daycare. Her and Sissy headed out and got into the car. They went to a nice bar and had a few drinks and laughed. It was a nice end to a stressful day for Elisa.

Elisa told Sissy about Guy, about Kyle, and about Brian's resignation. "I cannot believe he had the audacity to call you after the way he treated you and what he said to you." Sissy was referring to Guy.

"Oh yes, I told him that I would get back with him."

"Do you still like him and want to date him Elisa?" Sissy asked taking a drink. Elisa was stirring her martini. This was her second one.

"He apologized to me and promised to never say it again and that what he did was trite and menial." Elisa sighed. "He is great in bed." Elisa said and laughed.

"But that is no reason to give him another chance Elisa, only if you truly forgive him and want to see him again."

"I know Sissy, but sex is a major factor as well."

"Does he make you happy and satisfy you Elisa, other than sexually? I told you if you don't want him I will take him."

Sissy laughed and Elisa lightly punched her in the arm.

"Maybe after a few more martinis, I will make my decision."

"No, that just makes you hornier Elisa. It doesn't do anything for your decision making."

"Well thank you for that dear Sissy, but anyway, I will have a few more before heading home." Elisa drank her martini and ordered another one.

⚜

Kyle was putting the finishing touches on Elisa's dinner. He kept it warm for her and cleaned up. He had fixed him something to eat and took a shower. Cora had left. They actually ended up getting along. Kyle thought Cora was sweet and Cora thought Kyle was funny. He knew he was not supposed to do this, but he walked to Elisa's bedroom door. He opened the door and looked in. Elisa had a beautiful four poster bed with a beautiful cover. He walked in. He felt the bed. It was all silk sheets and cover. He looked around and saw a drawer with a mirror and chair. He walked over and saw all kinds of skin cream, perfume, and make up. He picked up some the perfume and smelled it.

He smelled one and it had been the same one Elisa wore the night she took him to dinner. He saw a bureau of dresser drawers with pictures on top of it. It was one of Elisa in a graduation gown, one of her with an older lady, had to be her mother, and one with Elisa as a child.

No pictures of a male, he wondered if her father had not died when she was young. It looked like that she was an only child. He saw her nightstand and he walked over to it. Elisa's lamp, phone, and alarm clock were on it. He opened the drawer and saw two envelopes. He saw one with the name Elisa on it and the other with the name Cara on it.

Who was Cara? Could she be a sister? A friend from school? An aunt? Elisa had never mentioned anyone by the name of Cara. He was about to pick them up when he heard some voices downstairs. He hurriedly shut the drawer and ran out of the room and quietly shut the door. He went to the top of the stairs and saw Elisa taking her coat off, another lady with her. It was the same lady with the blond curly hair he had seen trying to give him the hundred dollar bill.

"I will see you tomorrow at work." Elisa told Sissy.

"If you make it," Sissy laughed.

"Oh I will make it. You watch." The two women laughed and hugged each other and then Sissy left. Elisa looked up and saw Kyle. "Kyle."

"I am sorry Miss Drinnings. I did not mean to eavesdrop but your dinner is warm for you."

"Thank you Kyle. I will eat now."

"Okay Miss Drinnings. Goodnight."

"Goodnight Kyle." Kyle walked back to his room. Would she know that he was in her room? He left everything exactly as he saw it. He pulled out his purple heart he got from the military and the necklace his mother had given him before she died. Those were two items he kept from his belongings. He was glad that he had not given Janice the necklace or his purple heart.

He missed his parents. He wondered what happened to Elisa's parents. Could he bring himself to ask her about them or about the name Cara and who she was? Then she would know that he did something that he was not supposed to do. For right now, he would keep it to himself.

❈❈❈❈❈

Elisa took out her dinner, plopped her shoes off, and sat down to eat. It was delicious. She was satisfied. *Kyle may work out after all,* she thought. She finished her dinner and headed upstairs. The effects of the alcohol running through her body made her light headed.

She stood in front of Kyle's shut door and then went to her room. She got undressed and got a hot shower. It seemed to make her feel better. She blow dried her hair. She sat down at her vanity and put on her creams and brushed her hair. She got up and crawled into bed with the alcohol having its effect and putting her to sleep.

She had not come to Kyle's room so Kyle felt safe. She had not noticed anything out of order. He opened the door and walked to her bedroom; he peeked in through the small opening in her door and saw her sound asleep. Oh what he would not give to be able to go in there and lay right beside her and hold her.

He could imagine making love to her. He had not made love to a woman since Janice. He had to get these thoughts out of his head; this was his employer for goodness sake. He walked back to his room and shut the door. He got back into bed. He dreamed of him and Elisa being together and doing things together. He dreamed she looked up into his eyes.

She had the most beautiful eyes. He had a smile on his face.

※⊱⋇⊰※

The next morning, Kyle had Elisa's breakfast ready. He would eat after she left. "How was your evening Miss Drinnings?" Kyle asked her.

"It was marvelous. It was exactly what I needed. I needed to cut loose. I have so much going on." Kyle smiled. "Oh Kyle," Elisa said.

"Yes Miss Drinnings."

"Dinner was absolutely fabulous. You outdid yourself. You may prove to be a great cook and employee."

"Well I thank you for the compliment."

"Here is the menu for tonight."

Kyle looked at it. "I will have it ready for you."

Elisa got up. "I will call if anything changes about dinner." Elisa walked into the foyer. She grabbed her briefcase and coat.

"Do you need any help putting your coat on Miss Drinnings." She had not heard Kyle come out of the kitchen.

"Oh Kyle, you scared me. Um, no I am fine thank you. Remember, have dinner ready by five thirty unless something changes."

"I will Miss Drinnings." And with that, Elisa was out the door and on her way to work. Kyle watched the car pull away. He knew tonight how he would make the dinner very special.

He got back into the kitchen to fix him something to eat and clean up. It was so nice having an actual roof over his head and food he could fix himself. He liked this. Elisa had not mentioned anything about him being in her room or questioned him. Tonight Elisa wanted tilapia, fresh green beans, and a salad. Kyle would outdo himself again.

⊷⊱⊰⊱⊰⊶

Elisa got to work. Now that Brian was gone, it was one less designer for Pose, but Pose would still be successful. She had designers come and go and it did not affect Pose. It was Thursday and in three weeks it would be Thanksgiving and Elisa still had not figured out what she was doing for the holidays.

The fragrance line was up and running and they said it should be ready in time for the spring show in April. Elisa was ecstatic. Maggie Bench called her to keep her informed about it. "Oh Elisa, the fragrance line is doing absolutely wonderful. It will be a major success, and should be ready in time for the spring show in Paris. You could not ask for a better time. Well done Elisa!" Maggie exclaimed with jubilance. "Everything is going according to plan it sounds like. I have the spring show in a little over five months, the fragrance line, and the models lined up to do the commercial for the Pose fragrance line."

Elisa had told Maggie about Brian's resignation and the argument that hand ensued between them. "Do not worry about him Elisa; we have other designers who are just as talented if not better. I never did like him much anyway." Elisa agreed even though the London show with his designs had been a success.

She would not have infighting among her designers or those who worked for Pose Magazine. It would be detrimental to Pose. "Well dear Elisa, I must go. Eric is taking me to lunch." Elisa had not heard from Eric since she faxed him over the documents he needed and told her that everything for the fragrance line was a go.

"Well you have lots of fun Maggie."

"Oh I will." The women hung up.

That reminded Elisa of calling Guy back and giving him her decision about dinner. She did not like his attitude but he did apologize. He had acted like a fool. Elisa called Guy and told him that Saturday night would be fine. He said he would pick her up at eight o'clock. There Elisa had done it; she could not renege on it.

~~*~~

That evening Kyle had Elisa's dinner ready as planned. He had her bottle of wine out chilling, he had her dinner on the table, and a candle lit. He had found one in the kitchen drawer. When Elisa walked into her kitchen, she was taken aback. Kyle was a good cook but this was too much. He had gone too far. "I hope you like it Miss Drinnings."

Elisa turned around. "Well, yes Kyle, but you did not have to do all of this."

"A beautiful woman like you Miss Drinnings deserves nothing but the best."

"Are you flirting with me Kyle?"

"Oh no Miss Drinnings. I understand that I am just your cook. But I am sure that you have had a hard week and I wanted to do something to try and make it more soothing and subtle." He pulled the chair out for her.

"I appreciate it immensely Kyle. I really do.

My last cook never did this for me." "Well, I am different." Kyle said, opening her wine and pouring her a glass. "I shall go up to my room, but if you need anything else just holler." Elisa still could not believe what Kyle had done. He left and she turned back around. It was another part of Kyle she was learning about.

CHAPTER 21

It was Saturday, early evening and Elisa was getting prepared for her date. "I will not be here tonight to eat Kyle. I have a date. You have the evening off to do what you like." Kyle and Elisa were both at the top of the stairs.

Kyle thought about going to visit Mildred. "I think I will go and visit my dear friend Mildred. I was wondering if I could use your phone Miss Drinnings to call her. She should still be there finishing up."

"Yes you may Kyle." Elisa told him.

"Thank you Miss Drinnings." Kyle went to use the phone in the hallway. Elisa had gone back to her room to put some finishing touches on herself. Kyle wanted to tell Elisa how beautiful she looked, but he knew she would think that he was flirting with her again, so he kept quiet. Deep down inside he was jealous. He got on the phone and dialed the number to the hamburger shop.

"Hello, Bernie's Hamburger Shop, this is Mildred may I help you."

"Hey Mildred this is Kyle."

"Oh Kyle, how are you doing dear?" Mildred said excitedly.

"I am doing great Mildred. My employer has a date and has given me the night off. I wanted to come and visit."

"Oh Kyle, you can come and see me anytime. You do not need to ask. I always have time for you." Mildred said happily.

"Okay I will be there in a little bit, just let me change."

"Okay Kyle I will see you when you get here." Kyle hung up and Elisa walked out of her bedroom.

"Is everything okay Kyle?" Elisa asked him.

Yes Miss Drinnings. I was going to head over after I change." Kyle could not take his eyes off of Elisa.

"Well then, I will have my driver take you there." Just then the doorbell rang.

Cora had left early. "Well get changed then. I will get the door." Elisa went downstairs and Kyle curious, hung at the top of the stairs. Elisa opened the door and it was Guy.

"Oh my Mon Cherie. How I have missed you." He grabbed Elisa and kissed her wrapping his arms around her. Kyle saw this but made sure that neither one could see him. He felt a twinge of pain hit his heart.

Kyle could see that the man was handsome. He was very well dressed and Kyle could see that the man was high society as well. "We should be going Elisa. I have our usual table." They headed out the door with Kyle looking on. *He is a lucky man,* Kyle thought. Kyle sighed and went to get changed.

⊷⊶⊹⊱⊰⊹⊷⊶

"As usual Elisa you look stunning. I have thought about you often." Elisa smiled. "I am sure you have." Elisa knew she did not sound convincing but Guy overlooked it. He grabbed her hand and kissed it. They got to the restaurant. Elisa was wearing an off-white long sleeved and long dress with dazzling diamonds on it. She had her studded hand bag to match.

They walked into the restaurant and went to their usual table and ordered the usual bottle of expensive wine. "So my Mon Cherie, how have you been? What have you been up to?" *If you had not acted like a child and ignored me for two months you would know.* Elisa thought, but kept it to herself.

The waiter brought their wine and they both ordered. When the waiter left, Guy opened the wine and started pouring.

"Well," she said, taking a sip of her wine. "I have already decided who will accompany me to Paris in April; the fragrance line is going well and should be ready by the time of the spring show, and just the usual of running a very successful magazine."

Guy smiled. He grabbed her hands. "That is good to hear

Elisa. You sound like you have been busy. I have been busy myself with my stores. They are doing very well.

I not only called you to have dinner with you tonight Elisa, but to see what you were doing for Thanksgiving. I thought that we could go to the Bahamas, or Jamaica, or Cancun. We could be together and get out of this cold weather for a few days." That sounded enticing to Elisa. She could take the four days and relax on a sandy beach somewhere.

She could give Kyle that time off to let him see his friend or spend it how he wanted to. She remembered too that Sissy had invited her to her parent's house for Thanksgiving. "To be honest with you Guy, I have not really had time to ponder on it. Holidays are not pertinent to me nor are they something that I really dwell on."

"So what do you say Elisa. Let me whisk you off in my private jet again to one of the beautiful islands. We can drink, relax, swim, and make love." Guy was giving her a mischievous grin. She wondered if she should. He had not spoken to her in two months and now he wanted to whisk her off to some island. I mean she did accept this dinner date with him, what could hurt. She had no other plans.

Before she could answer, the waiter brought their dinner. When he left, Elisa responded. "Sure why not Guy, I would love to go." Elisa started eating.

"Where would you like to go?" Guy sounded happy that she took him up on his offer.

"I would like to go to the Bahamas and drink plenty of Bahama Mamas."

"It is settled then," Guy replied. "I will pick you up Thanksgiving morning and we will take flight to the Bahamas, but I will make sure to have you back Sunday in time for work Monday."

They finished their meal and headed back to her townhouse.

≈≈❈≈≈

Kyle was in Mildred's apartment. She had fixed him some dinner and they were sitting drinking tea. "Tell me Kyle dear,"

Mildred said, "how do you like your new job and how is she treating you?"

"Well she has me calling her Miss Drinnings." They both laughed. "Now that I work for her I cannot call her Elisa. She is treating me well Mildred. She had a date tonight with a very handsome and well to do man.

"I had to admit she looked beautiful as always and I wanted to tell her but I did not want her to think that I was flirting with her again. I had to also admit Mildred that I felt some jealousy at seeing this man hug and kiss her." Kyle looked down. "Kyle dear, are you falling in love with Elisa? Do you love her?" Mildred could see it in his eyes. He had not felt this way about any woman since Janice.

"Would it matter Mildred?" Kyle sighed and looked up at her. "I mean I am way out of her league. I am just her cook. I mean I lay there in bed imagining what it would be like to hold her and make love to her."

"Oh Kyle dear," Mildred took his hand. "It does matter Kyle. You have not loved another woman since Janice. You cannot torture yourself like this Kyle, but you also cannot deny that you have feelings for this woman.

You know the man I loved Kyle was killed in a work related accident. He was a contractor doing roofing for someone's house. He lost his balance and fell from the roof breaking his neck. He died instantly. I never let myself love again Kyle. I never let myself feel it again for another man. Sometimes I wonder if I had let myself love again, would I have married and had kids.

I would not be sitting here and living in this apartment working as a waitress. But then again, I may never have met you Kyle and our paths would never have crossed. I am lucky to have met you Kyle and been able to share so much. You love her and maybe one day you will get to show it, that is up to you."

Kyle knew she was right, it was good in words but in action, he did not have a snowball's chance in July. "Well Mildred, it has been great to see you again. Dinner was sumptuous as usual and having this talk."

"The same here Kyle. What are you doing for Thanksgiving Kyle?" He and Mildred stood up.

"I don't know Mildred. I am not sure what Elisa will be doing. I do not know if she would want me to cook a dinner for her or not."

"Let me know Kyle," Mildred told him as they walked to her door. "I can fix us both a small Thanksgiving dinner."

"I will let you know Mildred. I will call you. I would love to have you fix me a nice Thanksgiving dinner. I could even come over and help you, instead of just coming to eat."

Mildred laughed. "You can if you wish. You are a good man Kyle, never forget that."

"I will call you Mildred and I will come over early to help you fix dinner if I can, if Elisa gives me the holiday weekend off."

"I will be looking forward to it Kyle." They hugged each other and he left. He got back to Elisa's townhouse. He walked inside and walked upstairs. He could hear voices. He walked to where they were. He was standing in front of Elisa's closed bedroom door.

He could not see in but he could hear a female and male voice. He did not want to eavesdrop but he was curious now. "Oh Elisa I want to devour you all night." Guy said as he kissed her ferociously with Elisa breathing hard. "You bring out the animal in me." Guy entered her with all his strength and Elisa screamed out.

Kyle could hear them. He wanted to be that man in there now. He walked away from the door and back to his room. He changed and crawled into bed. He knew he could not give her all the material things that that man could give her, but he could give her something that money could not buy if she would give him a chance. *Yeah, good luck with that Kyle,* he thought. He fell asleep thinking about her.

⊹⊱✱⊰⊹

The next morning he was up early to fix her breakfast. He

could hear voices coming down the steps. He figured it was Elisa and her lover. "So my Mon Cherie, can we get together before Thanksgiving again. I want to make up for the last time and take you to a show. The Tran Siberian Orchestra is coming to Carnegie Hall and I would love to take you."

"I would like that very much Guy. They are my favorite orchestra band."

"They are playing the weekend before Thanksgiving and I of course can get the very best of seats." He held her and gave her a long kiss. "I will call you Elisa."

"Okay Guy." Elisa walked him to her door and let him out. Kyle had heard them in her bedroom this morning. They had made love again. Kyle had peeked and watched them in the foyer. He went back to making breakfast.

Elisa walked in. "Mmm, sure smells good in here." Elisa commented as she opened the refrigerator door and took out some orange juice.

"Yes Miss Drinnings I am making my famous blueberry pancakes."

"Sounds delicious," Elisa sat down at the table and flicked through a magazine. Kyle put the pancakes on her plate and set them down in front of her.

"How was your evening with your friend Kyle?" Elisa asked him as she poured syrup on her pancakes.

"It was good Miss Drinnings. We had a nice dinner and Mildred and I talked for most of the evening. She asked me what I was doing for Thanksgiving. I told her that I did not know what you would be doing."

"Well to answer you Kyle, I will be going away with Guy that weekend. He is picking me up on Thanksgiving morning. You can fix me dinner the evening before and then you will have the rest of the weekend off. I will not be back until Sunday evening. You will resume work on Monday morning. Is that sufficient for you Kyle?"

"Yes Miss Drinnings. I will let Mildred know."

"You will be receiving your first pay this week Kyle."

Kyle was excited. Finally some money that he did not have

to beg for, he would actually earn it the right way. "Thank you Miss Drinnings, and how are your pancakes?"

"They are delicious Kyle thank you." Kyle cleaned up and Elisa gave him the menu for dinner tonight.

Kyle wanted to ask her how her evening went with this man named Guy but he talked himself out of it. He went upstairs to his room and shut the door. Elisa had spent the day going over some work and preparing for work. Kyle came downstairs later and Elisa looked up. "Where are you going?" she asked him.

"I was just going for a walk. I just wanted to get some fresh air. Would you like to come with me?" Kyle hoped that she would say yes.

"Sorry I can't, I have a lot of work to do for tomorrow. And besides, I am your employer not your roommate. Just be back in time for dinner." Elisa gave him that look.

"Yes Miss Drinnings." Kyle opened the door and breathed in the cold air. *It is just a walk,* Kyle thought, but he did not insist or become persistent. He wanted to take in this neighborhood. He loved walking.

He got in front of a florist shop and walked in. He looked around. The owner came up to him. "May I help you sir?" Kyle turned around and stared at an elderly man.

"I am just looking around thank you." Kyle remarked.

"Well if you need anything just let me know." Kyle said he would. Kyle was wearing better clothing than he did before at the last florist shop. The man did not look at him with disgust as the other florist shop did.

He saw a dozen yellow roses and knew when he got his first pay he would buy them. He would use them each night for Elisa when he fixed her dinner. He would find a vase to put one in. He also saw a bouquet that he would buy Mildred for Thanksgiving.

It was a beautiful autumn bouquet and would look good on her table. He left the store and went into some other stores. He walked into a clothing store and a jewelry store. The prices he saw were outrageous and beyond his means. If he saved enough, he figured he could get Mildred something nice for Christmas.

This would be the first Christmas since losing everything and becoming homeless that he would have a job and making his own money.

It was exhilarating. He wanted to get Elisa something nice but what do you give someone who already has everything? He left to head back to her townhouse. He was getting another one of his migraines and had to sit down. The pain was excruciating. Kyle could not move. Everything was going blurry. The last thing he remembered was total darkness.

CHAPTER 22

Kyle heard a voice that sounded far away. He could not tell where it was coming from. "Sir, sir, are you okay?" He heard the voice again. He felt like someone was shaking him. He slowly opened his eyes. He squinted and it took a little bit for him to get to where he could see anything. The voice was coming from a passerby who had seen him. He was shaking Kyle.

How long had he been out? He did not know. "Are you okay sir?" Kyle looked at the person.

"What time is it? How long have I been this way?" Kyle asked the gentleman.

"It is four o'clock sir and I am not sure. I just found you passed out. Are you okay?" The gentleman asked again.

"What, oh yes, thank you. I have to get going. I need to get back home." Kyle started to get up. He felt wobbly.

The passerby helped him up. "Are you sure you do not need to go to a hospital sir?" Kyle did not have any medical insurance yet.

"Oh no thank you I am fine. I appreciate this." It was a few more minutes before Kyle was ready to leave.

The man who helped him had left. Kyle had to get back. He had dinner to fix for Elisa. The migraine was gone. He walked into the townhouse and Elisa came down the steps. "My, my, you sure do take long walks." Elisa said to him.

"Oh I am so sorry Miss Drinnings. I lost track of time. I will get dinner started." Elisa watched him walk into the kitchen. He prepared her dinner and set the table. He lit another candle and left it in front of her dinner.

He poured her a glass of wine. He walked out into the living room and told Elisa that her dinner was ready. "Thank you Kyle, I shall go and eat." Kyle went upstairs. He would eat later. Elisa walked in and saw the same candle he had used the other night lit up.

She shook her head. *"Why are you doing this Kyle?"* She said to herself. She sat down to eat and dinner was good as usual.

Later that evening with the candle incident forgotten, Elisa was soaking in a bath. Kyle was downstairs eating. He cleaned up and went back upstairs. He would not tell Elisa about the migraine. He walked to his room. Today had been scary for him. He had never blacked out from any of his migraines before. This was scary.

Elisa got out of her bath and wrapped a towel around her. She dried off and got dressed. She prepared herself for the evening.

⊛⊰⊱⊛

The rest of the week had been busy for Elisa. She had meetings. She interviewed a number of designers to take Brian's place. She had not decided on any of them. Sissy had been out sick with the flu, so Elisa did not have her assistant. That made double the work for her. The new fabrics that Elisa had shown her designers had been a go. The models had loved them and no allergic reactions that Elisa knew of.

Guy had called her again. He wanted to take her on an early Thanksgiving trip. He wanted to jet set her off to San Francisco this weekend. It was two weeks before Thanksgiving. She said she would be too busy to go. Guy wanted her to see his store there and have some fun.

She told him that this weekend would not be a good weekend and he hung up disappointed. Elisa knew it but did not care. She could not always just drop everything for Guy when he called. It was Friday and Elisa paid Kyle his first pay. It was more than what he made in a month working the sidewalk.

He was like a kid who had gotten that toy he wanted for

Christmas. He asked the driver if he could take him back to
the same florist shop that he had been to earlier that week. The
driver stopped in front of the shop and Kyle told him that he
would not be long.

Kyle walked in and the same elderly gentleman was there.
Kyle asked him about the dozen yellow roses and the elderly
man had gotten them and wrapped them up for him. The man
asked Kyle if he would like a note to go with the roses and
Kyle said no. The elderly gentleman asked Kyle if he would
like a vase to put them in when he got home. Kyle had decided
against a vase and would just put the rose next to Elisa's plate
along with a note.

He paid for the roses and left the shop. He went and got
some paper and a pen to write Elisa some notes. It would be
just friendly notes hoping that her day went well. He told the
florist that he would be back to get the bouquet for a friend of
his. Kyle got back to the townhouse and prepared dinner. Elisa
had not called to tell him no so he got started. He could not
wait until she got home tonight.

He was excited. He hoped that Elisa would like the rose
and the note to go along with her dinner. He did not want her
to think that he was flirting with her again or trying anything
which is why he got the yellow roses and not the red ones. He
hoped that she would not get angry at him. He just appreciated
what he had now and what she had given him; a new life.

He cooked the sauce to perfection and added the pasta to
the water. Elisa wanted fettuccine alfredo tonight with grilled
chicken. He had cooked the pasta to just the right consistency
and had the chicken ready to add. He drained the pasta and
added it to her plate. He put the sauce on and cut up the chicken
to put on top of the alfredo. He set her table, got her wine out
and poured her a glass, and took a yellow rose and set it beside
her plate with a note on the bottom.

After he got it done, he heard her walk in the door. *Perfect
timing* Kyle thought. He walked out of the kitchen. Elisa was
putting her briefcase on the table. He walked over and helped her
with her coat. "Oh Kyle you do not have to do that." Elisa said.

"I know Miss Drinnings but you must be tired and dinner is ready." He hung her coat up and she went upstairs to change.

"I will be down in a minute."

Later, Elisa came down and walked into the kitchen. She saw the yellow rose lying beside her plate. She walked over to the table and picked up the rose. She saw the piece of paper. She opened it and read it. *I hope you had a good day at work today and this yellow rose is for you as a token of my appreciation for what you have given me.~ Kyle.* Elisa looked around. She had never had anyone do this for her, not Emilio, not even Guy.

She saw Kyle standing there and then he left. She followed him out. "Why Kyle, why you doing this for me? The candle, the rose, helping me with my coat. Why?" Elisa asked him.

"Can you not tell by the note I had left with the rose if you had read it Miss Drinnings? I got my first paycheck today and it felt good to actually have money that you worked for and not had to beg for. To have more money than what you could make in a whole month, in a week.

"To be able to cook for you and do this, and to be able to have a place to stay. You have changed my life." *And I am in love with you Elisa. I have been from the moment I saw you and you acted like I did not exist.* Kyle was thinking to himself, but did not dare say it out loud.

"Kyle I am not sure what to say to all of this. I have never had anyone do this for me, not even Guy."

"Well maybe it is time Miss Drinnings that someone does. Enjoy your dinner." Kyle finished and walked up the steps before Elisa could say anything else. She headed back to the kitchen and ate. She stared at the rose and smiled.

Elisa walked to Kyle's door and knocked on it. He did not answer. She knocked on it again and called out "Kyle," but still no answer. She opened the door, it was unlocked. She walked in. She saw the bed made and some stuff on the dresser. She walked over to it. She saw a necklace and a purple heart. She saw no pictures. *Hmm I wonder why,* she thought. She picked up the Purple Heart and looked at it.

Elisa put the Purple Heart down. She picked up the necklace.

It was a locket actually. It was cylinder in shape and made of gold and on a thick chain. It looked like it could have been a stop watch. She saw a button on the top of it and pressed it opened and saw a picture on each side. It was a picture of a man and a woman. This has to be his mother and father. She heard a door open and hurriedly put the necklace down forgetting to close the locket. She ran out of the room closing his door and went to her room. Kyle walked back in.

He went to his dresser to get him some underclothes and that is when he saw it. The locket was opened. He knew he had closed it. He was sure of it. He would open it from time to time and when he was done looking at it, he would close it. Now it lay here on his dresser opened.

He also noticed that his purple heart was not lying in the same place as it was before. Was his mind playing tricks on him or had someone been in his room? He thought about Elisa, but she had not set foot in his room that he knew of since hiring him. He would ask Cora, but he knew when he left this room to take a shower that his locket had been closed and his Purple Heart was not laying where he put it.

In her room, Elisa was sitting at her vanity brushing her hair and putting on her night cream. She ran out of there and forgot to close his locket. She hoped that he would not say anything about it. She had not meant to snoop, but she just wanted to go and thank him for a nice dinner and everything. She would not bother him again tonight. She would see him tomorrow. She got up and walked over to her window and looked out.

⚜

The next morning Cora had gotten to work. Kyle saw her as he got to the bottom of the steps. "Good morning Cora," Kyle said. She was hanging up her coat.

"Good morning Kyle," Cora repeated.

"Hey Cora."

"Yes," she responded.

"I was just wondering. Last night I walked into my room and my locket that was lying on my dresser was opened and my Purple Heart had been moved. Would you know anything about this?"

"Oh no Kyle, I have not been in your room since I washed and changed your sheets five days ago." He knew that five days ago the locket had definitely been closed and his Purple Heart had not been messed with.

"Okay, thank you Cora." Kyle walked to the kitchen.

"You're welcome Kyle."

Elisa walked down the steps. "Buenos diaz Senorita Drinnings. Como estas?" "Buenos diaz Cora and estoy bien." Elisa replied.

"Bien, bien," Cora said clapping her hands. "I am here to pick up anything you need Senorita Drinnings."

"Thank you Cora, I will need my dry cleaning picked up today. I will need my outfit for work on Monday."

"I will go and get that for you. Um, your new cook Kyle asked me about his locket and Purple Heart. He asked me if I would know anything about his locket being opened on his dresser and his Purple Heart being messed with.

"I told him that I have not been in his room for five days, not since I had washed and changed his sheets on the bed." Elisa trying not to sound nervous replied.

"Oh I see. I would not worry about it Cora."

"I would never touch his stuff Senorita Drinnings. I only go in there to change the sheets on his bed."

"I know Cora. Do not worry about it, just go and get my dry cleaning. I have nothing else for you to do today. So after that you can go and enjoy the rest of your weekend. I will have my driver take you to the dry cleaners." Elisa smiled.

"Oh thank you. Thank you. My sister and I have made plans this weekend." Elisa got her driver and he took Cora to the dry cleaners. Elisa told her she was welcome and walked into the kitchen. She hoped that Kyle would not mention anything about the locket or the Purple Heart.

He had her breakfast ready for her. He made no mention of it and Elisa did not dare to bring it up. "Breakfast looks good Kyle."

"Thank you Elisa." He had made her an omelet with cheese and toast. Her coffee was already waiting for her. He had a rose waiting for her with another note underneath of it.

"Kyle, I just wanted to say again that the rose and the note last night were beautiful and I wanted to say thank you."

"You're welcome Miss Drinnings." Kyle was cleaning up.

"And here again you have done it for me. This is too much." Elisa said.

"You deserve it Miss Drinnings like I have made it clear before." Kyle said, giving her a half smile.

"If I did not know better, I would think that you.." but Elisa could not finish the sentence.

"You mean in love with you Miss Drinnings. Oh no, this is strictly professional and I enjoy it. I enjoy cooking and I have not gotten to do it as much as I would like." Kyle finished cleaning up. "And besides Miss Drinnings, I am just your cook and the chances of me and you having anything more than a professional relationship are unimaginable."

He left her to her breakfast. She watched him leave and opened the note. "*Here is another rose for a beautiful employer who has helped me.*" Elisa folded the note back. She just sat there staring at her breakfast. Suddenly, she was not so hungry. She pushed the plate away and drank her coffee. She had messed with his personal items without asking him while she told him that her room was off limits, he has been an exquisite cook, he has a romantic side to him, and yet professional at the same time.

Each day, Kyle was showing her a side of him that surprised her. And yet he was right, the chance of them ever having more than just a working relationship was unimaginable. They were worlds apart, yet she could not find herself getting upset at the roses, the notes, nor the candle lights. Like he said, he was not in love with her, but this was his way of showing his appreciation for the job. Or was he? She laughed at the thought.

CHAPTER 23

It was the week before Thanksgiving and Elisa had been working diligently to get ready for the holidays. She had gone shopping to pick out a new outfit she would wear Saturday night to the Trans Siberian Orchestra that Guy was taking her to. Maggie had called to ask if Elisa wanted to take a tour of the building they were using to produce the Pose fragrance line. Elisa said that she would love to. It would be after the Thanksgiving holiday.

She was busy typing on her laptop when Sissy walked in. "Hello Elisa, how is the new cook working out for you?"

Elisa looked up from her laptop. "He is working quite well. He is a good cook. No, a great cook. He has lived up to my expectations." She did not tell Sissy about the notes, roses, or the candle light that Kyle had done for her. She did not want Sissy to start in on her about it.

"That is great to hear. What are you doing for Thanksgiving?" Sissy asked her.

"Well I have decided to jet set off with Guy to the Bahamas for the holiday weekend. It would be nice to get out of this cold weather."

"Oooo romantic," Sissy said putting her hands together. "It sounds like you and Guy are back at it." Sissy gave Elisa a wink.

"Yes and no. He wanted me to go with him to San Francisco a week ago but I couldn't go. He got mad, but I know he will get over it. In fact," Elisa said holding up one hand, "we are still on for the Orchestra Saturday night and our nice holiday getaway as I have stated. Guy and I are going to *21* before the show."

"I am so jealous," Sissy said, playfully sulking. "I am just going to stay home and watch some movies and binge on popcorn. Oh fun." Sissy remarked, rolling her eyes.

"Sissy you really need to get out and find you a man and have a social life. Ever since that lawyer guy you have become like a hermit. It is not the end of the world. You are still young yet. How long ago was that, like two years ago or something?" Elisa asked her.

"It was a year and a half ago I remind you," Sissy said defensively "and I have not even been looking nor do I want to. My mom and dad keep asking me when I am going to get married and give them a grandchild; you know being the only child is hard sometimes. What is Kyle doing for Thanksgiving?"

"Well, I am going to give him that weekend off since I will be out of town until Sunday night. He has a friend on the other end of Manhattan who is a waitress in a hamburger shop. Her name is Mildred, sweet lady she is. He has known her for years. I talked to her when I was checking out Kyle's references."

"At least he will not be alone spending it by himself." Sissy said wholeheartedly. "I hate to see people spend the holidays alone. I know I would not want to, that is why I go to my parent's house in upstate New York." Sissy was always the sentimental one.

"Well, I am going to get out of here and do what I do best and that is being your assistant. If anything changes for Thanksgiving, let me know," Sissy reiterated, "My family will still welcome you for dinner."

"Thanks Sissy. I will keep that in mind in case Guy wants to act like a jealous child again who got told no by his mother." Elisa said sarcastically. "When my scheduled interview shows up, just send him on in." Sissy mouthed *okay*, waved, and left the office.

⊰⊱⊰⊱⊰

Kyle was in the kitchen going over the menu that Elisa gave him this morning. He was still thinking about the necklace and his Purple Heart being messed with. He had a feeling that Elisa had been in his room but why? He laid the menu down. He wanted to know more about this Elisa so he went upstairs. Cora had not shown up yet so he was safe.

He walked upstairs and to her room. He hesitated before walking in. He wanted to make sure again that he was alone. He walked in. The room was the same as he saw it last time. He looked over at the night stand and walked to it. He opened it and saw the envelope with Cara's name on it. He saw the envelope with Elisa's name on it.

He pulled out the one with Elisa's name on it and opened it. He took out the letter. He knew he should not be doing this but he was curious. He knew nothing about his employer, except that she had given him a job, a place to stay, took him to dinner, bought him clothes, and he was now earning an honest living.

He opened the letter and started reading it.

My dearest and sweetest daughter Elisa,

I do not want to leave you but there comes a time when our time is done and we must say goodbye. Know that I will always love you and know I have not truly left you. After your father walked out on us, I tried to do the best I could to give us a good life. Though we were not rich, we had each other. You and Cara were my life and I even now; do love your sister even though she blamed me for your father leaving. I wish that I could have made Cara understand and explain why her father left and that I did everything I could to keep him here. I couldn't. She was so angry and hurt and then she up and left.

I never saw her again after that but I never stopped loving her. In the letter I have written her, I hope she sees that I tried to do everything I could do to hold this family together. You grew up Elisa and made me very proud. You went on to college, worked hard, and made a good life for yourself. You kept your promise to take care of me. You have got to stay strong Elisa, even after I am gone. You need to remember that we all choose our own destiny that we all choose how we want to live every day we are given, and that life will throw us a few curveballs but we just have to learn how to hit them.

I remember when you were little how you would dress up and act like you were a model, or read those magazines and learn about the latest fashions. You grew up to be a beautiful woman Elisa. You became a successful woman. I wish that I could have been like you and gone to college and became successful, but I married your father right out of high school and then had you.

I always pushed you to be successful. I remember one evening we were out on the porch and you asked me this question: "Mother do I make you proud?" and I said, "Every day." Though you and I were closer than Cara and I, I loved you both just the same. Don't forget where you came from Elisa and where you are now. We all have battles to fight; we just have to know which ones to fight. When you get down or lonely Elisa, remember, someone else may have it worse than you. Remember this song I use to sing to you and your sister Cara, "Oh Star in the Sky" Oh, Star in the Sky, how you shine so bright, oh how you light up the sky, Oh Star in the Sky shine on me tonight. Blink, blink, blink so bright, oh star in the sky. Oh Star in the Sky you give off your beautiful light, Oh Star in the Sky shine on me tonight.

Elisa I am sure your career keeps you busy, but remember this: "Don't drive through life so fast that you miss the scenery." My time is almost up and I am getting weaker but I will always love you. I must go now.

Love,
Mom

Kyle's eyes were watering. So Elisa had a sister named Cara, which would explain the envelope with her name on it. Her father left them and her mother died. It explained why there were no pictures of a male and another girl. He was still holding the letter and thinking when Cora walked in. "Oh my gosh!! Cora put her hand to her mouth.

Kyle jumped off the bed with the letter still in his hand.

"Cora." Kyle had the look of a deer in headlights.

"Kyle, you must not be in here. Senorita Drinnings would be very upset if she knew you were in here. I only come in here to get her clothes to dry clean, change her bed, and to pick out her clothes to wear, but never have I gone through any of her personal items."

"I am so sorry Cora. I should not be in here. My curiosity got the best of me. Please do not tell Elisa I was in here. I cannot afford to lose this job. I do not want to go back to living how I was. Please Cora do not tell her." Kyle had those pleading puppy dog eyes. Cora knew he was putting her in a bad spot. She had worked for Elisa for five years and loved what she did and loved Elisa.

If Elisa found out about this and knew she had not told her when she caught Kyle doing this, she could lose her job. She could not afford this. What was she going to do? Kyle folded the letter back up and put it away. Cora was still silent. "Please Cora; can you keep this just between us?" Kyle did not even hear Cora come in or upstairs.

"Kyle I have been loyal to Senorita Drinnings for five years. She trusts me. Kyle you have put me in a bad position." Cora said nervously. They both knew they could lose their jobs. Kyle more than her, he had only been there for three weeks. Cora put her head down and left the room. Kyle wasn't sure if she would tell Elisa.

They were getting along but she was more loyal to Elisa than him. He left the room making sure to put everything back as he found it. He walked back downstairs. He saw Cora and she said nothing to him as he walked back into the kitchen.

A handsome young dark haired man walked up to Sissy's desk. She was writing stuff into an appointment book. She looked up to see who it was with the very sexy accent. Standing in front of her was the young dark haired man. Sissy could not take her eyes off of him.

"I am Renaldo Cansini. I am here to see a Miss Elisa

Drinnings. I am her scheduled interview for the designer position." He smiled at her and showed the whitest teeth. He was well groomed, clean shaven, and smelled good. Sissy could not speak. "Miss, hello," he waved his hand in front of her face.

"Oh I am sorry sir, excuse me. She said to just send you on in."

"Thank you Miss."

"Um, you can call me Sissy," Sissy stood up smiling and straightening her skirt.

"Okay Sissy it is nice to meet you." He took her hand and kissed it. Sissy had to catch her breath.

He walked into Elisa's office. Elisa looked up. "Excuse me sir may I help you?" Elisa asked him sounding annoyed that he would walk in her office like that.

"Yes, I am here for the designer position with Pose. Your secretary or assistant said to just send me on in."

"Yes come on in and have a seat please." Elisa saw that he looked so young. He had a baby face. Elisa decided that he had to be in his early twenties at least. "I am Elisa Drinnings, Chief Editor of Pose Magazine, but you can call me Miss Drinnings."

Renaldo sat down across from Elisa. She had to admit to herself that he was very handsome. She was sure that Sissy noticed it too. Elisa made it a pact not to get involved with her designers or anyone at Pose Magazine. "Okay Miss Drinnings. I am Renaldo Cansini."

He had a wonderful accent. "Okay Mr. Cansini."

"Please call me Renaldo," he told her.

"Okay Renaldo, please tell me about yourself and why you want to work for Pose Magazine."

Elisa was seated in her chair staring straight at him. Any woman could get lost in those eyes. "I was born in Italy, but my parents immigrated here when I was three. They own a restaurant here in Manhattan. A nice Italian Bistro. I am the youngest of three kids. My two older sisters are married and help my parents with the restaurant. I worked there for a while but got bored with it. I wanted to do something more exciting.

"I went to school and started designing my own clothes. I went to the New York Art Institute and got my degree in fashion. I would like to work for Pose Magazine because I believe that I can offer a lot to Pose. I have here my portfolio and my resume if you want to look at them." He handed her his portfolio and his resume. Elisa looked over his resume.

"You may think I look so young, but I am twenty-nine. I went to business school as you can read from my resume to help run my parent's restaurant but then I decided to go to learn fashion and design. My father was disappointed but supported me."

"Yes, I can see here from your resume." Elisa said looking at him. "Of course I will need to verify your references and check out your portfolio. Pose Magazine is a very successful magazine and I want to keep it that way. I have interviewed quite a few before you Renaldo and they did not impress me."

"I promise you Miss Drinnings, if you give me a chance I will not let you down." He flashed his smile that he flashed at Sissy minutes ago.

That smile may get you all the women you want but it won't land you this job. Elisa thought. "According to your resume, you have not worked for another fashion magazine; Pose would be your first, am I right?"

Elisa had her hands folded on her desk. "That is correct Miss Drinnings. If you take a look at my portfolio I am sure you would be more than impressed." Renaldo told her confidently.

"I will be the judge of that. Many schools send me their so called finest designers, but I have the final say.

Thank you for your time Renaldo, I will take a look at your portfolio. I will get back with you next week before the holiday weekend." They both stood up and shook hands. He had a firm grip. He was very well built as Elisa could see.

"I look forward to it Miss Drinnings." He left her office. Sissy ran in there soon as he was out of sight.

"Are you giving him the job? Did you hire him? Where is he from? Don't you think he is sexy?" Sissy said, hardly containing her hormones.

"Sissy control your hormones, I am going to look at his portfolio now and get back with him next week before the holiday weekend. He is from Italy. His parents own an Italian Bistro here in Manhattan. He has two older sisters whom are married and help his parents run the restaurant.

"He ran it for a while but got bored with it and decided to design clothes. He went to the New York Art Institute like me."

"Oh, that is more than enough reason to hire him." Sissy emphasized.

"Um, no it is not, and he is only twenty-nine years old. He is ten years your junior." Elisa said to her, grabbing his portfolio to go over it. "This will tell me if he is good enough reason to hire him."

Elisa held up his portfolio to show to Sissy. "Not that his portfolio would need any help I am sure. And who cares if he is ten years younger than me. I go for the young men too." Sissy said with a wide grin.

"You are such a cougar Sissy." Elisa said laughing. Sissy laughed. Sissy put her hands together as to beg Elisa to hire him.

"I will let him know next week Sissy. Now get your hormones under control and get back to work." Elisa said, throwing a paper ball at Sissy.

"I will be forever at your mercy Elisa if you hire him."

"Go Sissy," Elisa said, pointing to the door. Elisa tried to sound stern but couldn't.

"Okay, okay, I am going. Gee whiz." Sissy left and shut the door. Elisa poured over his drawings. The other designs she went over lacked class and style. She liked what Renaldo offered. He seemed to be a natural. She spent the rest of the day going over his portfolio.

⊰⊱✧⊰⊱

Kyle was busy fixing dinner and knew Elisa would be home anytime now. He and Cora had not mentioned about the incident earlier in Elisa's bedroom. He made her dinner, got a rose, and wrote a note. He got her wine out. He was finishing up when he heard Elisa's voice.

"Good evening Cora how was your day?"

"It was a good day Senorita Drinnings. I have all my work done so I shall go now."

"Well Cora you have a good evening and I am going to go and change before dinner." Cora watched her walk upstairs. She hurried up and grabbed her coat and headed out. She turned and saw Kyle in the kitchen doorway. They said nothing, but the look on both of their faces said it all.

Cora walked out the door and shut it. Elisa came down in a pair of sweats and a New York Art Institute sweatshirt. She walked into the kitchen and saw the rose with the note. *Oh Kyle.* She thought as she sat down. She read the note. *I hope you enjoy this meal. I cooked it from the heart. Kyle.* She sat staring at her food. She took a sip of wine. Kyle was watching her from the doorway. She had not heard him and did not realize that he was watching her.

Even in her present attire she looked beautiful. He felt bad about what he did today but now he knew a little bit more about her. From the letter, he knew that she did not have a pleasant childhood. He was falling in love with her more and more each day. All the money in the world could not buy what he wanted to give her. He left her to her dinner and walked upstairs.

CHAPTER 24

Saturday night came and Elisa had on a black velvet evening gown. Her hair had been put in a French braid on top of her head. She had on her black velvet shoes to match and her handbag. She had told Kyle that he had the evening off. Kyle came out of the kitchen and saw Elisa coming down the steps. "Wow you look stunning Miss Drinnings. This guy is a lucky man."

"Thank you Kyle. He will be here any minute so go and do whatever it is you do on your night off."

That meant I do not want my date/lover to see you and know you exist. Kyle took that as a cue and headed back into the kitchen. A few minutes later Guy showed up. "Oh my Mon Cherie you look so beautiful. Shall we go?" Guy took her hand.

"Yes, I am ready." Elisa said walking out the door with him. Kyle had been peeking making sure they did not see him.

He went out into the foyer and watched the car leave. He was all alone in the townhouse. It had started snowing. Kyle could see snowflakes falling to the ground. He wanted to go into Elisa's room again and read the other letter but decided against it. He walked into the living room and turned on the TV to see what was on.

He flipped through the channels and could find nothing on. He lay down. His migraine was back and his vision was getting blurry. The room felt like it was spinning. Before he knew it, he had passed out.

❧◦❧◦❧

Elisa and Guy had a great dinner at *21* and headed on to

the Orchestra. As usual, Guy had gotten them balcony seats. "These are great seats Guy." The show was about to start.

"Nothing but the best for my Mon Cherie." Elisa smiled at him and they enjoyed the rest of the evening.

After the show, Guy walked with Elisa to her door. They walked in together. Elisa was about to go upstairs when she saw Kyle on the couch. She did not want Guy to see him. What would she do if Guy saw him in the morning when he came down? "You know what Guy. I am very tired. I had a wonderful evening. Thank you. I am looking forward to our trip next weekend."

"Are you sure you don't want me to stay Elisa. Is everything okay?" Guy saw she was acting funny.

"Yes everything is okay. I have a headache and it has been a long and strenuous week. So I am just going to go upstairs and change and get into bed." She gave Guy a kiss.

"Okay my Mon Cherie. I would love to stay the night, but if you're not feeling well, I will go."

"Thank you and I will see you next week." Elisa opened the door to let Guy out.

"Goodnight Elisa."

"Goodnight Guy." Elisa watched him leave. She shut and locked her door. She went into the living room. "Kyle get up," she shook him but he did not stir. She shook him again, this time harder and practically screamed at him. "Kyle get up!!

Kyle you get up this instant. Kyle!!" He stirred and when he opened his eyes he looked up at Elisa. He had to adjust to get his eyes into focus. "What?"

"Kyle get up and go to bed. You fell asleep on my couch."

"Oh what," Kyle sat up and looked around.

"You need to go to your bedroom. I had to ask my date to leave when I saw you on the couch."

"I must have fallen asleep. I am so sorry Miss Drinnings."

"I had a hard time getting you up Kyle. You would not budge." He tried to get up, but fell back down on the couch.

"Are you okay Kyle?" Elisa asked him.

"Yes, just give me a minute."

"Do you need me to take you to the hospital or see a doctor Kyle?" Elisa asked him sitting down next to him.

"No, I am okay Miss Drinnings."

Just having her near him made him weak. "I think I can get up now."

"Are you sure Kyle?"

"Yes." Kyle got up and slowly walked to the stairs. "Goodnight Miss Drinnings. I will see you in the morning."

"Goodnight Kyle." Elisa said. She got up and watched him slowly walk up the steps holding on to the railing.

When he made it to the top, she walked up the steps. She watched him walk into his bedroom and shut the door. *I wonder what is wrong with him.* Elisa thought. She did not know what to do. He refused medical care when she asked him. She went to her room and got herself ready for bed.

In the guestroom, Kyle was lying on his bed. He needed to see the doctor but did not want to tell Elisa about the migraines. They were getting worse now to where he would black out. He was afraid that if she found out, she would get rid of him. *She would get rid of him if she found out that he had gone in her bedroom and meddled in her stuff.* He closed his eyes and before he knew it, he was out again.

Kyle was up and in the kitchen when Elisa walked in. "How are you feeling this morning Kyle?" She asked him.

"I am feeling better, thank you Miss Drinnings."

"You scared me there for a bit Kyle when you did not wake up right away. I brought my date in here and saw you on the couch. I had him leave. Did you fall asleep or pass out?" She had grabbed her a cup of coffee and was flicking through a magazine while Kyle was fixing her breakfast.

He made whole wheat toast, eggs over easy, and a fruit salad for breakfast. "All I know is that I lie down and the next thing I knew, I was out. I do not remember much after that." Kyle was getting her plate out of the cabinet.

"Does this happen frequently?" Elisa looked up from her magazine.

"From time to time yes," Kyle replied, setting her breakfast in front of her.

"Have you thought about seeing a doctor over this?"

Elisa picked up her toast and started eating it. "I did not have any insurance to go so I never went. With no job, no disability payments, no way to pay a doctor I never went." Elisa was listening intently as Kyle talked. "I have been getting them for a while, but they just started getting worse. I use to never just black out before."

"Tell me Kyle; are they headaches, migraines, or what?" Elisa asked him. Kyle had eaten earlier before Elisa woke up. He was way up before Elisa anymore. He was used to it being in the military and being up so early. He wanted to get his day started. Kyle sighed. He really didn't want to tell Elisa this, but he could not back out now. The conversation had progressed too far.

"They started out as just headaches but advanced to migraines. I woke up one morning under the bridge and had the most blinding pain. Everything to me was blurry; it took me a while to get my vision adjusted. I lost some of my vision when I got shot in the head in the military. They come and go Miss Drinnings. I will be fine."

"Are you sure Kyle? Why don't you go to the doctor's now? You have a job." Elisa finished her breakfast and Kyle took it for her and rinsed it off and put it in the dishwasher.

"Would you like more coffee Miss Drinnings?"

"Yes Kyle, but please answer my question first." Kyle got her more coffee and presumed to answer her question.

"If I had medical insurance I would, and doctors are expensive. I know you will not give me medical insurance for at least another couple of weeks." Kyle finished up. "I am going to head out and take a walk." Kyle said. "Give me your menu for the evening if you want to have dinner here. Also, I will need to go to the grocery store before the holiday weekend."

"Okay Kyle I will give you my menu and I will have my driver take you to the grocery store. I will make out a list of things for you to get me Kyle. I will also give you medical insurance early. You seem to be doing a great job and though you have a little over two weeks left on your probation, I want you to call my doctor. His name is Doctor Rhines He is a very good physician and I have had him for years.

"I will set up your medical insurance this week. Why did you not tell me about your medical condition before I hired you?" Elisa stared intently at him.

"You did not ask."

"Is that why you inquired about the medical insurance after you got the job?" Elisa could tell in his eyes that it was yes.

Kyle hesitated, "yes Miss Drinnings, that is why."

"You should have told me Kyle it would have helped me..", but before she could finish Kyle interrupted her.

"Helped you do what Miss Drinnings, have second thoughts about hiring me. Hiring a man who has frequent black outs or migraines?" Kyle was upset.

"No Kyle, but it would have been better. I would have enacted your medical insurance right then and there if you would have told me.

"I would like for my employees to take care of themselves and you could have gone to the doctor's by now. Look, if I give you the medical insurance now, would you call Doctor Rhines and make an appointment? His number is right by the phone. I keep all my emergency numbers there. You can call him Monday before Thanksgiving. Tell him you work for me."

Kyle stood silent for a minute. "Please Kyle; I would not want you to have a seizure or something. As an employee of mine, I am responsible for your well-being as long as you work for me and now with you living under my roof I am even more responsible."

"So this is not because you care Miss Drinnings, but it all comes down to responsibility. I will make that phone call when you implement the insurance and see this Dr. Rhines. I would not want you to feel guilty if something happened to me." Elisa was hurt by the remark; she did care for her employees and had always taken care of them.

"I will have you know," Elisa said now angry and pointing her finger at him, "I do care about my employees. You can ask Cora. Your remark offended me. It is the responsibility of every employer to make sure that their employees are well taken care of. I hired you because you were honest and up front with me and your references checked out and you have so far been an absolute wonderful cook.

"I appreciate the little things you do to make my dinners special but I will not stand here and have one of my own employees patronizing me in my own home. Do you understand me Kyle?"

Kyle had not meant to offend her. "I am sorry Miss Drinnings. I never meant to offend you. It is just that the last woman who said she cared about me and who I deeply loved left me."

"It is okay Kyle."

"I am going to go for a walk. I hope you enjoyed your breakfast." Kyle walked out of the kitchen and grabbed his coat. He walked outside. The weather was cold and there was light dusting on the ground. The sun was peeking just a little bit. Kyle sucked in the cold air and walked.

Elisa stood at the door and watched him.

❦

It was Sunday evening, and Kyle had finished dinner and was pondering if he should tell Elisa about what he did in her room before she wasted her time giving him insurance. He hated putting Cora in the middle of it. He would call Mildred and talk to her before he did anything.

Elisa was in the living room when Kyle found her. "Miss Drinnings I was wondering if I could use your phone to call Mildred?"

Elisa looked up from her work. "Sure Kyle."

"Thank you." He went upstairs to use the hall phone so he was out of ear shot of Elisa.

Mildred picked up on the third ring. "Hello," Mildred said. She sounded tired.

"Hello Mildred it is Kyle."

"Oh Kyle how are you doing my dear. I miss you. I know

you cannot get to the shop like you use to. Is everything okay?" Mildred heard concern in his voice.

"Well, yes and no. Elisa wants to give me medical insurance early because of my condition. She came home Saturday night and she found me passed out on the couch.

"I never mentioned it to her before she hired me and we had it out, but she said she would take care of it and for me to call her doctor and set up an appointment."

"Kyle that is great to hear. You needed this. You should go and have that checked out. You have been living with this for a long time now. You see deep down inside she is a good person." Mildred said kindly. "So what is the problem?"

"No problem there. I just well, I broke one of her rules twice now and her housekeeper caught me and I asked her not to tell.I did not want to put her in this situation."

"What did you do Kyle?" Mildred asked him now with concern in her voice.

Kyle hesitated and looked to see if Elisa was coming up the steps. When he did not hear or see her, he continued. "I did something that was off limits. I went into her bedroom twice and looked around and messed with some items.

I saw some pictures on her dresser and I saw her nightstand. When I opened the drawer to that, I saw an envelope with the name Cara on it. I was going to read it when she came home with one of her friend's. The second time I did it, I read the letter with the name Elisa on it. It was a letter from her mother. I wanted to know more about her. I mean Mildred, this was her personal life I read about.

She has a sister named Cara, whom I am assuming she has not spoken to in a long time. Her mother I would assume is dead and her father walked out on them. Should I tell her Mildred?"

Mildred let out a long whistle. "I think Kyle that she has entrusted you to her home. This was her personal life you intervened in. If you tell her, she may fire you and her trust for you will be destroyed, but you Kyle have to make that decision."

"If it were you Mildred what would you do? I mean I need this job and it was a life saver." Kyle sounded desperate and Mildred could hear it in his voice.

"I would hate to see you get fired right before the holidays and with Christmas coming up. But Kyle, you need to be up front with her. I would tell her eventually, when is up to you." Kyle knew she was right. Mildred was so wise.

"Are you still coming here for Thanksgiving?" Mildred asked him.

"Yes I am. I would not miss it for anything Mildred." Kyle said happily.

"Okay, but I am going to hold you to your end of the bargain and help me cook dinner." Mildred said, laughing.

"I promise you I will help you cook for Thanksgiving." Mildred and Kyle talked for a few more minutes and then hung up.

The tumultuous decision to tell Elisa about him going into her room and reading her letter was weighing on him. He loved this job and it kept him close to Elisa, but he did not know how much longer he should keep this a secret. The longer he waited the more he would get Cora involved and he liked Cora. He had to take that chance. He could wait until after he got the medical insurance and saw the doctor.

Then he would feel like he was using her just for that reason. He could screw up everything and he knew it, but Mildred was right he would have to eventually tell her. He went back downstairs and she was still sitting on the couch. "Miss Drinnings." Kyle was standing in the entrance to the living room.

"Oh Kyle you scared me." Elisa held her hand to her chest. "Yes, what is it?"

Elisa put what she was working on down. "I have something to confess to you before you go and get that medical insurance going and see your doctor." Elisa had a confused look on her face.

"Sit down Kyle please and tell me. Yes, you kept your medical condition from me but we got it resolved."

Kyle sat down, his hands were shaking uncontrollably. "I am not sure where to start or how to begin."

"Just say it Kyle. Start from the beginning." Elisa had kept her legs underneath her and now had her arms across her chest. Kyle took a deep breath and started talking.

CHAPTER 25

"YOU WHAT!!" Elisa screamed. "How could you? That is my personal space and you had no right Kyle. I trusted you in my home and you broke one of my rules."

"I am very sorry Miss Drinnings. I just got curious and I did not mean to intrude."

"Kyle Rimmer you are fired. You will have your stuff out tonight. I will call you a taxi and you can have him take you to where you want to go.

"All of this time you were in my home you were going through my things in my bedroom. I cannot believe you Kyle. You were doing so well. You did not steal anything did you?"

"No Miss Drinnings I did not."

"Good, because I will check. You will take only the clothes you have on and whatever you did not throw away before I hired you.

You will take nothing that I bought you. I am glad that you did not wait to soak any medical insurance out of me. I will not condone this from my employees. Emilio knew that and so does Cora. Does she know anything about this?" Elisa was fuming.

"No, she doesn't know a thing. She is innocent in all of this."

"You will go upstairs now to your former room and you will be out tonight. Do you understand?" Elisa still angry and yelling asked him.

Kyle was rubbing his head. "I will go now."

"And do not take your time; I want you out of here pronto." Elisa hollered up at him as he was walking up the stairs.

He got to his room and looked around. *Well,* he thought, *you have managed to screw up a good thing again,* first his marriage and now this.

He walked over to retrieve his Purple Heart and necklace and that is when everything went blurry and he started feeling dizzy. He fell to the floor and started shaking. The room was spinning and he could not speak. Elisa was downstairs waiting. She wondered what was taking him so long. Still perturbed by this, she stomped up the steps and hastily went to Kyle's room. That is when she saw him on the floor shaking.

"KYLE!!" She screamed.

"What is happening? Are you okay?" Elisa ran over to him. She looked down at him. "Kyle what is it?" He could not speak. He was just staring. "I am calling the paramedics." She ran to the hall phone and dialed 911. "Hello, what is your emergency?" The lady on the other end asked. "Hello, this is Elisa Drinnings and one of my employees is on the floor of his bedroom shaking uncontrollably and he cannot speak. I think he may be having a seizure."

"What is your address ma'am?" Elisa gave the lady her address. "We have the paramedics on their way now."

"Please hurry." Elisa cried.

"They will be there as soon as they can. I need you to stay calm ma'am." The lady told Elisa. The phone was cordless and the lady on the other line told Elisa what to do until the paramedics could arrive.

Elisa listened to her and did everything the lady told her. Elisa had never experienced anything like this. She was scared. Elisa could hear sirens in the background. "I hear sirens in the background," she told the lady.

"Okay, stay with him until they come to your door." Elisa stayed until she heard the knock and told the paramedics what was happening and took them upstairs.

"They are here now," Elisa said to the lady on the other line.

"Okay ma'am I am going to hang up. You did a wonderful job." Elisa was crying.

"Thank you." Elisa hung up the phone. The paramedics

were checking his vitals. They put him on the stretcher. "Is he going to be okay?" Elisa asked one of the paramedics.

"He has suffered a severe seizure. His vital signs are low. We need to get him to the hospital now."

"I am going with you." Elisa replied.

"Are you his wife?" "No, I am his employer. He is my cook. Please can I come with you?"

"Okay ma'am but you need to remain calm." They took Kyle out and put him in the ambulance. They raced towards Trinity Memorial Hospital. Elisa felt so bad. She felt she was to blame for him having this seizure.

They got to the hospital and they wheeled him into the emergency room. The doctor on call came running along with a bunch of nurses. "He had a severe seizure and his vital signs are low." The paramedic told the ER doctor. The ER doctor was a woman who looked to be in her late forties and had a pointed nose with some gray in her brown hair. She was slim. Elisa was beside Kyle.

"Ma'am we are sorry, but you are going to have to wait out here. You cannot come back here." Elisa watched as they pushed him through a set of double doors and he was gone. Elisa sat down in one of the chairs and stared out the window. If Kyle died, could she ever forgive herself?

She had to call Mildred. She wondered if Mildred would be up at this hour. She remembered that Kyle had given Cora Mildred's number to call her to contact Kyle. Elisa remembered the number, she dialed it.

⊰⊱⊰⊱⊰⊱

As she suspected, Mildred had been sleeping. "Hello, who is this?" Mildred asked into the phone groggily.

"Mildred it is me Elisa. Do you remember me? We talked about Kyle before I hired him."

"Oh yes, Elisa, hello. Is everything okay?" Elisa did not know where to start.

"I am at Trinity Memorial Hospital. I had to call the paramedics for Kyle. He had a severe seizure. I am in the ER and they took Kyle back. The doctor has not been out to talk to me yet. I need you to come." Mildred started crying. Through her tears she told Elisa that she would be there. The ladies hung up.

Elisa sat back down. There was an elderly man in a wheelchair hooked up to an oxygen tank and he smiled at Elisa. Elisa smiled back. There was a mother with her son at the ER desk. Elisa could overhear them talking. She was telling the ER nurse that her son had been throwing up with a high fever. Elisa hated hospitals. The last time she was in the hospital was when her mother was in one before they told her that there was nothing more they could do for her and sent her home under Hospice care.

It would be a long night and Elisa had to work tomorrow. An hour later, Mildred came through the door and spotted Elisa. Elisa got up and ran over to the older lady and they just hugged. "Has the doctor told you anything yet?" Mildred asked her.

Elisa could see that she had been crying. "No, they have not been out yet." The ladies sat down.

"What happened Elisa?" Mildred asked her softly taking Elisa's hand.

Elisa looked at the elderly man who was now talking to another man, possibly his son. "We had a fight tonight Mildred. He told me something that betrayed my trust in him and I fired him. I told him that he had to leave tonight and to get his stuff. He would take what he brought and go with the clothes on his back. He went upstairs and it was taking so long so I went up there and that is when I found him on the floor shaking.

I called 911 and told them what was happening and the lady had me stay with him until the paramedics came." Elisa was crying and Mildred hugged her. Elisa continued to tell Mildred what happened and why they were fighting.

Mildred let go and looked into Elisa's eyes. "He called me before he told you. He felt guilty and wanted to know what he should do. I told you you need to be up front with her. That it was up to you when you told her but you need to tell her.

He knew the risks. He knew you would lose your trust in him and he would lose this job. He loved this job. I told him that you entrusted him in your home. He told me about a letter from your mother he had read. I told him that he intervened in your personal life. Kyle was nervous and scared, but he made the right decision.

"Kyle is not perfect. No one is Elisa, but he is a good man. If he did not feel guilty or cared, he would not have told you what he did. I know the holidays are coming up, but he made the choice to tell you."

"I screamed at him Mildred. It is my fault he is here. It is my fault he had the seizure." Elisa said with tears in her eyes.

"No Elisa dear, it is not your fault. Kyle's migraines had worsened over time. I have never seen him go into a seizure or heard of him going into one until tonight. You know he was shot in the head in Afghanistan?"

Elisa shook her head. "His headaches progressed. I feel it was from his injuries he sustained over there. It has nothing to do with you Elisa or what ensued tonight. Kyle will not blame you Elisa. I know him."

"If he makes it, if he dies I feel it would be my fault." She looked at Mildred.

"Oh no Elisa, stop saying that. Don't put this on yourself."

"He never told me about his condition until this morning when I brought it up. He was lying on my couch Saturday night when I got home from my date and I tried to wake him up. He did not respond and I kept shaking him. Finally he woke up.

"I asked him why he never told me about this. He told me that I did not ask. He told me he would be alright."

Mildred laughed. "Yep, that is Kyle always the tough one. I am wondering if they did not get the entire bullet out while he was in the hospital. I asked him about that and they told him they did." At just about that time, the same doctor that Elisa saw earlier walked out with another female doctor.

She saw Elisa and walked up to her. "Hello I am Dr. Alice Regan the ER doctor and this is Dr. Olivia Spears, she is a neurosurgeon." Dr. Spears was a tall black woman with her lips painted red, high cheekbones, and a beautiful complexion. She had her hair pulled back and her lab coat on.

Elisa shook both of their hands. "Are you his wife?" Dr. Regan asked Elisa.

"No, I am his employer. He was my cook. Why?"

"Do you know if he has a living will?"

Elisa was wondering why the questions. "I don't think so. I mean he was homeless before he worked for me." Elisa stated.

"What about family? A mom? Dad? Brother? Sister?"

Mildred spoke up. "No doctor. His mom and dad are dead and he was an only child. Why?"

"Who are you?" Dr. Regan asked Mildred.

"I am his longtime friend Mildred Hirth." She shook Dr. Regan's hand.

"I will let Dr. Spears here talk to you ladies."

"Hi, I am doctor Spears." She shook Mildred's hand.

"We took a CT scan and it showed a mass near the Temporal lobe."

"He was shot in the head while fighting in Afghanistan." Mildred spoke up. "He has had headaches for years and they have progressed into migraines but I have never seen him have a seizure. He has lost some of his vision.

"I was wondering if they had gotten the entire bullet out from his wound," Mildred told the Doctor.

Dr. Spears continued. "We did not see any fragments of a bullet." Mildred sighed with relief. "The temporal lobe is important for the processing of speech and vision. The injury sustained to it by this bullet would have affected his sight. His vision will only get worse."

"Are you saying he could go blind?" Elisa asked the Dr.

"Yes. He could lose his sight completely at any time. There is nothing we can do."

"Why," Elisa asked the doctor stunned. "Can you not help him?" Doctor Spears looked at Doctor Regan and then back at the women.

"I am afraid to say this, but it must be said, how Kyle has not lost his vision by now is a mystery; especially going this many years with no medical help. The mass we saw on the CT scan is a brain tumor. The headaches and severe migraines stem from that. The seizures will only get worse. I can prescribe some medicine to control the seizures, but I am afraid that there is nothing else we can do. Had he gotten medical help before now we could have detected it and removed it."

"What are you saying Doctor," Elisa was looking at the doctor with fear in her eyes.

"This is hard to say. Kyle has an inoperable brain tumor. There is nothing we can do now. It has spread too much, that is why he has been battling these severe migraines and now black outs. The tumor was growing."

Mildred sat down and was sobbing. Elisa sat down beside her.

"Did he have anyone in his family die of a brain tumor?" Doctor Spears asked them. Mildred blew her nose.

"Yes, his mother died of a brain tumor before Kyle graduated High School."

"Has he had blurry visions?" Doctor Spears asked them.

"Yes," Elisa said. "He told me that he has had blurry visions. He told me it took him a while to get his vision adjusted to where he could see.

Would the wound in his head from being shot have helped this tumor along?" Elisa asked Doctor Spears.

"Getting shot in the head did not help, but head injuries have not shown to be a typical factor in brain tumors. But we are going to have to keep him in here for a few days before we can release him, just to monitor him."

"How long does he have to live Doctor?" Elisa asked looking at Mildred.

"He will be lucky to make it to spring, maybe summer. The more the tumor continues to spread, the more likely he will lose his speech as well."

"Can we go and see him?" Mildred asked them.

"Yes, but he will not know you are there."

"We still want to see him," Mildred said firmly.

"Okay, Doctor Regan here can take you back." Dr. Regan

led them back to Kyle's room. When they walked in, they saw monitors. He had an oxygen mask over his face and the heart monitor was keeping track of his heart rate. Mildred walked over to him and took his hand. She kissed it.

"Oh Kyle my dear, losing you would be like losing a son." Mildred broke down and Elisa walked over to her and put her hand on her shoulder.

Mildred took Elisa's hand and held it. They stared down at Kyle. Elisa spoke up. "I am sorry Kyle. I have a confession to make myself. The locket and Purple Heart on your dresser, I messed with it. I was in your room that night. I opened your locket and saw a picture of a woman and a man whom I assumed was your mother and father.

"I am so sorry Kyle. You broke one of my rules and invaded a personal space of mine, but I did the same. I forgive you Kyle and I wish that you could forgive me." Mildred looked up at her and Elisa looked down at Mildred. Both of the women smiled at each other. "Do you think he can hear us Mildred?" Elisa asked her.

"I don't know Elisa. I don't know."

Chapter 26

It was Wednesday morning, the day before Thanksgiving. Elisa had called Sissy and told her what was going on; Sissy said she would take care of everything. Elisa said she would not be in today. She told her workers that they could leave early for the holidays and they were ecstatic and thanked Elisa. Kyle was awake. Mildred was holding his hand. "Hello Kyle," Mildred said tenderly. Kyle looked at Mildred and smiled, and then he turned his head and saw Elisa, and then turned back to Mildred.

"Do you remember anything Kyle? Anything at all?" Mildred asked him.

"I don't. I can't remember what happened or why I am here." Kyle looked around and saw the monitors around him.

"You had a seizure Kyle. Elisa here called 911 and brought you here. She found you on the floor of her home." Mildred stated

"Why was I on the floor?" Kyle asked Mildred, looking pensive and looking more like a little boy who had just found out his dog died than a grown man.

"Like I said, you had a seizure. Elisa found you."

"Why did I have a seizure?" Kyle was looking at her, frantic. Mildred sighed. She did not know how to say this. She wished that the doctor would come in. "I will get the doctor and let her explain it," Mildred said, patting his hand.

"No," said Kyle, "I want you to tell me why I am here, why I had a seizure, and why are these monitors hooked up to me? Why is she here?" Kyle was pointing to Elisa.

"Dear, she had called the ambulance and she came with

them who brought you here."

"I want you to tell me Mildred please." Kyle was squeezing Mildred's hand.

"Kyle the migraines that you've been having, the black outs, and seizures, well," Mildred looked at Elisa who nodded her head as if to tell Mildred to continue. Mildred continued. "Kyle the doctors did a CT scan on your head and there is a mass near your Temporal lobe."

"A mass, what do you mean Mildred?"

"You have a brain tumor Kyle. The doctor said it is inoperable." Kyle's eyes got wide.

"So what does that mean Mildred? They cannot operate to remove it? There must be something they can do." Kyle was shaking his head back and forth and his eyes were watering. Mildred wished that she could tell him that the doctor was wrong, but she could not. She has always been honest with Kyle.

"No Kyle, I am afraid not. There is nothing they can do. The migraines you were having meant that the tumor was spreading. You could eventually lose your eyesight completely and your voice."

"No, no, no." Kyle cried. "There has to be a mistake." Just then, Dr. Spears walked in.

"Good morning Kyle and all. I was coming to check on Kyle but it seems he is awake."

"Tell me doctor," Kyle begged "that there is something you can do, that you can remove this brain tumor." The Doctor looked up from her chart at Kyle. She looked at Mildred then Elisa. She walked over to Kyle's bed.

"The brain tumor has spread too much, had we been able to catch it sooner, I could have removed it." Was it from being shot in the head while in Afghanistan doctor?" Kyle asked feeling defeated.

"Getting shot in the head caused you to lose some of your sight yes, but it would not have caused this. Head injuries do not factor in to brain tumors. According to a biopsy we did, it is malignant. I consulted with a pathologist and he agreed with me. There were other extensive tests done and they showed that the cancer has spread to other vital organs; his lungs, liver. It has progressed beyond the surgery stage and it occurs frequently in the frontal and temporal lobes. It is three percent of all brain tumors. It can cause behavioral changes in a person. It can cause weakness and paralysis. We found it in the frontal lobe, once in the temporal lobe; this is where his eyesight and speech will be affected more. Even if there was something we could do, it would only prolong the inevitable.

❦❖❦

It was the brain tumor that had eventually taken his mother's life. His mother had just brushed off the massive migraines until it was too late. Before she had lost her speech completely, she had told Kyle that she loved him and was proud of him. She had lost her eyesight there at the end.

Kyle remembers rushing into his mother's bedroom and seeing her shaking. His father had already passed away by then. It was all coming back now. "Mother!! Mother!!" a young high school Kyle screamed. "What is happening?" He grabbed the phone and dialed 911.

"911 what is your emergency?"

"My mother, she is shaking uncontrollably and I cannot get her to respond to me. She is just staring and not moving her eyes."

"Stay calm young man and you are?"

"I am her son." Kyle said into the phone crying.

"I need you young man to listen to me until the ambulance can arrive."

"Okay," Kyle said. He gave her the address and did everything that he was told to do until the ambulance arrived. They took his mother to the hospital and that is when he found out about the tumor. It was the middle of his senior year. He hoped that she would live to see him graduate, but unfortunately she did not. She passed away that April.

Kyle did not want to finish school and get his diploma, but his grandparents encouraged him and eventually he did. He went to school, married Janice, and then joined the military. Kyle's mother believed in another place, and told Kyle someday she would see him again, and that she would see his father and tell him that Kyle says hi.

It was a warm April day when they buried his mother. He held the necklace that his mother had given him before she died. As these thoughts ran through his head, he was trying to absorb it all. He could not believe what was happening to him, he had lost so much, and now he was going to die. It seemed like a dream, and when he would wake up, everything would be okay and he would get on with his life as normal, but he knew it wasn't to be.

⊷⊶⊹⊱⊰⊹⊷⊶

"I gave you a prescription medication that will control your seizures. I am releasing you today. I will have you sign some paperwork. I am so sorry Kyle; I wish that I could do more." It was just another storm in the midst of many that he had to face. He had to face a lot of storms in his life and had always come through, but this one would be the most challenging one and he knew who would win in the end.

"Doctor," Kyle asked softly. "How long do I have?" Mildred and Elisa were crying.

"I am afraid spring, summer at the most." He would not live to see another winter. "I will go get that paperwork for you to sign and then you can go home." The doctor walked out.

"This is the same tumor that killed my mother. I only have months to live. My mother did not make it another year and she died in April before I graduated."

Mildred hugged Kyle. The argument that Elisa had with Kyle before the seizure was forgotten. It did not matter what he had done, it was trivial compared to what Kyle would go through for the next few months of his life. Elisa would keep him on as her cook. She could not abandon him now, it would not be fair. She would take care of him, because in an unusual sort of way, he had taken care of her.

Elisa's phone rang. She picked it up. It was Guy.

"Hello my Mon Cherie. Happy Thanksgiving."

"Happy Thanksgiving to you Guy." Mildred and Kyle heard her. She remembered that they had their vacation planned for this weekend. She would leave tomorrow.

"I hate do to this my Mon Cherie, with it being the holiday weekend, but I have an emergency I must take care of. One of my stores had caught fire and I need to go and talk to the insurance company. Of all weekends, I am so sorry my Mon Cherie."

"It is okay Guy I understand. Go and take care of it as soon as possible."

"I will make this up to you. I promise."

"I know Guy." They both hung up.

Elisa turned around. "Well it looks like that my plans for Thanksgiving has been squashed." She still had Sissy she could call and have dinner at her parent's house for Thanksgiving.

"Well," said Mildred. "Kyle and I were going to have Thanksgiving at my place there is always room for one more."

"I do not want to intrude Mildred. I mean I can call my assistant and have dinn..," but before Elisa could finish, Mildred interrupted her.

"Nonsense, there is always room for one more right Kyle?" Kyle was not in a very festive mood. He had just found out that this would be his last Thanksgiving. "Yeah sure Mildred," but not even he could convince himself.

Mildred heard the doubt in this voice. "Oh Kyle, let us enjoy this holiday."

"I am not really in the festive mood right now Mildred, I mean this will be my last Thanksgiving with you." He looked away. Elisa and Mildred looked at each other. It would be even harder when Christmas came around.

"Let us not worry about this now, tomorrow is Thanksgiving and we can all be together and.."

"Do you not understand what the Doctor just said Mildred?" It was the first time that Kyle had ever raised his voice to Mildred. She was hurt by it, but she understood. Who gets told every day that they only have months to live?

"I am dying! Dying! Dying! I will not be around next year to enjoy it. Why don't you both just go away?"

Elisa heard the consternation in Kyle's voice. Mildred just stood there with her mouth open and nothing to say. The Doctor came back in and had Kyle sign the papers. "I want you to start on that medication as soon as possible." The Doctor left the room.

"Why bother," Kyle grumbled. "It won't keep me alive and change the situation. I am going to die regardless. You ladies can go; I will have a taxi take me."

"Take you where Kyle?" Elisa asked him.

"Back to the place that I have lived for years so I can die there. Maybe after I die, they can save money and just throw my body in the water."

"Kyle stop this now," Mildred was angry now.

"You will come to my place and that is final. You will have dinner with us. You will not spend this holiday alone. No one should. I have always been there for you Kyle and I will not let you do this.

"I will not let you keep feeling sorry for yourself and let yourself not enjoy the time you have left. I love you and I have always loved you as my son. Your mother would not want this. We will all have dinner together and make it full of life not death."

Elisa had not known Mildred that long, but saw that she could be tough when she needed to be. Kyle made a grunting sound but knew not to cross Mildred. He reluctantly agreed to share Thanksgiving with them, but no matter what to him, death was in this holiday air.

Thanksgiving Day, Elisa had her driver take her to the restaurant and she went to the apartment Mildred had told her to go to. Elisa knocked on the door. "Oh Elisa darling, I am so glad that you could make it." She walked in. It was a tiny place but cozy for Mildred. She saw a worn couch with a scratched up table in front of it, a rocking chair, and a stand with a lamp on it. "Come in and sit down Elisa, Kyle is in the kitchen getting the bird ready." Elisa took off her coat. She was wearing a red cashmere sweater with black dress pants. Her red hair was down and she was wearing black heeled Prada boots.

"Oh you look amazing Elisa." Mildred said as she took Elisa's coat.

"Thank you Mildred."

"Sit down and I will get you something to drink." It was mad with the Macy's Thanksgiving Day Parade going on that Elisa's driver had to reroute to get her here.

Kyle came out of the kitchen. He was wearing faded worn out jeans and a tan sweater. "The turkey is in the oven. It will take a few hours to get done." He saw Elisa.

"Hello Kyle."

"Hello Miss Drinnings."

"You can call me Elisa Kyle."

"Okay Hello Elisa, Happy Thanksgiving."

"You too Kyle."

He could not help but notice how beautiful Elisa was. "You look radiant Elisa." Kyle said.

"Thanks Kyle you look nice too." She did notice that he had shaved.

Mildred brought out the water for tea. "Now let us sit down and have some tea while the turkey cooks. We can fix the other food later." Mildred sat down in her rocker and Kyle sat at one corner of the couch while Elisa sat at the other. Kyle had taken the money leftover that Elisa had paid him to get his medication. It was expensive without insurance.

Mildred sat down and poured the water for the tea. Kyle sat down on the other end of the couch from Elisa. Kyle had gotten his medication filled before the pharmacy closed for Thanksgiving. Mildred had made sure of that and that he took it. Kyle looked a lot better than he had yesterday in the hospital. Elisa was glad to see he was a bit more cheery than he had been.

"Thank you Elisa for saving my life. If it weren't for you, I would probably have died there on your floor. I cannot remember how I got there or what happened before." Elisa had not told him what had led up to it. "What happened before that Elisa?" Kyle asked her while she sipped her tea. Elisa looked at Mildred. Mildred gave a small smile and a reassuring look at Elisa.

Elisa sighed. "We had a fight Kyle. Um, you had done something that I asked you not to do when I hired you as my cook. You do not remember any of this?" Kyle shook his head no so Elisa continued. "You had gone through some of my personal items in my nightstand drawer that was in my bedroom. You had read a letter that my mother had left and saw a letter that she had written for my sister Cara that I have not spoken to in over five years.

"I felt you had violated my space and I told you to get out. I told you that you were fired and to get only what was yours and leave what I got you there. The clothes, the shoes, etc. I waited and waited but it took you a long time so I went upstairs and found you on the floor shaking and that is when I called 911." Kyle remained silent as he listened and looking down at the floor. Mildred had wooden floors that were old and had a rug underneath her coffee table that she had picked up at a thrift store.

"But I have a confession to make." Kyle looked up at Elisa with a puzzled expression. "The day you came into your room and found your necklace lying open and your Purple Heart moved, and had questioned Cora about it because she asked me about it. I did that Kyle." Kyle sat motionless and expressionless. "I was in your room and had opened the necklace and saw a picture of what looked like your mother and father."

Kyle sat so still and remained silent, that Elisa thought he did not hear her or did, and was trying to find the right words. Finally he spoke up; he had no anger or malice in his voice. "I had a feeling Elisa, but said nothing. I knew Cora was telling the truth and there was only one other person that it could have been. I had not been at my job long and I," he searched for the words. "I liked you too much Elisa to be mad. I had no business going in your room but I was curious. I wanted to know more about you."

"You could have asked me Kyle." Elisa interjected.

"Would you have told me then Elisa? Would you have revealed your personal life to a stranger like me, who was only your cook, who had not even been there a month?" When Elisa did not answer right away, Kyle had his answer. He continued. "My mother had given me that necklace before she died and I got my Purple Heart from being injured in the military and for exemplary service.

It was okay Elisa that was all I had left from my belongings that I took with me."

"No Kyle, it wasn't okay, I had invaded your space after I told you not to invade mine. I was no more in the right." Mildred sat there listening not saying a word. She wanted them to work it out. She would only give her advice if they asked for it. "I want to take this opportunity to ask if you would like to come back as my cook. Same pay with insurance and your room back." Elisa saw that Kyle was contemplating what she was asking him.

After a few minutes, he spoke up, "I will be dead in a few months Elisa, do you want a cook who could possibly lose his speech and eyesight. Do you want someone that you will eventually have to take care of and may not be able to cook for you anymore? Think about it Elisa."

"I already have" she said softly. "I want you to come back Kyle."

"Why Elisa?"

Now it was Elisa who was searching for the words to say.

"Well for one you're a marvelous cook, two, I miss the notes, three the candle and the roses were lovely, and finally you're not like any other man I have ever met."

"What do you mean Elisa?" Kyle sat his mug on the coffee table and put his hand between his knees.

"You are a good man Kyle and I have seen that. You are sentimental, kind, you have a romantic side, you're not haughty, condescending, you have been through so much in your life and survived and I admire that. I have been through a lot in my life too and I have survived.

"The only difference is that life has been much kinder to me than you and while it is unfair, you made the best of it. I want you to stay with me Kyle and be my cook for as long as you can. I will take care of you. I want to take care of you."

"No Elisa you don't have to."

"Yes I do Kyle and I want to. I am in a position to do that and I want to. Please let me." Elisa had a soft look on her face and her violet eyes were somber.

"Is this because I am dying Elisa?" It cut Elisa to the quick.

"Oh no Kyle, it has nothing to do with your illness. I was unfair to you and I was wrong.

I do not want you to go back to the streets or living under a bridge when you can have so much more." Kyle got up and walked to the window. Mildred got up and took the dishes into the kitchen. Kyle walked back and sat down.

"Are you sure Elisa? Are you sure you're ready for this? Ready to take on someone who is about to die?"

"Yes Kyle, I did it for my mother and I want to do it for you."

"Okay then, I will come back." Elisa hugged Kyle.

CHAPTER 27

Kyle felt Elisa's embrace and he took in the scent of her. "Hey kids," Mildred said. "The Macy's Thanksgiving Day Parade is going on why don't we watch it, or you two can go and watch it in person."

"Have you ever watched the Macy's Thanksgiving Day Parade before Kyle?" Elisa asked him.

"My parents took me to it a few times until I got older."

"Why don't you two go and watch it?" Mildred asked. "The turkey will not be done for a while and then we can make the fixings for it."

"What do you say Kyle?" Elisa looked at him.

"Why not." Kyle responded. "Would you like to come Mildred?" Kyle asked her.

"Oh no dear I will stay here and keep an eye on the turkey and besides it is crowded and I have a hard enough time getting around as it is. You two go and have a good time." They grabbed their coats and Mildred shooed them out. Mildred had gotten Kyle a coat at the same thrift store where she got her rug. Elisa and Kyle took a taxi and got to where the parade was.

Mildred had watched them leave and was happy. Kyle deserved to be happy and if this woman could make him happy, then Mildred was content. They watched the parade as best as they could and then headed out to get something hot to drink. They found a vendor and got some hot chocolate. "How did you like the parade?" Elisa asked him.

"Well, it was nice from what I could see of it. I remember my dad putting me on his shoulders to watch it." They walked around.

"What all do you remember of your father Kyle?" Elisa asked him, her hair shining in the sun.

"I remember him playing ball with me, giving my mother flowers, writing her little notes and she would write him notes back and put in his lunch box. I remember him taking me fishing each spring and summer in upstate New York on the lake. I remember each Christmas he would make the ham and mom would cook the rest of the food.

"We would sit around the Christmas tree and sing and he would tell my mom and me stories, that is, until he got sick. He had served in Vietnam and not too long after that he got ill. He was buried with a 21 gun salute. That is where they fire the guns 21 times. They gave the flag to my mother and she gave it to me before she died. When Janice left me she took it with her." Kyle pulled out something from under his coat. "I got my dad's dog tags with mine. That is one thing of my father's that Janice did not get." Elisa saw the shiny metal dog tags. "I have not taken these off since I put them on." Elisa had not seen them until now. Maybe because she had never seen Kyle without his shirt on and he kept them hidden.

"I want to take you somewhere Elisa." She was confused now. He grabbed her hand and managed to flag down a taxi. They got in and he told the driver where to go.

"Where are you taking me Kyle?" Elisa asked him.

"It is a surprise." Elisa had no idea where he could be taking her. When they got there, Elisa paid for the taxi and got out.

"Where are we going Kyle?"

"Be patient Elisa," Kyle reiterated. He took her to a bench where he would sit and feed the birds. They stopped. Elisa looked around. She had never ventured to this part before.

"I don't understand Kyle, what is it that you're showing me."

"This is it Elisa." Elisa was still confused and Kyle saw it.

"It is where I would come and feed the birds before I would go back to where I lived."

Kyle and Elisa sat down. "The birds were my friends Elisa. They, like me, were free. They could go where they wanted to and they were a part of nature. The birds would not judge me, mistreat me, or look down on me because of my status. They were the same as me. They, as you and me, are part of this circle of life no matter if we are rich or poor. When I saw you Elisa for the first time you caught my eye, but I knew I could never get next to you because of our different worlds. I thought I had a better chance of trudging up the mountains of Afghanistan than be with you.

"I never thought at this moment in time that you and I would be sitting next to each other on this park bench. I never thought that I would see your world much less be in it. I am sure you never thought that you would be sitting next to a man you despised for the longest time because you felt that I was, as the others felt, just another homeless man, a panhandler, and not worth much to society. But you have proven me wrong; our worlds collided maybe by fate, chance, or whatever you want to call it.

"I got that job as a cook and that was a window opening for me where a door had closed. I never thought that in a million years that I would be working for you. You saved my life more than once Elisa and I hope that one day before I die that I can pay you back."

Elisa's eyes were watering. "You don't have to Kyle. I needed a cook and no one else worked out or responded so I gave you a chance. And anyone would have dialed 911 and saved your life."

"If that had happened on the street, maybe, or maybe not, but even after the argument you said happened you still saved me, even after I violated your space."

"We were both wrong Kyle it is in the past now so let it be." Snow had begun to fall. It was in Elisa's hair.

"I want you to walk with me to another location." As they walked, Kyle asked her about Cara. Elisa stopped and they stood in front of each other.

"It is so complicated. I am not sure where to begin or even if I can. I know you read the letter from my mother and you know that she died and that my father left us. Cara, my sister, dropped out of high school when she was seventeen and went to Hollywood.

"She wanted to become an actress. When our mother was diagnosed with ovarian cancer, I hired a Hospice nurse to take care of her and I spent the last few weeks with her. That is the only time where I took a substantial amount of time off of Pose. My mother wanted me to get a hold of Cara before she died. She wanted to see Cara." They started walking again. The snow was still falling. "I did but Cara could not get away from her work. Her producer said if she left she would be dropped for the lead role. She put her career over our mother. I told her that she was dead to me and that she was no longer my sister.

"I told her that I would not let her know when our mother's funeral was and I never did not that she would have showed up. My mother and father had a fight one night. He had lost his job and the bills were piling up and no money or food. My father came home drunk one night and he and my mom got into a fight and he hit her. I ran out trying to protect her and told him I hated him. He dragged me back to my room and my mother told him that she did not want him coming home like this.

"That is when he left and never came back. From then on, Cara never forgave my mother to this day. She died sad but not alone. I took care of the house and made sure we ate when we had the food while my mother worked two jobs and I went to school. I vowed that I would not end up like her." Elisa was crying and Kyle held her.

"I am so sorry Elisa. I was lucky to have the parents that I had, but to go what you went through, I could not imagine. My father loved my mother dearly until the day he died."

Kyle released Elisa. "I never told Cara about the letter."

"Do you ever think that you could forgive her Elisa?" Kyle asked her softly. Elisa stopped walking and stared up at Kyle.

"Do you ever think that you could forgive Janice if you saw her again?" When Kyle took too long to answer Elisa knew the answer.

"This is not about me and Janice, Elisa, this is about you

and your sister. I do not know where Janice is or even if she is still alive. You have some idea of where your sister Cara is. If she is still in California then you could look her up." She did not tell him that she had her new agent's number already.

"This is about you Kyle, if Janice was standing here now could you forgive her, or forgive your best friend for what they did to you?" Kyle put his hands in his pockets. The snow was accumulating.

"It was a long time ago Elisa and I have moved on."

"Yes or no Kyle?" Elisa was waiting on an answer.

"Yes Elisa." She looked into his face and there was no smile. He was serious.

"Then you are a better person than I Kyle." He and Elisa started walking again.

Kyle grabbed Elisa and turned her around. "If I can forgive Janice and my ex-best friend for what they did to me Elisa, you can forgive your sister Cara?" Elisa shrugged her arms free.

"You have no idea Kyle of what all went on. She abandoned us. She made her choice. She will have to live with it."

"So what made you bring her up Elisa?"

"Because you asked about her and you saw the letter to her from my mother. I have answered your questions Kyle. Now take me to what you want to show me or I am going back."

"Why don't you just try and contact her Elisa?"

"That is enough Kyle. This conversation is over." The look in her eyes said she was done talking about it. They got to where Kyle had stayed.

"Why did you take me here Kyle?" Elisa asked him.

"This was my refuge. It was my own "place" I came to every night and could look up at the sky. It was my home for years." Elisa could not imagine what it would be like to live homeless, though they could barely pay the rent sometimes.

"This was my world for years Elisa. This was the side that you don't see because you live on the side that doesn't give this side a second thought." She looked around. "Now you know Elisa."

She looked up at him. "How did you survive all of these years?"

"I had to. I was in the military, and in a war zone, and got shot and survived. I was facing the enemy every day. I watched my buddy die as I held him in my arms. When you face adversity, you learn to survive. What doesn't kill you makes you stronger. You should know about that Elisa."

She knew what he meant by that. Her past had made her stronger. The snow was falling harder now. "Let us go Elisa," and he grabbed her hand and they got a taxi back to Mildred's. When they got in, Mildred had started on the other fixings for dinner.

"Wow, I thought that you two had gotten lost. I was about to send the whole New York Police Department to find you guys."

"We are fine Mildred." Kyle hugged her. "I was just showing Elisa around and we had a good talk." He looked over at Elisa and she smiled.

Mildred's table could not hold all of the food so they had to use up what kitchen space she had. Mildred's kitchen was small with a round wooden table. The bouquet that Kyle had bought for her was sitting in the middle of it. Mildred had loved it. Elisa had felt guilty for what she did to Kyle's bouquet to her.

"Well help me cook and the sooner we can eat." Kyle helped Mildred with the food and Elisa was helping to set the table. When the turkey was done, Kyle started slicing it. They had mashed potatoes, corn, stuffing, deviled eggs, salad, dinner rolls, which were homemade by Mildred, cranberry sauce, and Mildred's homemade pumpkin pie. Kyle ate like he hadn't eaten in weeks. Elisa was enjoying herself and was kind of glad that Guy had to cancel though she hated hearing about his store catching on fire.

After dinner, Elisa helped Mildred with the dishes and they all sat down to play checkers and cards. Elisa was beating Kyle. "Hey where did you learn to play checkers so well Elisa?"

"My sister Cara and I would play when we could." Kyle saw the look in her face when she mentioned Cara's name. They played Rummy until late. Mildred gave some food for them to take home and told them to be careful as the roads may be slick.

"Thank you so much Mildred for dinner it was delicious."

"Don't just thank me, thank Kyle."

"You two keep it safe." Kyle and Elisa got back into the car and back to her townhouse. It was a Thanksgiving that Kyle would never forget and one that Elisa was glad she did not miss.

Elisa had taken the tour of the building being used for creating the fragrance line for Pose. She spoke with the people who were responsible for making it and she saw all the equipment being used. She spoke to the people who would be responsible for shipping it. She looked at Maggie and gave her a thumbs up. To Maggie, that meant that Elisa was happy with it and the progression of the fragrance line.

It was two weeks after Thanksgiving, and Emilio had kept in contact with Elisa. He told her that Thanksgiving went well and that his mother was getting around. Emilio had cooked dinner for them all and he asked her what she was doing for Christmas. She told him that she had no immediate plans yet. Guy had not gotten back a hold of her so she had no idea what was going on there. She told him about Kyle and what happened and Emilio had told her he was sorry.

Emilio's whole family had been there for Thanksgiving which made his mother so happy. Emilio was happy that she had given Kyle another chance. He said it sounded like Kyle was a good man and if Elisa was happy then he was happy. He wanted Elisa to be safe. She told him that Guy had to cancel his engagement for Thanksgiving but had been invited to Kyle's friend's house for Thanksgiving and had a good time. Emilio was happy that she did not have to spend it alone.

Emilio said that if she had no plans for Christmas that she could spend it there with him and bring Kyle if she wanted to. Elisa had thanked him profusely. She missed Emilio and was glad to see he was okay and his family despite his mother's condition. It was a Saturday evening and Elisa and Kyle had eaten dinner. She had started allowing him to eat dinner with her. They were sitting on the couch, her drinking and him drinking grape juice since he could not have alcohol with his medication. Kyle had gotten his insurance and it helped with his medication which Elisa made sure he took. Every day was uncertain with his condition, but they took it one day at a time.

Since he did not have medical insurance at the time of his hospitalization, Elisa had paid for his stay. There was no way that Kyle could pay it. Kyle had started a fire in the fireplace and was sitting with Elisa on the couch. The weather had gotten worse just like Kyle read. They had gotten a massive accumulation. It was nice to sit by the fireplace. Kyle noticed that it made Elisa's hair glow.

She had on a silk blouse and beige dress pants. Kyle was in new jeans that Elisa had gotten him and a nice wool sweater. He had cleaned up and shaved. His hair was cut and styled. It made him look younger and Elisa watched him as he stared into the fire; with the fire lighting his face up. In the few weeks since Thanksgiving, he had not brought up Cara, but it was on the forefront of their minds. The medication was helping his seizures and he had no more scary incidents like the one before.

"So what are you going to do for Christmas Kyle?" He turned to her.

"I will probably spend it with Mildred. How about you Elisa?" She had allowed him to call her that.

"I am not sure Kyle. If Guy ever calls me or gets a hold of me I may spend it with him. My former cook invited me and you to his house."

"Me," said Kyle. "Why, he doesn't even know me. He met me once."

"Yes, but I have told him about you and he says that you seem like a nice guy."

The fire was cackling. It had been a busy few weeks with the fragrance line moving forward and the spring show in four months. She wondered if Kyle would make it until then. "I want to make this Christmas even more special Elisa since it will be my last." He looked at her somberly. She took his hand.

"It will be special Kyle."

"It would be more special if I could spend it with you, and

only you Elisa." Elisa was speechless. Kyle had always been the gentleman and had not tried to force anything on her.

She was still seeing Guy. "Maybe I will get lucky and this Guy will not make plans with you." She laughed. At that moment, there was a knock on the door. Elisa and Kyle looked over. Elisa was wondering who that could be at this time of night. She got up to answer it.

"I will get it." Kyle said. He got up and walked to the door before Elisa could catch up with him. He opened the door and there stood Guy.

CHAPTER 28

"Was I interrupting something?" Guy said with a hint of annoyance to his voice.

"No Guy, we were just talking." Elisa answered.

"You expect me to believe that?" Guy asked giving Kyle a once over.

"Yes Guy, nothing is going on. He is my cook."

"Well, do you always have evening chats with your cook Elisa? And I might add, dressed so nicely." He eyed her up and down. "I have to cancel our Thanksgiving holiday because of my shop catching fire, which by the way, the insurance will cover everything and you get cozy with another man, whom is your cook."

"It is not like that Guy. Kyle is a gentleman." Guy smirked. "I am sure he is. Isn't that what you like Elisa?" Elisa was getting upset. "I will leave you two alone." Kyle started to leave but Guy stopped him.

"Oh no Kyle, I am not staying. I was just going to see what Elisa was going to do for Christmas but I have some idea."

"You usually call me Guy, why not tonight?" Elisa asked him boldly.

"I wanted to surprise you and make up for Thanksgiving but seeing this, I am glad that I came. My assumption about you cheating had been right all along." Guy crossed his arms. Kyle did not like this man.

"I have never cheated on you Guy. I have never slept with Kyle."

"At least not yet," Guy grimaced. "Where did you happen to find him and what benefits are you giving him?" Guy was assessing Kyle. He felt threatened that another man had invaded his turf.

"He needed a job so I gave him one and the benefits that you have in mind are not so."

"Well Elisa, you turned down my proposal for marriage now I see why."

"You are a liar Guy. You know exactly why I did not want to get married, not just with you but with any man."

"Save me the story Elisa I have heard it enough. You could have had everything with me. I could have given you the world but yet you settled for this." Guy pointed his hand towards Kyle who was getting furious.

"I have given you what you wanted Elisa and this is the thanks I get. Well Kyle, is that is your name, you can have her; she is nothing but a slut; a money hungry cheating slut."

"That is enough!" Kyle shouted. "I will not have you talk about her like that."

"What are you going to do about it Kyle." The way Guy said his name, made Kyle lunge forward at Guy and he hit the door. Elisa screamed.

"Stop this please!" She screamed. Kyle was on top of Guy before Elisa could get to them.

"You son of a bitch!" Kyle yelled. "You do not deserve a woman like Elisa." Kyle had hit Guy in the mouth and his lip was bleeding.

"Both of you stop it now and I mean it or I will call the police!" Elisa told them.

"Guy you need to leave now!"

Guy was still rubbing his mouth. Guy put his hand on the door and looked at Kyle, "you can have her. I was getting tired of her anyway. There are other fish in the sea."

"Same here Guy," Elisa said staring straight at him with glaring eyes. "I never want to see you again."

"Consider your wish granted Elisa." Her name slid off his tongue like venom. He opened the door and slammed it, the cold air coming in. Kyle was standing there rubbing his hand.

"Let me see that Kyle." Elisa started to look at his hand.

"I am alright Elisa."

"Please Kyle let me look at your hand."

"I said I am alright." Kyle turned around and walked into the kitchen with Elisa following behind him.

"Why did you do that Kyle?" Elisa came up behind him.

"Do what Elisa?"

"You know what I am talking about Kyle, hit Guy like that."

"For what he called you and I was not going to listen to how he was treating you Elisa and saying to you."

"It is not for you to protect me Kyle. I would not be surprised if he doesn't file assault charges on you."

"I don't care Elisa." Kyle was still holding his hand. Elisa got some ice out of the freezer and put it in a towel. She put it on Kyle's hand.

"Here keep this on your hand." It did not look cut, but it was starting to bruise.

"Let him file assault charges on me. It was worth it. You were worth it." Elisa looked up at him and he looked away.

"Kyle why do you say that?"

"I think you know why Elisa." Kyle walked away and went upstairs. He went to his room and sat on the bed. Elisa came to the door and walked over to him sitting on the bed beside him.

"No man has ever done this for me Kyle," Elisa looked up at him. "No man has ever stood up for me ever, not even my dad."

"Because they are all stupid Elisa, they never knew what they had or lost." His words touched her heart.

"I will go and get the first aid kit." Elisa turned back to face him.

"If he does press charges, I will say he started it." Kyle smiled. She came back with the first aid kit and wrapped his hand.

"There that should do it; if it gets worse I will take you to the hospital." Kyle had enough of hospitals.

"Thank you Elisa," Kyle told her.

"No, thank you, Kyle and your welcome." Elisa turned to go.

"Elisa."

"Yes Kyle." Elisa stood in the doorway to his bedroom and turned her head.

"Did you ever love him?" Elisa looked down with one hand on the door frame. She looked back up at Kyle.

"No, Kyle, goodnight."

"Goodnight Elisa." Elisa left and Kyle lay back on the bed and smiled. The next morning, Kyle had their breakfast ready and a rose lying beside Elisa's plate when she walked in.

"I thought I smelled something good cooking."

"I want you to sit down. I will get everything for you."

"Okay," Elisa sat down at the table and Kyle got their drinks and breakfast and set it on the table.

"I want to make a toast," Kyle said.

"To what?" Elisa asked.

"To us and how far we have come, and for the opportunity to be here at this moment in time." They clinked their coffee cups together and took a sip. Elisa took a bite of her breakfast.

"Mmmm this is good as usual Kyle."

"I have outdone myself again." Kyle said with delight.

"Kyle remember when we were talking last night before we got interrupted." Kyle still had the bandage on his hand.

"I asked you what you were doing for Christmas." Kyle stopped eating.

"Yes Elisa, why?"

"I have a spring show coming up in April for my magazine in Paris and I would love for you to come but," Elisa paused.

"But you feel that I will either be blind or dead by then." Kyle finished for her. She did not say it, but she was thinking it.

"I just thought that for Christmas we could go to Paris together." Kyle almost choked on his food. "Kyle you okay?" Elisa got up.

"Really I am fine. I just can't believe that you would want to do that for me."

"Why not Kyle?" Elisa sounded almost offended. "You defended me and you had done so much for me that this is my Christmas gift to you."

"Elisa, I was not expecting this. I was not asking for anything when I defended you. Any decent man would have done the same." Kyle looked into her eyes.

"Maybe Kyle, but please let me do this for you."

"I should be the one to do this for you Elisa; I mean you have done more for me. If I could afford it, I would take you." Kyle wished in his heart he could.

"This is not about money Kyle. This is a gift. Please accept it."

Kyle touched Elisa with his good hand. "You are so beautiful Elisa. Guy was a fool." He rubbed her face. She took his hand, kissed it, and then looked back up at him. He pulled her face to his and kissed her. It felt so good. He had wanted to do this for a long time. He had not kissed a woman since Janice. His whole body was tingling. He released her. "Oh Elisa I am so sorry. I did not mean to."

"It is okay Kyle." They both got up and he picked her up. "Kyle what are you doing and what about your hand?"

"Something that I have wanted to do for a long time and my hand is fine."

He took her up the stairs and laid her gently on his bed. He took her head, pulled her to him, and kissed her again. He untied her robe with his good hand. She had on underneath, a silk red chemise that matched her robe. Her breasts were firm and her skin soft. He could feel himself get hard. He took his hand and rubbed it up her leg, pulling her chemise up and showing her panties.

Kyle had on his boxers and he started pulling them down. He could not believe that he was doing this. He had imagined this for months. Even though he had not been with a woman for years, this felt natural. He got on top of her and started kissing her throat and breasts. Elisa moaned. He took her panties and slid them down. He pulled her chemise up and rubbed her breasts. He played with each nipple and licked it. He was taking his time. He wanted this moment to last.

He was kissing in between her breasts His powerful hands rubbing and touching her all over. He kissed her up and down her legs. He scooted back up and kissed her on the lips. He took his hand and started playing in her womanhood. She was getting wet. By this time, they both were naked. They were sweating and breathing hard. The snow was falling hard outside. "Oh Elisa you are so beautiful." Kyle whispered. "I want this moment to last forever." He took his time doing everything just right.

She rubbed her hand over his chest. It was muscled. She rubbed it over his stomach and it was flat. She could feel his hardness. He put his hand under her buttocks. She looked into his eyes. "Take me Kyle." He entered her and Elisa cried out. He was gentle. He was moving with ease taking his time. He didn't want to hurt her. She was fragile to him like a China doll. He was looking into her deep violet eyes.

She put her hands on his face and they kissed again as he slowly kept the pace. "Elisa, Elisa," he moaned. "Oh, Elisa."

"Yes Kyle."

"I want you. I love you." He whispered in her ear. It was the first time he loved another woman since Janice, but it never felt like this with her. Elisa looked in his eyes. They were telling, they were beautiful, and honest. "My only hope before I die Elisa is that I will hear those words from your lips to me." Her eyes were watering and he kissed each one.

She did not want to be reminded of his impending death. They would just take one day at a time. He moved together until they finally climaxed. They both looked at each other and smiled. "You were wonderful Kyle," Elisa let out a long breath.

"So were you my dear." Kyle kissed her nose. They lay in his bed for most of the day.

"Kyle."

"Yes Elisa."

"I don't want to think about you dying. I do not even want that to be mentioned."

"It is inevitable Elisa."

"I know but we do not have to remind ourselves every day of it. Let us just enjoy the time we have Kyle."

"I second that Elisa. What would you like for dinner tonight?"

Elisa had one hand propping her up. "I was thinking that we could go out and eat tonight or we could order in. I am giving you the night off."

"Oh you are."

"Yes, I am, and you have not given me an answer to my gift."

"I would love to go to Paris with you Elisa. I would go anywhere with you; anywhere in the world with you." Kyle held out his arms and Elisa fell on top of him.

They made love again until they were spent. "How about we order in? I was thinking pizza." Elisa said.

"I am all for that."

"So pizza it is. What would you like on it?" Elisa sat up to get dressed.

"Everything but anchovies."

"Good call," Elisa stated and walked out of the room to order the pizza.

They said with the weather it could be an hour before they got their pizza, and Elisa said that was okay. She told Kyle that and he said that it would give them an hour more to do what they wanted. "Can I ask you something Kyle?" Elisa asked him taking her finger and going up and down his chest. He had one arm behind his head. "You said you loved me, do you mean it and if Janice wanted you back would you go back to her?" Kyle sat up.

"Why you asking me this Elisa, of course I meant it when I said it, and that is two questions not one, I love you and no, if Janice wanted me back, I would not go back to her. She is the past. I said I would forgive her not go back with her. She made her choice years ago and I have had to accept that. I do not think that I have to worry about that. What about you Elisa? If Guy came back and wanted you back, would you go back to him? He could give you so much more than me. Why did you not love him or want to marry him or any man for that reason?"

Elisa turned to look at the wall. "Elisa please do not turn away. I am sorry."

"It is okay Kyle. I would not go back to Guy. He was wealthy and we had fun together but that is all it was Kyle. There was never anything more. There was nothing more I could give him. It was never about the material things Kyle. I was on top of the world and had everything that a woman could want.

"My dreams had come to fruition. They were a reality. But Guy was becoming possessive and jealous. He seemed to have changed. You saw him last night and the way he acted. And besides, when he was married he had mistresses. It would have been a sham marriage anyway. It would have been more for publicity than love. He said he loved me, but I am sure he has told other women that. He would have, like he said to me last night gotten tired of me and found some new model. I never wanted to marry because I saw what my father did to my mother and I hated him for it. I still do even after all this time. I would never let a man control me.

"I was too busy building a career anyway and Guy knew that. He knew I did not want marriage. I was honest and up front with him from the beginning. So have I answered all your questions?" Elisa asked him.

"Yes Elisa." They heard the doorbell and Elisa went down to answer it. It was the pizza delivery man. She paid him and ran the pizza upstairs.

"You are going to let us eat up here?" Kyle laughed.

"Um, well, I was thinking, how about we take a bath together and eat pizza?"

"You do not have to ask me twice on that." Kyle hopped off the bed and grabbed the pizza which was hot under his hands and Elisa ran the bathtub.

They had a bottle of grape juice and ate pizza while they soaked. "Elisa sometime when the weather gets better, I want to take you fishing at the lake where my father used to take me. I have not gone there since he died." Elisa was leaning back on his chest. "It held too many memories for me."

"Then why would you want to take me back to it Kyle?"

"I want to show you where I was happiest, and my happiest times Elisa. I want to share that with you. Do you know how to fish?"

"My father was Native American and he had taught me some, but I have never taken to it."

"Your father was Native American? Why you don't look Native American Elisa. I would think that you would." Elisa chuckled.

"Well my mother was Irish and I got her looks, and my sister Cara got the darker skin and eyes, she took after our father. Where I would burn in the summer, she would tan."

It was the first time that Cara had been brought up for a while. Kyle was rubbing her stomach. "After my father left, I put him out of my heart and mind. I moved on. Cara took some of the pictures of him and the rest I destroyed. There were pictures of me and Cara as young girls in our photo albums. I threw them away."

"But you kept the letter from your mother to her Elisa. Why?"

Elisa leaned up and put her arms around her chest. "If you never intended to talk to her again, why did you keep the letter?" Elisa had never asked herself this question.

"To remind me of what she did, and how she was so selfish to not try and come to see our mother on her death bed when my mother wanted her to. It was my mother's last words to her; just maybe because it was my mother's last words to her." Elisa got out of the tub and dried off.

She got dressed and put her robe on. Kyle got out, dried off as well, and got dressed. "I am tired Kyle. I have to work tomorrow." She gave him a kiss and walked to her room.

"I will have breakfast ready for you in the morning Elisa."

"I know," Elisa said and smiled. He went into his bedroom and shut the door. He laid on the bed that he and Elisa had made love on hours ago. He took in her scent and it put him to sleep.

CHAPTER 29

Elisa had made the reservations for her and Kyle to Paris. She had sent Emilio and his family a Christmas card and told him of her plans. The Christmas card contained a check for a substantial amount and Emilio was aghast. He did not expect it and said he could not give her any money, but his mother had made her a beautiful scarf for Christmas. Elisa said it was beautiful and she would take it to Paris with her.

Emilio sent her one back and told her to have a good time and stay safe. His mother was looking tired, but her spirits were up. They would spend Christmas with the whole family, and of course, Emilio would cook the Christmas dinner.

It was his favorite time of year. He said his father was working as hard as he could, and the money that Elisa sent really helped his family out. Emilio told her that his family would be forever grateful to her. It touched Elisa. His father would stay up late with his mother and get so little sleep. Emilio would stay with her while his father worked. Elisa had kept him up to date on what was going on with her, what had ensued between her and Guy, and what Kyle did for her.

Emilio said that was admirable of him, and if he could, would shake Kyle's hand. Emilio knew that Elisa was a good woman and did not deserve that. Emilio said had he been there, he would have done the same thing. No one treats his daughter Elisa like that. Elisa laughed reading the letter. Fortunately, Guy never pressed charges and never called nor came back around to her place.

Elisa was finishing up reading the letter when Sissy came in. "Oh, Elisa, hey girl. What is going on and what are you doing for Christmas?" Sissy had a red dress on with a Santa hat and black boots. She had decorated her desk. "Are you not going to decorate your office Elisa?" Sissy asked her. It was Sissy's biggest holiday.

"I have not even put up a tree Sissy; you know how I feel about Christmas."

"Oh Elisa, I was hoping that things would change this year."

"Well they have some." Elisa remarked.

"Elaborate please." Elisa had told Sissy what happened with Guy and Kyle, and Sissy commended Kyle and said that Guy was a pompous asshole, which Elisa agreed with her. Elisa told Sissy about her and Kyle going to Paris for Christmas for a few days, and be back before New Year's Eve so they could watch the ball drop in Times Square."

"Oooo," Sissy said.

"You and Kyle are going to Paris together for Christmas. Is there something going on that I should know about? Huh huh?" Sissy gave her a wink. Elisa told her about Kyle saying he loved her, but kept the part out about them making love, she and Sissy were best friends, almost like sisters, but there were some things that Elisa did want to make Sissy privy to.

"I figured as a Christmas gift from me, I would take him to Paris. The spring show is there in April and we were not sure if he would make it until then." Sissy knew what Elisa meant. Elisa told her about Kyle's tumor and what the doctor said. He was still taking his medication and he had not had a seizure since the week of Thanksgiving. Sissy's heart went out to him, and thought that Elisa taking him to Paris for Christmas was a noble thing.

"I am so proud of you Elisa for doing this for him. You have made him a happy man. I am sure Kyle is overjoyed."

"He told me that I did not have to do this. He said he should be taking me and wished that he had the money. I told him that it was not about the money. It was a gift from me."

"Well, I hope you two have a glorious time." Sissy said sincerely. "So what about you and Renaldo?" Sissy and Renaldo had been getting closer over the weeks and Elisa had noticed.

"Oh you would not believe this Elisa, but he wants to take me to Italy for Christmas."

"And of course, you said yes, right Sissy?" Elisa asked like you would be crazy not to go.

"Oh, of course, don't be stupid Elisa."

"Have you met his family yet?"

"Yes, and they do not mind that I am older than him. They loved me and welcomed me into the family in no time. They are good people Elisa and so kind.

"He took me to eat at his family's restaurant and I must say it was absolutely mouthwatering. All their dishes are family recipes. You will have to take Kyle there sometime. Hey I got it, why don't we just make it a double date after the holidays. What do you say?"

"I will ask Kyle when we get back from Paris."

"Good," said Sissy clapping her hands together. "Does this mean that you will give love another chance there Sissy?" Elisa asked before Sissy walked out the door.

"I am considering it, so let us see what will happen." Sissy gave her Cheshire cat grin and left.

The snow was falling and she had worn her designer snow boots. They were calling for more snow over the Christmas holiday. Well, at least it would be a white Christmas and she would be spending it in Paris. She had Kyle's passport expedited. She had managed to pull some strings and get it even though it usually took weeks to get it. The lady who did the passport was a big fan of Pose magazine and loved it, so she had done Elisa a favor. Elisa had given her a ticket to the spring show in Paris, and the lady was on cloud nine.

The designs for the spring show were in high gear. The models were getting ready for the spring show as well. Elisa, for the next few days before Christmas, had made sure everything was set before she left for her trip. They would leave a couple of days before Christmas so they could enjoy Paris on Christmas, and leave on the twenty-ninth to be back in time for New Year's Eve.

She had Cora pack her stuff for her trip and Kyle and her had gone shopping for him and would do more shopping in Paris. Kyle still could not believe that Elisa was doing this for him. He would believe it once they were on the plane and in Paris and even then, he would have to pinch himself. The night before they left, they were lying next to each other after making love. "Are you ready for tomorrow Kyle?" Elisa asked him.

"I still cannot believe this is happening to me, but yes, I am. Anywhere with you Elisa is where I want to be."

They had continued to share dinner, talk by the fire, and make love. They were packed except for a few things that Elisa would need to pack in the morning. "I have to pinch myself Elisa to make sure that this is not a dream. Three months ago, I was living under a bridge, begging for money, getting by, and then you came and changed all that Elisa. I will never forget that, and I will forever be grateful."

"I know that I never treated you right Kyle. I never gave you a chance, but now I have seen differently, and who knew that our worlds would collide, or we would be lying here. You have changed my perspective on things." Kyle kissed her and they made love with the snow falling. The next morning, they headed out and to the airport. They pulled up to JFK airport and Kyle got their things.

They went inside and the airport was busy. They got in line at the ticket counter and each checked a bag. The ticket agent smiled at them as she handed Elisa the tickets. "I am sorry to say Miss," the ticket lady said, "but the flight is delayed due to weather. We are not sure when it will leave. They are calling for more storms coming from the north." Elisa thanked her and went to security. The line was long.

"The last time I was in an airport was when I came back from Afghanistan," Kyle said. He saw some soldiers hugging their families, some leaving back to a war zone, and some coming home on leave for Christmas. His heart went out to the ones who were leaving, who had to spend the holidays in the unforgiving mountains and deserts of Afghanistan and Iraq. His father had spent Christmas in Vietnam, so he knew it would be heartbreaking for their families.

Elisa was watching him and grabbed his hand. He looked at her and smiled. He was glad to not have to go back to a war zone.

He would be in Paris with Elisa. They got through security and to their gate. People were talking to the ticket agent. Some angry, some looking tired. The airport was decorated for Christmas and there was a Santa walking around handing out candy to the kids.

The kids were all running up to Santa. Elisa stopped believing in Santa a long time ago. She stopped believing in Christmas altogether. The ticket agent came over the intercom and said the Captain had decided to leave and get this plane out before the storm. There were cheers from the crowd. We will begin boarding for flight 2989 to Paris. Elisa had first class seats. They boarded and took their seats.

The flight attendant came up and offered them some drinks and something to eat. Elisa let Kyle have the window seat since it had been a while since he had been on a plane, and it was her Christmas gift to him. After everyone was boarded, the flight attendant made her speech. They taxied out and headed down the runway. They took off heading to Paris. When they finally landed in Paris, it was bustling with people. Elisa and Kyle grabbed their bags and took a limousine waiting for them.

"Wow a trip to Paris and a limousine. I am in Paradise." Kyle said enthusiastically. They got in and got to their hotel. It was a five star hotel in downtown Paris. They checked in and Elisa had made sure to get the executive suite. Kyle was looking around. This sure as hell beat his past living quarters.

The hotel was done in marble and there were chandeliers being held up with pure gold fixtures. *This has to cost a fortune a night,* Kyle thought. "Madam," the hotel manager said. "Your room is ready for you."

"Merci," Elisa said, and the concierge took them to their room. He opened the door and Elisa and Kyle walked in. The carpet was a plush white and there was a couch and chair. Kyle walked into the bathroom and there was a bathtub with a Jacuzzi.

"Wow, this bathroom has a Jacuzzi," Kyle said jubilantly. The bed was soft as Elisa sat down on it. It had silk pillowcases.

"I hope that everything is fitting for you Mademoiselle Drinnings." There was a bucket of ice with a bottle of expensive French wine it.

"This will do quite well Monsieur. Thank you." Elisa gave him a hearty tip and the concierge bowed and left. Elisa walked over to the window which had a balcony that over looked the city of Paris. The Eiffel Tower was in the background.

Kyle walked up behind her and put his arms around her. "I could get used to this."

"I hope Monsieur, because this is just the beginning." He kissed her and they made use of the bed. He took her gently. Her skin was so warm and soft.

He entered her so gently and took her arms and put them above her head. She looked at him and the fireplace in their room was burning. After they had both climaxed, they went to the Jacuzzi and soaked.

"Thank you again Elisa for this. I am not sure how I will ever repay you." Kyle was kissing the back of her head.

"Don't worry about that Kyle, you do not have to pay me back." He knew he could never out do this.

He carried her to the bed and made love to her again with the Eiffel Tower in the background all lit up. The next morning they had breakfast at a café and then started to do their sightseeing. They went to museums, went up in the Eiffel Tower, they strolled through the snow in the park, they kissed and hugged a lot. They got a lot of pictures, and got some of the locals to get their pictures. Paris was beautiful in the winter and especially at Christmas.

They would eat dinner at a fancy French Bistro and other restaurants. They would come back to the hotel room and make love every night after soaking in the Jacuzzi. Since Kyle could not have alcohol, Elisa had ordered club soda or juice. They had ordered room service one night and just stayed in. They shopped and shopped, and Elisa got him a gold watch and some designer clothes. Being Chief Editor of a fashion magazine, Elisa knew what styles were in season.

Kyle looked handsome as ever and Elisa looked stunning in her evening gown. It was the night before they were leaving, and Kyle was sad, and so was Elisa. "I do not want this night to end Elisa. I have had the most wonderful days with you. I will not be able to get this moment back."

Elisa turned to face him. "Thank you Kyle for giving me this time and for letting me give you this gift. We have made so many memories."

"I love you Elisa, and I always will." He would take her love to his grave.

It was a trip that neither one of them would forget. They made love on their last night in Paris and fell asleep in each other's arms. They got up the next day and packed. Elisa took some more pictures of the Eiffel Tower and one with Kyle in front of it standing on the balcony. They got the concierge to take one of them together on the balcony. Elisa tipped him well.

They got to the airport for their long flight back to the states. There were no delays and they landed in New York without a problem. The snow was coming down. There was sleet and ice on the ground, so the driver took his time getting them back home. Once back, they made some hot chocolate and curled up in front of the fireplace.

Cora was on vacation for the holidays and Elisa and Kyle had put their things away. "We need to get to Times Square early tomorrow. They cordoned the streets off after it gets full."

"So are you used to all of this snow Elisa?" Kyle asked her as they were sipping their hot chocolate.

"Oh hell yes," Elisa laughed. "I am from Ohio. That is the state that can have all four seasons in one week. You could wake up with sunny skies one day, and the next have an inch thick of ice on your car, and snow buried up to your trunk."

"So you are from Ohio, from which part?"

"Troy, it is a nice city, but I wanted to be in the fashion business and New York was the place. My mother is buried there at Riverside Cemetery. I have not been able to make it out there for a while to visit her grave." Elisa said sadly.

"Well, why don't you find the time to do that." Kyle stated.

"I think I will."

They went to bed after a long trip. They were exhausted. Elisa would be flying back to Paris in less than four months for the spring show. Elisa and Kyle were in her bed holding each other, and fell asleep with visions of Paris dancing in their heads.

CHAPTER 30

New Year's Eve Elisa and Kyle were down early at Times Square. It was already filling up. Elisa and Kyle had gotten some hot chocolate and were pigging out on hot dogs and having a good time. Kyle had called Mildred and asked if she would like to join them, and Mildred had declined, she told them to have a good time and she would look for them on TV. Kyle wished her a Happy New Year's.

There were bands, streamers, and people walking around in party hats. Christmas had come and gone and it would be a new year. Kyle had enjoyed Christmas, and it was the best one he ever had. Elisa was happy to see Kyle happy. The trip to Paris had been great. She wanted Kyle's last Christmas to not be filled with sorrow. He had been through enough.

It was getting late, and the people getting antsier to ring in the New Year. The New York Police Department started to cordon off the streets as they were full. "Did your parents ever take you here for New Year's Kyle?"

"Yes, my father took me once and it was enough for him." Kyle laughed. "How about you Elisa?"

"No, my mother wanted to take us girls, but my father said no, the holidays were a drag for us, especially after our father left and my mother had to work two jobs. Holidays in our family were like any other days."

"I am sorry Elisa." Kyle told her and hugged her.

"How about this year Elisa?" She looked up at him.

"Honestly,"

"Yes, honestly Elisa."

"I never did put up a Christmas tree, but they are better than previous years."

"How about we do this Elisa, why don't we put one up tomorrow?"

"A Christmas tree, but Christmas is over." Elisa gave him that look like you must be out of your mind."

"I know that Elisa, but it could be a New Year's tree or a winter tree, we decorate it with, instead of Christmas ornaments, just things that have brought us joy throughout the year, our good memories."

Elisa thought about it. "Well, okay we start tomorrow."

"Cool," said Kyle. "I can get Mildred's tree which would look so small in your townhouse, but suits Mildred's small apartment."

"Okay, tomorrow we go to Mildred's and get it, and I would like to invite Mildred over for New Year's dinner," Elisa told Kyle.

"She would love that Elisa, great idea." Kyle kissed Elisa.

The ball was about to drop as the partiers counted down, starting with ten and going all the way to one until the ball reached the bottom, and rang in the New Year. "HAPPY NEW YEAR," Everybody chimed and started singing.

"Happy New Year Elisa."

"Happy New Year Kyle," they kissed long and hard and held each other singing with the crowd. It was the best New Year's for both of them.

That night they celebrated more by drinking sparkling grape juice and making love. It was a new year, and a time to put the old behind them. "Elisa," Kyle said softly.

"Yes Kyle," Elisa responded.

"What is your New Year's resolution?"

Elisa just never thought of one. "I don't know Kyle. I never really gave it any thought." "What is yours?"

Kyle turned on his back and looked up at the ceiling. "How about we make one together Elisa?"

Elisa leaned up. "Really?"

"Yes Elisa really."

"Hmm okay, so what will it be?"

"That is the point Elisa, we make it together." They both were thinking.

"We make an impact on other people's lives." Kyle said.

"What do you mean by that Kyle?" Elisa asked him.

"I mean Elisa, in whatever way we can; we make an everlasting impact on other's lives. You made an impact on mine, and I hope that I have made one on yours."

"You have Kyle, and it sounds like a great resolution." Elisa smiled and kissed him, but how would she make an impact on others?

They fell asleep until New Year's Day. The next day, Elisa and Kyle were at Mildred's, and she let them use her tree that she had taken down. It was not too small and not too big, it was medium height, and it would look very small in Elisa's townhouse, but they did not care. Mildred accepted their invitation for dinner.

They all got to Elisa's townhouse and Kyle put the tree up. Mildred looked around Elisa's apartment and took it all in. "My, my!" Mildred exclaimed, "About five of my apartments would fill this townhouse. It is absolutely stunning. It is gorgeous Elisa."

"Thank you Mildred. I had some work done after I bought it." Mildred loved the fireplace and the carpeting.

"Now we can start decorating it." Kyle proclaimed, proud of himself for doing such an arduous task.

They took their pictures of Paris and put them up. Kyle put his necklace on it. Elisa took pictures of her mother and her and put them on there. Mildred had some lights to go on it and she strung them up. After they were done, they stood back and admired it. It was a beautiful tree, filled with times of joy and happiness. Mildred got a picture of them all standing in front of it. "Well, I am going to start dinner." Kyle said.

"I will help." Mildred said.

"No Mildred, you're our guest. Why don't you and Elisa stay in the living room and talk and I will do the cooking."

"Are you sure Kyle that you will not need any help?" Mildred asked him.

"I am sure."

"He will be fine Mildred," Elisa reiterated. "Come and sit down." Mildred sat down on Elisa's leather couch. It was nice.

They were drinking hot apple cider. "So Elisa, have you lived in New York all your life? Were you born here?"

"No, I was born and raised in Troy, Ohio and I moved here after high school to pursue my dream of fashion."

"What about your parents Elisa? Do you still see them?" Elisa stared at the fireplace.

"I am sorry Elisa, if you do not want to answer those questions."

"No Mildred, it is okay. My father walked out on us when I was twelve, and my sister Cara, when she was ten. My mother died of ovarian cancer and I took care of her for the longest time."

Mildred saw the expression in Elisa's face. "No, it is a complicated story."

"I see," said Mildred.

"I am sorry Elisa; you seem like such a nice young lady."

"Thanks Mildred, but I and my sister have not talked for over five years, almost six." Elisa held her cup between her hands, the warmth of it warming her hands.

Elisa had her legs underneath her. "Cara, my sister, blamed my mother for my father leaving and never forgave her. When she was seventeen, she dropped out of high school and left for Hollywood to become this budding actress. My mother became ill, and I made sure she was taken care of as I promised her when I was young. I worked and went to college. I used most of my money to send to her and then in her final weeks, I was right beside her.

"She wanted to see Cara and I called her. She was too wrapped up in her career to come home. Her producer would not let her. My mother died a week later, and I told Cara that she was no longer my sister and she was dead to me. I never told her about the funeral. My mother wrote us both letters and I never told Cara about it."

"But there must be a reason why you kept it Elisa." Mildred

said, hurting for this beautiful woman.

"I guess to remind me of what she did."

"Have you ever thought about contacting her?"

"I never told Kyle this, but I have a designer whose father is a Hollywood producer, and I had him find out some information without breaking a law. He got me her agent's new name."

"Have you tried calling this agent?" Elisa sighed.

"No. Why?" By that time, Kyle called and said it was time for dinner.

"If nothing else Elisa, make a resolution to do that and rectify that. She may have wronged you and your mother, but she is still your flesh and blood. I was an only child. I never had a sister to share with, love, and grow up with."

They got up to eat, and as usual, it was delicious. Afterwards, they all cleaned up the kitchen. Mildred stayed a little while longer, and she got up to leave. She had to get up early the next morning to open the restaurant. "Elisa darling, you will have to come by the restaurant, you and Kyle and have lunch sometime."

"I will, I promise Mildred."

"I will hold you to that Elisa." Mildred said shaking her finger at her.

"And she means it," Kyle chuckled.

"I know Mildred. If you promise her something, she will see you keep it." Elisa hugged Mildred and Mildred whispered in her ear. "Remember what we talked about earlier." Elisa pulled away and looked at Mildred. Elisa smiled and nodded her head in response. Elisa had her driver take Mildred back home.

"I have to be up early for work the next day myself. It has been a busy day, and holiday for that matter. I want to take a hot bath and sleep."

"Mind if I join you?" Kyle asked.

"Not at all Kyle." They walked upstairs and got a bath together. They got out and Kyle carried her to her bedroom. He laid her down and took in the scent of her.

Her hair was still wet and her skin smooth. "So what did you and Mildred talk about?"

"Oh, just girl talk," Elisa laughed, and Kyle pulled her head to his and enveloped her in his kiss. He made love to her gently. She ran her fingers through his hair, and he had one hand on her thigh moving her in rhythm to his movement. Afterwards, they fell asleep intertwined with each other.

—————

The winter seemed to drag on as January turned into February. The fragrance line was in full production and would be available in time for the spring fashion show. Maggie and Elisa had lunch, and Maggie was proud to hear that Elisa was using the fabric for the spring show. Sissy and Renaldo were on it hot and heavy, and asked if her and Kyle wanted to have dinner with her and Renaldo for Valentine's Day at his family's restaurant.

Elisa talked to Kyle about it and Kyle was all for it. The two models who would be commercializing the fragrance line were practicing their lines. Elisa had talked to them again, and they would be paid well for their time. Elisa even offered them a full time position as Pose models, and they said they would give her their decision after doing the commercial for the fragrance. Elisa told them fair enough.

"How was your time in Paris and your New Year's?" Sissy asked Elisa one day in her office. They were having lunch in her office.

"It was the best holiday I have ever had." She told Sissy about Paris, New Year's Eve in Times Square, the tree they had put up, and the resolution they had made together. "It sounds like you and Kyle enjoyed your time together and you made him forget about his illness."

"Yes Sissy, we did not even think about it. I am still wondering how I can make an impact on others' lives Sissy." Elisa said, pondering about their New Year's resolution.

"You have already made an impact on Kyle's life, and I am sure Elisa that you will find a way to make an impact on many more." Sissy took a bite of salad pointing her fork at Elisa.

"So how was Italy?" Sissy smiled like a child and blushed.

"Come on Sissy, I told you about my trip. Now tell me about yours." Elisa was not going to let her off the hook.

"It was so romantic Elisa. Italy was so romantic and Renaldo. We should think about having a fashion show in Italy."

"Dually noted," Elisa remarked.

"Now continue." "We did a carriage ride instead of a gondola ride being winter, we walked holding hands in Rome, we shopped, and he bought me this bracelet." Sissy showed Elisa the bracelet Renaldo bought her.

"It is beautiful." Elisa commented. It was a tennis bracelet with diamonds and red hearts going around it.

"We ate at the finest restaurants, drank the finest wines, visited the vineyards, he took me to where he grew up, we went and toured the leaning tower of Pisa, and we took a lot of pictures. He kissed me under an Italian sky. We made love every night. Oh, Italian men can be so romantic."

"Don't look now," Elisa laughed. "But I think that 'Miss I will not fall in love again' is falling in love. Is that true Sissy?"

"Well, Renaldo is hard not to love, and we have only been seeing each other for a few months now."

"You're dancing around the question Sissy." Elisa did not want to let Sissy go on this.

"I think I am falling in love with Renaldo." Sissy finally said.

"You think Sissy?" Elisa had her hands under her chin and staring down Sissy.

"I don't think, I am Elisa." Elisa got up and was delighted. She came over and hugged Sissy, and they jumped up and down. "So, Saturday night we have a double date Elisa." Sissy reminded her.

"I won't forget. Kyle is excited about it too."

Sissy got back to work. Elisa was so happy for Sissy. She deserved someone good, and she hoped that Renaldo would not break her heart.

⊰⊱❈⊰⊱

By the end of the week, Elisa was ready for the weekend.

She and Kyle went shopping for him to have something to wear for Saturday night. Kyle had some money; they were walking on the sidewalk, and saw a man with some red roses. Kyle went over and bought her a dozen. "Oh Kyle, you did not have to."

"I wanted to Elisa, and stop saying I don't have to, beautiful roses for a beautiful woman."

Elisa got home and put the roses in a vase. She set them on her table in the foyer. "Perfect," she said.

"Just like you Elisa." Kyle came up behind her and put his arms around her. Elisa turned around.

"No I am not Kyle. I am not perfect."

"To me you are." Elisa had tears in her eyes and Kyle kissed them away.

"Let me make you a nice Valentine's Dinner since we are going to this nice Italian Bistro that your friend and assistant are going to with her man."

"Sounds like a good idea to me."

"Then it is settled." Kyle made his meatloaf, whipped up some cheddar and sour cream mashed potatoes, and fresh green beans."

"You are going to make me fat Kyle." Elisa said stealing a green bean.

"You would still be beautiful Elisa." Kyle had gotten two long candles and lit them. Elisa set the table. Kyle served dinner. Elisa was wearing jeans and a New York Institute sweatshirt with her red hair pulled up in a ponytail.

"I am not exactly dressed for dinner Kyle."

"This is casual dress and you look good in anything Elisa." Kyle poured wine for her and juice for him, Elisa blushed. "I wrote you this Elisa, for Valentine's Day."

"I would love to hear it."

Kyle cleared his throat and started. "If I woke up and couldn't talk, would you be my voice? If I woke up and could not see, would you be my eyes? If I woke up and could not hear, would you be my ears? If I knew I would not wake up, would you make this the most memorable night of my life?"

Kyle got done reading and Elisa was crying.

"What made you write that Kyle?" Kyle took Elisa's hands and looked into her tear streaked face.

"I know we have been avoiding this, but my time is limited. Can you make me a promise Elisa? I want to be able to say what I have to say now before I do wake up and can't talk. I want to be able to keep your face in my memory before I wake up and can't see." Elisa was sobbing.

She held her napkin in her hand circling it in her fingers. He got up and got her something to blow her nose with. "Kyle, I do not want to talk about this. We have gone all this time and not talked about it."

"I know Elisa, but it is inevitable. I need to say what I need to say now. All the money in the world Elisa will not change this." She knew he was right. They had evaded it for a long time, but Kyle knew that time was their enemy.

"I want you to promise me that after I am gone, you will contact your sister to try and mend things. I cannot do that with Janice and Jerry Lites, my ex-best friend, but I have forgiven them in my heart. You still have this chance Elisa. Please promise me."

Elisa cared for Kyle deeply, but this was on promise she didn't know if she could make, let alone keep. "I don't know Kyle. I mean it has been almost six years."

"Dammit Elisa, listen to me. You are not dead. I am the one who is dying. I will be dead in a couple of months. Cara may still be alive and you can have that chance with her."

"I know you are dying Kyle, do you have to remind me?" Elisa got up and paced the kitchen putting her hand to her forehead.

She put her hands on her hips and looked up at the ceiling. "Even if I give you this promise Kyle, if I make it, it does not guarantee anything. She may not even talk to me or want to see me."

"Maybe, maybe not Elisa, but you will not know until you try. There are no guarantees in life except death and taxes. That is why it is called taking chances. Please Elisa, don't do this just for me, but for you. Take that chance." Kyle stood in front of her with his hands on her shoulders.

"Who knows, you may have an impact on her life. She may need you. Hell, she may be thinking about you or wanting you to contact her." Kyle stipulated. "If she was Kyle, I am sure she could find me. I mean, Pose magazine is sold all over the nation and the world. My name is listed as Chief Editor and headquartered in New York."

"Maybe she is waiting for you to make that first move. You are the one who told her that she was dead to you and no longer your sister. Maybe she is scared. Your words cut her and she has just never attempted to."

"You're not making this easy for me Kyle."

"Nothing ever is Elisa, which is why they call it life." Elisa laughed and playfully hit him. "Sometimes I hate it."

"I know Elisa, but you know that is the bitch of things, and it is too short.

This will be my last request before my time is up Elisa. I promise you that." She looked into his eyes and saw nothing but love and kindness. How is that five months ago she treated this man as a leper, and now here he was in her kitchen after making this scrumptious Valentine's dinner and sharing what all they have shared, and being the man she never gave him the chance to be?

She owed him this. It was a long shot. "Okay Kyle, I promise. I will try, but no more requests."

"I promise, scouts honor," Kyle said, holding up his right hand. She hugged him and the rest was history.

CHAPTER 31

They were all sitting around the table at Renaldo's family restaurant sharing salad, wine, (except for Kyle) bread, and hearty pasta dishes. "I must say Renaldo, your family recipes are to die for. They are delectable."

"Why, thank you dear Elisa. My family has had these recipes for generations."

"Isn't he cute and so darling?" Sissy asked Elisa, acting giddy. Elisa thinks maybe it was the wine taking affect. It did that to Sissy.

"So Kyle," Renaldo said. "Elisa here tells me that you are a superb cook."

"Well," Kyle answered shyly. "I do love to cook, and well, yeah, I guess you could say that Elisa is right." Elisa love tapped him on the arm and giggled. They had ordered desert and another bottle of fine Italian red wine. Kyle just had water.

Kyle was having a great time. "I am sure Sissy shared with you our trip to Italy."

Elisa looked at Kyle. "Well she shared it with me," Elisa said. "But it sounds like you too had a romantic and absolutely memorable time there." Elisa gave a wink to Sissy and she gave a wink back. Their deserts came and they started eating it. Elisa ordered the scrumptious brownie delight, Kyle ordered the cheese cake with chocolate syrup, and Renaldo and Sissy both ordered a chocolate cake.

Sissy bit into her cake and came down on something hard. "Ouch," Sissy screamed out in pain and the other patrons were looking on. "I think I broke a tooth." Renaldo looked and pulled out a four carat diamond ring.

"No darling, my love, I think you will be fine. You just bit down on this." Renaldo showed her the ring, and Elisa and Kyle stopped with their forks in the air. Sissy's eyes got wide. She was not expecting this.

"Sissy," Renaldo began in his most romantic Italian voice. "I know that we have only known each other for a few months, but these last few months have been amazing with you Sissy. You're bright, funny, caring, loving, and beautiful." Sissy was crying. "Sissy Epson will you marry me?" Elisa sucked in a deep breath and took a gulp of wine. Kyle saw her and smiled.

Sissy got out of her chair and was jumping up and down and said, "Yes, I will marry you Renaldo." The whole restaurant was clapping. Elisa was so happy. Sissy had found love again.

Elisa got up and hugged her. "Oh my gosh Sissy, you are getting married. When is the big day?" Elisa inquired.

"I would like it to be in Italy next June." Renaldo said. "Would that be too soon for you Sissy?"

"Oh no, that would be great and it is perfect." Sissy was admiring the ring on her hand.

"My family of course already knew I was going to ask her. They gave us their blessing, made the cake with the ring in it, and made sure that she got the right piece. You are both invited." Renaldo said, looking at both Elisa and Kyle. They both knew that Kyle would not be around to see it. They left the restaurant in good spirits. Sissy was getting married. It has been a joyous night.

Kyle was silent. Elisa knew what he was thinking. He would not see the wedding. He stared out the window. "Kyle, you okay?" Elisa asked him.

"Sure Elisa, I am fine." She knew he was lying. The ride home was awkward. They got back to her townhouse and Kyle went upstairs. She found him in his bedroom holding his necklace.

"I am so happy for Sissy."

"Me too Elisa," Kyle said without looking up.

"It is about the wedding isn't it Kyle?" Elisa put her hand on his shoulder.

"Only that I will not be there to see it, but I hope that you have a good time and it goes well. I wish them the best." The rest of the night was somber. There were no words that could change the situation. Kyle and Elisa held each other late into the night.

⊷⊶⊱✲⊰⊷⊶

Winter had been horrendous on New York, but February gave away to March and the weather was breaking. It was a beautiful sunny day in March, and Kyle wanted to keep his word and take Elisa fishing. Elisa had talked to Sissy about how Kyle would be gone before the wedding, and Sissy had a great idea. "Why don't we get married here and have the bigger wedding next June?" Elisa told her she did not want Sissy to have to change their plans. Sissy said it was "okay," Renaldo was fine with it, and Kyle would get to see it.

Elisa told Kyle about it, and Kyle was surprised that they would do that for him. "They would do that for me? Really?" Kyle said enthusiastically.

"Yes Kyle, how many times do I have to tell you? They will do it for you. They will get married next week and have a little ceremony, and then they will have the real wedding in Italy next June."

Kyle was happy as a kid that was ready for summer vacation from school. They went to the store, got some fishing gear, and headed to the lake where Kyle's dad would take him fishing. Elisa had on some fishing clothes and she looked cute with her hair tied up and under the hat. "You look like a fisherwoman." Kyle told her.

"Is there such a thing Kyle?"

"There is now."

Elisa wanted to drive, so she rented an SUV and they headed north to spend the day fishing. They got to the lake and got their fishing equipment set up. "Now this is how you bait the hook." Kyle got behind her and showed her how to bait it. "Now take it like this and throw the line in like this." Kyle took her hand and threw out the line.

"You have to be patient my father would say. When you feel the line jerk, reel it in slowly, but maintain control especially if it is a big fish."

Elisa waited and waited but nothing. "How long does this take?"

"Patience my dear Elisa." Here Elisa was, Chief Editor of a highly acclaimed fashion magazine fishing in upstate New York. Who knew?

They spent the rest of the day fishing. "My line is jerking!" Elisa exclaimed. "Okay, okay reel it in slowly." She did, and she was having a hard time. Kyle helped but by the time she got her line, whatever was on the other end got away. "Oh," Elisa said frowning.

"Don't worry Elisa my love. There are other fish in the sea, not just that one." Kyle smirked.

Elisa looked at him, "Ha ha, very funny Kyle. No pun intended right"

"No pun intended whatsoever." They finished their day and headed back to New York.

"How about we stop and see Mildred, and get us some juicy cheeseburgers loaded with a milkshake?" Kyle asked her.

"Go in this." Elisa asked, taking her hands moving them from head to toe.

"Elisa we are going to a burger shop, not a five star restaurant.

Elisa shrugged her shoulders and walked on. They loaded up the SUV and headed back.

They got to the restaurant and Mildred was working. "Well, well, well. Look who it is. Elisa you look different, but nice in that gear." Mildred said pleasantly.

Elisa had dried her eyes by then, "yeah, it is not my style of wardrobe, but Kyle here took me fishing upstate and, well, it was fun."

"Good, I am glad you two had a good time." Mildred said, putting her hands together.

"It is dinner, not lunch for us Mildred." Kyle said smiling.

"Close enough," Mildred smiled back.

"Let me get you a menu Elisa."

"We already know what we want Mildred, two cheeseburgers with all the fixings, fries, and shakes."

"Coming right up," Mildred said walking away. They took their seats. It was busy in there. A child was fighting his mother about putting on his jacket, and two elderly gentlemen were carrying on and laughing.

"Trust me Elisa, you will love this. These cheeseburgers are humungous." Kyle stretched his hands out to show her.

"I trust you Kyle."

Mildred brought out their milkshakes. "I will make them extra special for you both." Mildred took her pencil and put it back behind her ear. She went to go and take another order.

"So what am I going to wear to this wedding?" Kyle asked Elisa.

"Well it will be informal, so dress pants, a nice shirt, and tie. You will be okay Kyle. I have no doubt." Mildred brought them their food and they started eating. "Mmmmm, this is great Kyle."

"I told you so." Kyle reiterated. He wiped some ketchup off the side of her mouth. Elisa did not realize how hungry she was and finished it all. Mildred came over to their table.

"How was it?" "It was fabulous Mildred; give my compliments to the chef." Elisa said.

"Did you hear that Bernie?" Mildred shouted back. "This pretty young lady says give you her compliments." Bernie the owner waved his spatula and went back to cooking. "He is a good man until you do him wrong. He is a smart business man. This is on me." Mildred told them.

"Oh no Mildred, I cannot have you do that," Elisa said.

"Oh yes you can, and you will. I will tell Bernie, and he will take it from my pay. It is no biggie. I am just glad you two came."

Elisa and Kyle got up and both hugged Mildred. It had been an eventful day. Elisa returned the SUV and headed home. The tree was still where Kyle had put it; decorated the same. Elisa could not take it down. They agreed to keep it up, though now they would call it a "spring" tree. Elisa and Kyle both changed, and sat on her couch with Kyle rubbing her feet.

"Thank you Kyle for today." Elisa had her hand up against the side of her head.

"It was my pleasure Elisa." Kyle had his feet propped up on the coffee table, something that Elisa would have never allowed before, but now did not care. He had the necklace that his mom had given him before she died of her and his father. "Elisa, dear, I want you to have this before I die." He showed her the necklace. Elisa's eyes got big and she put her hand to her chest.

"Oh no Kyle, I cannot take it. It is something your mother gave you before she died and it has sentimental value."

"Yes Elisa, but I want you to have it to remember me by." Kyle handed it over to her. She took it in her hand and tears started to come down.

"Are you sure Kyle?" Elisa asked him, looking at him to be sure.

"Yes Elisa. I don't want you to forget me. It was a part of me and it will be a part of you now." She leaned over and kissed him.

"I will never, ever forget you Kyle." He kissed her back.

⊰⊱

The next week, Renaldo and Sissy had their small ceremony so Kyle could attend and they both looked stunning. Sissy was wearing white slacks, a cream colored silk blouse, and had a headband in her hair. She was letting Pose design her wedding dress. Renaldo was wearing black dress pants and a white dress shirt. Elisa had picked out Kyle's clothes and he looked handsome. Elisa was wearing a Vera Wang peach colored suit. It had been a wonderful and beautiful day.

The temperature had held for them. After the ceremony, Kyle and Elisa came back and made love. "I had a good time and it was a beautiful ceremony."

"Yes it was Kyle. They are happy that you were there."

"I am happy that I was able to enjoy such a splendid event."

Kyle remembered his wedding to Janice; it had been a small ceremony with just a few people.

Time moved on, and they took walks in Central Park, and she and Kyle even started feeding the birds again. Kyle was losing his eyesight more and more and Elisa noticed. She would help him, and even got him a cane to help him around. He was getting weaker and weaker as well. The spring show was two weeks away and Elisa decided not to go. She wanted to be here with Kyle.

She told Sissy this one day at the office. "You're not going?" Sissy said with disappointment.

"No Sissy, I think it is best if I stay here with Kyle, he has taken a turn for the worse." "You have worked so hard for this Elisa."

"I know Sissy, but Kyle needs me."

"I understand Elisa, and tell Kyle that Renaldo and I are thinking of him."

"I will Sissy, he will be glad to hear that." Elisa said emotionally. Sissy came over and hugged Elisa. Elisa sat down in the chair. "I know he will be gone Sissy, but I am still not prepared. He has changed my life."

"I know Elisa, it never gets any easier. But he will be happy knowing that you will be there in his final moments. He will not die alone, just like your mother did not die alone."

"I know. I knew my mother could go anytime, but it did not make it easier after her death. Kyle doesn't deserve this Sissy, bad people deserve this, not people like Kyle who have a good heart."

"I know Elisa it is not fair, but we do not get to make that choice." Sissy had not been a churchgoer, and Renaldo's family was Catholic, so she had gone to some services with him.

They would have a Catholic wedding next year in Italy. Sissy had not yet fully converted to Catholicism and his family had not pressured her. "I will though, make damn sure he gets a full military funeral. They denied him disability pay. Had they taken care of him, the doctors could have found this tumor out a long time ago and saved him."

"I know Elisa, but we cannot change the past."

"He asked me to make him this promise after he is gone."

"And what is that Elisa?" Sissy was holding Elisa's hands in hers. "He made me promise to try and contact my sister Cara."

"Wow," Sissy said.

"And what did you say to this Elisa."

"I was reluctant at first, but Kyle can be pretty convincing." Elisa laughed through her tears. "I told him there was no guarantee that she would talk to me. And Kyle being Kyle said that there are no guarantees in life but death and taxes."

"And he is right Elisa. So what else?"

"I finally told him that I would do it." "I am so proud of you Elisa and I am sure Kyle is too. You have to keep that promise to him."

"I will Sissy." Sissy patted Elisa's hands and got up.

"Will you tell the others about you not going to the spring show in Paris?"

"Yes, I will hold the meeting today."

"Should I make the announcement?" Sissy asked her. "Go ahead." Elisa said blowing her nose.

Sissy said she would and walked out.

"I have called you all in here for an emergency meeting. This is hard for me to say and I know we have prepared for this all year, but due to unforeseen circumstances and personal issues, I will not be going to Paris this year for the spring show." There were whispers and loud gasps. "Contrary to what you may want to think for my decision, I feel that it is best, and I will not regret it. My assistant Sissy here will be the interim Chief Editor, and will be representing Pose in Paris. Thank you all, you all have done a great job to get us ready for this. This meeting is adjourned."

Elisa walked out of the conference room before anyone could say anything. She walked back to her office and packed up her things. Sissy was behind her. "You sure you want me to do this Elisa?"

"Of course Sissy, I trust you and I know you can handle it."

"I won't let you down Elisa. This will get rave reviews."

"I believe in you Sissy." Elisa hugged Sissy and walked out of the office.

The fragrance line for Pose would be aired at the Paris show before it would be available to the market. Elisa had tested it and gave her mark of approval. Maggie would be disappointed that Elisa would not be at the Paris showing, but she did not care. Kyle needed her and he was growing worse day by day. He had lost his eyesight like the doctor said he would, and his speech was almost gone as well.

She got home and Kyle was sitting on the couch. "H-H-How w-w-was w-work Elisa?" It was a tedious task to get him to talk.

"I had a meeting today with the staff. I told them that I would not be going to the spring showing in Paris this year." Elisa sat down on the couch.

"W-why E-Elisa?" "I want to be here for you Kyle. I need to be here for you. I will take care of you Kyle like I said I would." She did not hire a hospice nurse to take care of him. She did it.

"P-P-please E-Elisa g-go."

"Kyle no I won't."

"Y-Y-You are a st-st-stubborn woman E-e-lisa." Each word was getting harder and harder for him to say.

"You know it Kyle," she laughed. She put her hands up to his face. She kissed him lovingly with tears in her eyes. She sat down on the couch and put his head to her shoulder and rubbed his arm.

⊰⊹⊱

Maggie called Elisa at the office and gave Elisa hell. "What the hell do you mean you're not going to be at the spring show in Paris? My gosh, are you crazy? You have worked too long and hard for this. I will be there, the whole goddamn world will be watching. You represent Pose. I mean the new fragrance line will be airing. It will be a success. You cannot miss this Elisa. You are obligated to be there." Maggie's anger permeated through the phone.

"I have some personal issues to deal with here, and I am not obligated to be there. I am having my trusty assistant Sissy go in my place and be interim Chief Editor and represent Pose. I think that she will do just fine."

"Sissy, are you out of your mind?" Maggie fumed.

"No Maggie, I feel that Sissy is quite capable of handling this despite what you think of her.

I have more important things here to tend to than this spring show." Elisa fired back. "I cannot believe this. What could be more important to tend to Elisa than this spring show that will be a pivotal event, especially now that the fragrance for Pose will be debuted at the show?" Maggie was huffing. *Maybe it was from one too many cigarettes,* Elisa thought.

"I cannot talk about it Maggie, but I feel that I have made the right decision that is why you gave me this job Maggie. I am in charge of Pose Magazine now, not you. I have made my final decision." Maggie was still going on when Elisa hung up the phone. Sissy walked in.

"I could not help overhearing your phone conversation. You really put it to her."

"Yeah, she will get over it. Let us talk about this more over lunch."

Elisa turned her laptop off and grabbed her purse. "My treat," Elisa said. "I know a great place to get a cheeseburger."

"I am there." Sissy grabbed her purse and was behind Elisa.

CHAPTER 32

It was the week of the spring show. Elisa and Kyle were lying next to each other in her bed. Kyle had completely lost his speech and could not speak. They knew it was just a matter of time before the tumor would steal his life. Elisa was crying. Elisa leaned up and looked Kyle in the eyes. "I want to say this to you Kyle. I should have said it a long time ago, but I didn't. I love you Kyle."

Even though he was blind now, his eyes showed a little life. "No Kyle, I am not just saying this because you are dying. I mean it. I do love you truly. You have been the best thing in my life. You have changed my life. I will keep my promise that I made to you over Valentine's dinner, and I will find a way to stick to our New Year's resolution."

Kyle was smiling and his eyes were watering. "Kyle I will be your eyes, I will be your voice, I will be your ears, and I am going to make this the most memorable night Kyle as if it were our last." She started to undress him, and kissed his eyes, his face, and throat. She kissed his chest and stomach. She made love to him ever so gently as he did with her. After she was done, she lay next to Kyle.

She talked to him long into the night. She held him with her arm over his chest. The next morning, Elisa woke up with the sun shining in her window. She got up and looked outside. "It is going to be another beautiful day, Kyle. Let us get up and enjoy it." But Kyle was lying very still. "Kyle come on." She jumped on the bed and shook him but no response. "Kyle please wake up. Please." She was crying and she felt for a pulse, and did not get one. "KYLE! No, don't you die on me."

She grabbed the phone and dialed 911.

"What is your emergency?"

"I need an ambulance now. My boyfriend has no pulse. Please hurry."

In no time, the ambulance was there and the paramedics were in her room. They tried and tried forever to revive Kyle, but it was no use. He was dead. He had died in his sleep, just like his mother did, and just like Elisa's mother had. The paramedics called it. "I am sorry ma'am, but there is nothing we can do. He is gone."

"No, no, no!" Elisa screamed. "Kyle!" The paramedics left and Elisa was sobbing.

Elisa had to call Mildred. Mildred picked up sounding tired. "What is it dear Elisa? What is wrong?"

"It is Kyle, Mildred. He's, he's dead." Elisa heard the phone drop and crying. "

When Elisa?" Mildred asked getting back on the phone.

"He had to of died in his sleep. I tried to wake him, and he would not get up. I could not find a pulse, so I called 911, the paramedics could not revive him."

"I will be right over Elisa." Elisa hung up the phone. The paramedics had taken Kyle's body to the morgue. Elisa lay on her bed and sobbed. Had she of gone to Paris, she would not have been here for his final moments. She went over in her head all the times they shared. She closed the curtains, hiding the sunlight.

Mildred came over as fast as she could, and Elisa answered the door. She could see the tear streaked face on Elisa. The two women hugged each other. Mildred had lost a son; Elisa had lost a dear friend, and the first man she had given her heart to. They sat in her living room with the tree still there. "You want me to fix you anything Elisa?" Mildred asked her.

"No Mildred. I am not hungry or thirsty."

Elisa got up and walked over to the tree. She looked at all the pictures on it. She was so angry at the world, at Kyle, at life, at everything. It was not fair. She knocked the tree over making everything fall off of it. Mildred ran up to her. "Elisa honey, no."

"It is so unfair Mildred. It is so unfair." Elisa cried and Mildred just held her. Mildred agreed, but could not change it.

"What will they do with his body? He has no family who will claim it." Mildred and Elisa were on her couch again.

"I will see to it Mildred that he gets a military funeral. I will have to go through his things and I will donate them to a homeless shelter. He gave me his necklace of his mom and dad his mother gave him. He wanted me to have it, to remember him by. I will never forget him Mildred, no matter what." Elisa hugged Mildred who was crying also and held her.

Elisa had done everything she could to make sure he got a military funeral with a 21 gun salute. It was a rainy day for the funeral. The American flag was draped over the casket. Elisa had on her black dress and a black hat with a veil. After the ceremony, they folded the flag up and handed it to Elisa since he had no next of kin to give it to. Elisa gave the flag to Mildred. Mildred cried. "You should have this Mildred. Kyle would have wanted you to have it."

"Thank you dear Elisa." Kyle was buried with his Purple Heart.

Emilio had come to the funeral and was standing next to them. Elisa had written a letter to him and he came.

⊰⊱❈⊰⊱

They were walking back to the car. Emilio had stopped to talk to Elisa. "I am so, so sorry for your loss, Elisa."

"Thank you, Emilio. Kyle was a good man. I wish that you could have gotten to know him more."

"What will you do now Elisa dear?"

"I will carry on like Kyle would want me to. He changed my life Emilio. He was this homeless man that I despised and would never give a second thought, but he came into my life and changed it. He showed me a side that otherwise I would never have seen."

"You know dear Elisa; people can do that from all walks of life. You lived in two different worlds yes, but you gave him a new life and he gave you a new perspective. It was his final gift."

"Yes he did. I made him a promise Emilio before he died."

"And what is that?"

"That I would try and contact my sister Cara. There is no guarantee she will talk to me or want to see me, it has been years and my last words to her were in anger."

"Yes dear, Elisa," Emilio responded. "I am glad to hear that. Like I said, when everything else is gone, family is all you have. There may have been some angry words spoken and things said out of anger and hurt Elisa, but as we have seen with Kyle, time is not our friend, no matter how much we want it to be." Emilio was right. She would do what she needed to do and keep her promise to Kyle.

"How is your mother, Emilio?" Elisa asked, changing the subject.

"She has taken a turn for the worse. She may not make it through the summer, maybe one or two months at the most."

"I am sorry, Emilio. Let her know that I am thinking of them and give your family my love."

"I will dear Elisa." He gave her a kiss on the cheek, a hug and walked away. Elisa walked back to the car with Mildred in it and drove away.

⁕⁕⁕⁕⁕

The next few days and weeks flew by. The weather had warmed up considerably and Elisa had donated all of Kyle's clothing and shoes to the homeless shelter. Sissy had given Elisa her condolences and said that the spring show was a success. The fragrance line was a success, and it was being sold all over now. It was raking in the money for Pose.

Elisa looked in the paper which she rarely does, and saw a photo of Guy Drakes standing next to a beautiful young woman. *Probably young enough to be his daughter,* Elisa thought and laughed. She read the article below it. It was an announcement of his engagement to this woman. "Cheers to you," she said out loud. She didn't care. It had been over for a long time. She wished them both luck.

She would sit in her office; not being able to concentrate.

She would look out her window and hope to see Kyle there, or she would start to call him to tell him she would not be home for dinner, but then realize he wasn't there, or call out his name when she got home, or walk into the kitchen expecting to see her dinner that he fixed her with a rose and a note, but no. Her nights were lonely now. Cora had given her sympathy to Elisa. Cora could not make it to the funeral. She had to go out of town with her sister that day, but she had loved Kyle as a dear friend.

Mildred would come over and they would have long talks. Mildred had helped Elisa take Kyle's items to the homeless shelter. Mildred had placed his flag on her dresser in her bedroom. Elisa knew she had to make that call, the one she promised Kyle she would make. She picked up the phone. She had the paper with the number of her agent in her hand.

Here goes nothing, she thought. California was three hours behind her so right now it would be five pm there. Elisa dialed the number and waited. She almost hung up, but someone came on the line. "Hello" a female voice said.

"Hi, my name is Elisa Drinnings, and I would like to speak with a Ricky Raines. He is an agent out there."

"Okay, do you have an appointment with him?"

"Um no, but I would like to inquire about how I could get into the market." It seemed like a plausible excuse.

"I will check to see if he is available." For what seemed like an eternity, a male voice got on. He sounded as though she may have interrupted his dinner.

"This is Ricky Raines. What can I do for you?"

"Hello, my name is Elisa Drinnings." There was a pause before he spoke.

"Are you by any chance related to a Cara Drinnings?" Ricky asked her.

"Yes, I am as a matter of fact, I am her sister." Another long pause. "Has she ever mentioned me?"

"Um no," Ricky Raines said. *Why should she, you disowned her.*

"May I speak with her?" Elisa asked her.

"I do not know. She is pretty busy, and I will have to ask her. I see that you are in the fashion business Miss Drinnnings. Is it Mrs. or Miss?"

"It is Miss Drinnings."

"Okay," Ricky responded. "I will talk to her, but I cannot guarantee anything."

"Here is my number." Elisa gave him her number and they hung up. Now it was a waiting game.

⊰⊹⊱

In California, Ricky was staring at the number. Ricky had been Cara's agent now for five years. He thought it strange that after all of this time, Cara's sister would be calling. Ricky had gotten her some low budget film gigs, but nothing big like she had when she first set foot in Hollywood at seventeen.

Ricky had lost some clout in the Hollywood stage. He had been busted for drug possession. He took the number and went back to Cara's condo to give it to her. "Hello, I am home darling." Cara was sitting on the couch.

"Hello dear," Cara came up to him and kissed him. She still had the long dark hair and skin, but she had taken up a bad habit.

"Daddy's got some candy for my baby." He pinched her ass.

"Oh let me see it." It was a bag of cocaine.

Cara put some on her finger and put it in her mouth. "You're still the best Ricky."

"I know sugar." They sat down and Ricky took a razor and sorted it out. Cara took a sniff and tilted her head back.

"This shit is the shit." Cara laughed.

"You will never believe what happened to me today baby."

"What," Cara said as she went to get them a beer. She took the lids off and handed one to Ricky.

"I got a phone call from a woman in New York." Cara pursed her lips.

"Oh no, it is nothing like that baby." Ricky had a reputation as a womanizer.

"She said her name was Elisa Drinnings." Cara held the bottle to her lips before removing it. "She said she was your sister."

"Is she?"

"No, she disowned me years ago. I have no sister."

"Well, she gave me her number. She is in New York. I know she is in the fashion business because I asked her."

"Well I don't care. I do not know an Elisa Drinnings." Cara took the paper that had Elisa's number on it, crumbled it up, and threw it on the floor. "Now let me give you some sugar." Cara said to Ricky.

"Daddy likes that."

❧◦✿◦❧

Elisa could only wait and see. She had done her part. She had kept her promise to Kyle. "It is all you can do Elisa." Mildred said to her, as they sat in her apartment. Kyle would be proud of you." "I know Mildred. I thought about calling again, but I do not want to push it. I said there was no guarantee she would want to talk to me. I basically disowned her."

"Yes Elisa, but you have to let her make that decision. Let her make that first step. You left the ball in her court." "Yes, Mildred, you are right. It is all I can do." Elisa said as she stared out the window.

❧◦✿◦❧

June came and still no call from Cara. Elisa had gotten a letter from Emilio stating that his mother had passed away. She went to the funeral. After the service, Elisa spoke with Emilio. "I am so sorry Emilio." Elisa had met the family and they all gave her hugs and told her they were grateful to her.

"She is at rest and in no more pain."

"What will you do now Emilio?"

"I do not know Elisa. I have thought about opening up a Guatemalan restaurant, but it is still too soon to know.

My father needs to rest too. I want to do what I can for my family now. Did your sister ever call you Elisa?"

"No Emilio and I do not blame her."

"Give her more time, Elisa."

"I have given her time Emilio. It is evident that she will not call."

"I want you to take care of yourself Elisa, and if there is anything you ever need, my family and I will be there for you."

"Me too, Emilio."

"I have to go. My family needs me."

"I understand."

"I love you Elisa."

"I love you too, Emilio." They hugged, and he kissed her on the forehead this time and left. Elisa watched him walk away, his future uncertain, and hers too. Elisa had thought about selling her townhouse and resigning as Chief Editor of Pose, but she is not sure what she would do or where she would go, everything was a whirlwind.

She left to go home. Now that summer was approaching, the days were longer and the nights shorter. For her, the nights had been too long and lonely. Guy had married the woman in the paper. They were going to go all over the world for their honeymoon. Elisa was happy. He got what he wanted.

CHAPTER 33

The summer was well under way. Pose was busy as usual getting the fall fashion and winter fashion lines for the upcoming seasons. The two fragrance models had decided to stay on at Pose. Elisa had decided they would have a winter show in Italy. Sissy was ecstatic and Renaldo was too. They had invited Elisa back out for their engagement party, even though they were not going to get married for another year.

Elisa was looking at some new designs for the fall and winter line when Sissy came to her door. Elisa looked up. "Yes Sissy."

"You have someone here to see you."

"Who is it?"

"Um, I think you should see for yourself." Sissy moved out of the way and Cara walked through the door. Elisa had dropped the designs on the floor where she stood.

"Cara," Elisa was shocked.

"Elisa." Cara said flatly.

"What brings you here, Cara?"

"Well, you contacted my agent and here I am," Cara said turning around, "in the flesh."

"How did you find me, and you never called me back?" Cara sat herself down.

"I have done a lot of thinking Elisa. I will never forget what you said to me on the phone years ago, but I thought that it would be more 'endearing' if I came in person."

Cara crossed her legs. She had her hair pulled up in a knot. "It was not hard to find you Elisa. Your magazine is only sold all over the nation and the world, and the address is on there."

"When did you fly in, Cara?"

"I flew in just this morning. I have some things that I need to say Elisa. You threw me out of your life, you said I was dead to you, and I was no longer your sister. I have made it as an actress, but here, lately, things have been drying up for me."

"Cara, you walked out on mother and me. She still loved you, but you blamed her for daddy leaving. It wasn't her fault. She had to work two jobs to support us. Daddy walked out.."

"No Elisa," Cara interrupted. "He walked out on us because mother told him to. He loved me. I was his native princess, but mother threw him out. Mother loved you more than me, Elisa. You were her favorite, and I was Daddy's favorite."

"You could not even give Mother the dignity of seeing her before she died Cara that is why I said what I said. She wanted to talk with you. She wanted both of her daughters there with her in her final days and you ignored it."

"I had a big movie I was working on and I could not leave."

"Yeah, you made that very clear to me Cara. Your movie was more important than our mother. You always put yourself first, Cara. Thought about you first, nothing else mattered."

"Well it seems you have made a good life for yourself Elisa. Chief Editor of a highly rated fashion magazine, you always did have an eye for fashion."

"Don't try and change the subject Cara and turn this on me. The least you could have done was show up for mother. She died sad, but she did not die alone. She knew you never forgave her but she still loved you, Cara."

"Whatever, it was a mistake to come here. I am getting the next flight back to Los Angeles." Cara got up out of the chair.

"Mother wrote us each a letter. She wanted you to know her final words. I have it Cara. I kept it because it reminded me of what you did and how you were undeserving of our mother's final words."

"Why are you telling me this Elisa, you are trying to hurt me like you did six years ago. Well, it is not going to work. Mother always loved you more than me. You were the perfect daughter, the one to be most successful."

"Is this about jealousy Cara over me and mother's relationship?"

"No Elisa, it is about the one person who loved me the most, the one person who cared for me, and the one person who believed in me who I lost." Cara put her purse over her shoulder and walked out of Elisa's office.

Sissy watched her leave. Elisa shut the office to her door. She sat down. She needed her mother here more than ever. Her mother and Kyle died. Her mother could solve all of this. *I have failed you all, I have failed you all.* Elisa thought, crying.

Elisa had done something that she had never done in all her years at Pose. She called off sick. She was sitting on her couch. Cora was busy cleaning. "Senorita Drinnings, you have a visitor." Cora told her.

"Who is it?" Cara walked in. Cora left.

"Cara, I thought that you were leaving back to Los Angeles and how did you know where I lived?" Elisa asked her curiously.

"I was Elisa. I was at the airport and had my ticket, but something stopped me. How I got your address is not important." Cara said nonchalantly.

"You said you had a letter from our mother. I would like to read it."

"I will go get it. Cora can get you whatever you like." "I cannot stay long Elisa. I rebooked my flight back to Los Angles for tonight." Elisa stopped on the stairs.

"I will get that letter." Elisa came back down and Cara was standing by the fireplace.

"You have a beautiful place here, Elisa."

"Thank you, Cara. I had some remodeling done after I bought it."

"You always had the eye for it," Cara laughed. Elisa handed her the letter. Cara stared at it.

"If you want to wait until you leave tonight Cara and read it on the plane you can. I have not opened it to read it. I am not sure what mother said in it."

"No, it is okay. I will read it now." Cara sat down on the

couch and opened up the letter, her mother's final words to her. She sat reading it.

My dearest Cara,

I know you miss your father. I do too. I loved him even after everything that has happened. I am sorry that you blamed me for your father leaving, you were only 10 years old and I know you did not understand. I tried to do the best that I could for you and your sister Elisa. You had it in your heart that you would not forgive me for your father leaving, but I loved you still.

A mother never stops loving her children Cara no matter what they do or say. You may think that I loved Elisa more, but I loved you both the same. You were your father's favorite, I know. The night that he left, he was drunk and had been drinking for some time. He lost his job and we argued about me working to pay the bills and put food on the table. The bills were piling up and I did not want my family going hungry, that is why I worked two jobs after he left.

I know I was not around much because of working two jobs, but I did it for you and Elisa so you could have a better life. I will always love you Cara and be proud of you. Your father made his choice, you made yours, and we all make choices in life. I never wanted him to leave. I just didn't want him coming home drunk in front of you guys anymore. I pleaded for him to stop drinking, but he would not.

I loved your father still. Ask Elisa about the song I use to sing to you both at night. Elisa will know the words. I have written her a letter too. As I write this, I am getting weaker, but remember that I will always love you Cara and I forgive you. I hope in time you can forgive me.

Love
Mom

Cara was sobbing now. "You see Cara; she loved you just as much."

"I am so sorry, Elisa. I am so sorry."

"It is okay, Cara."

"No it is not, I wish that I could have been there for her in her final days. I was so selfish and I cannot make it up to her."

"No you can't Cara, but you can go and see her."

"How Elisa?"

"We can make the trip back to Ohio, visit her grave and you can talk to her there.

I can go with you Cara if you like. I need to go and see her." "What is that song Elisa she sang to us? She said that you would know the words." Elisa started singing the song and Cara cried.

"Now I remember. She would sing it before we went to sleep."

"Yes, Cara." Cara started singing along with Elisa.

⊕❍⊛❋⊛❍⊕

Cara had extended her stay in New York, and her and Elisa went shopping, eating, and watching shows. Elisa took her to all the tourist sites. The days were hot. They were sitting at a café having lunch. "Elisa, will you come to Los Angeles? You would love it there, palm trees, sunny weather, the beach, and the walk of fame."

"Actually, I have been thinking of resigning as Chief Editor of Pose Magazine and selling my townhouse."

"Why would you give up so much? You have all of this." Cara was waving her hands around.

"For Kyle and the New Year's resolution that we made together."

"Who is Kyle?" Cara asked her.

Elisa told her who he was and how they met. She told her how he had changed her life and wanted to do something in his name. She had invested wisely with a good financial advisor even when the economy was getting bad. "He sounded like a good man, Elisa."

"He was Cara. I want to start a foundation in his name. I will call it *The Kyle Rimmer Homeless Veterans Foundation.* What do you think?"

"I think if he were here, he would be proud."

"Cara, I have been thinking. I would like to come out to Los Angeles and stay there. I want us to be close again and I could work on my Foundation out there. What do you think?"

"If that is what you want Elisa. I would love to have you, and we have so many years to catch up on."

"Yes we do," Elisa reiterated and they drank to that.

"I have an announcement to make that is why I have called this meeting. I love Pose and I have worked faithfully here for years. After some long and arduous thinking, I am resigning as Chief Editor of Pose Magazine." There were some gasps again. "Like I said, this was not easy for me, but I have other things planned, and I would not have time to devote myself to Pose as I would like."

People were looking around. "I know you must be wondering who will be your next Chief Editor of Pose. I have elected Sissy Epson. I believe that her dedication and hard work to Pose is to be recognized, and she will fill my shoes, effective immediately." Sissy put her hands to her mouth. She had always wanted this, but hated to see Elisa leave.

"I will miss you all. You have been the success of Pose and have seen her become successful. I applaud you all and I am proud of you." Everybody who had worked for Elisa came up to give her a hug, she had been tough, but they respected her.

Sissy came up to her. "You will come back to New York right?"

"Yes I will Sissy."

"You will always be welcome here, and if you like, you will always have a ticket to our shows." Sissy said hugging her.

"Thank you Sissy. I know you won't let Pose down, and this was your dream. It has come true."

"I hate to see you leave Elisa, but I understand." Sissy knew the reasons why and had kept them to herself. "You will still come to mine and Renaldo's official wedding right?"

"I would not miss it for the world." The two ladies hugged again.

"Elisa, I have a confession to make."

"What is it Sissy?" Elisa looking concerned now.

"Your sister Cara came to my office to see you and I told her that you called off, she asked me for your address and I gave it to her. I hope that you are not upset at me." Sissy had that worried expression on her face.

"Oh no Sissy, in fact, I am glad that you did, because we shared a good moment. I let her read the letter from our mother and she cried. It was what we needed."

Sissy was so glad to hear that. "Good, I was so worried about that, but I am happy to see you two working things out." Sissy and Elisa hugged each other again.

Elisa had packed up her office, and now the sign on the door said Sissy Epson Chief Editor. She would interview for her new assistant.

Elisa walked outside. She looked at the place where she had first seen Kyle and saw another man there. She pulled out her pocketbook and put some money in his can. She saw his dog tags hanging and was once again reminded of Kyle.

"Bless you child." The man said. Elisa smiled and left. She had sold her townhouse and given Cora a nice severance pay with good references for her to find another job. Cora hugged her and said she would miss her. She had been with Elisa for six years now. She had talked to Mildred about her plans and Mildred told her that was admirable of her. Kyle would be happy. Mildred would miss her, but Elisa said she would not be a stranger, and Mildred told her you better not be.

The two women hugged, and Elisa got back into the car and waved to Mildred. She wrote a letter to Emilio, he wrote her back, and said she would always be welcome at his family's home and Cara too. He was happy to see Elisa and her sister mending their fences.

He had opened a small restaurant in lower Manhattan and

his dad was retired now. Elisa had come a long way from the woman she was before she met Kyle. He had taught her to see outside the box. He showed her that her world was not the only one out there, that there was more, and he opened up her eyes. She had come full circle. He gave her what money could not buy. She had his necklace and it was around her neck.

Her flight to Los Angeles was getting ready to land. Cara said that she would be waiting for her outside of security. When her plane landed at LAX, she got off the plane to get her bags. It was warm in the airport and she could see the palm trees that Cara talked about.

Cara had gotten herself into rehab because she wanted to start fresh with Elisa. Cara still had her mother's letter. Cara told Elisa about the drug habit and Elisa had begged Cara to get help. Elisa said she would go with her. Cara had gotten rid of Ricky Raines and had a big movie deal coming up with a new agent. Elisa was proud of Cara.

Elisa saw Cara and ran up to her. "Oh my gosh, it is so good to see you again Cara."

"You too Sis, let us go and get your bags." Elisa followed Cara to baggage claim and got her bags. They walked out of the airport into the California sunshine smiling, happy, and together.

CPSIA information can be obtained at www.ICGtesting.com
Printed in the USA
LVOW13s1957060913

351160LV00005B/13/P